THE GHOST OF SANI ABACHA

The Ghost of Sani Abacha

Chuma Nwokolo

COUNTY BOOKS
2012

ISBN 13: 978-978-2190-10-9

County Books

www.african-writing.com

Cover image by Victor Ehikhamenor; author photo by Andrew Ogilvy.

Publication History

The Redemption of Pati Mugodo, Orange Crush and *The Fall of Phiri Bombai,* have previously appeared in African Writing Magazine Nos. 9, 7 & 8 respectively.

Seer & Sons and *Urban Architecture* have featured on the author's blog [blogs. african-writing.com/chuma].

Billy Goat was first published in MTLS Magazine No. 3.

A Roman Job Offer was featured in the New York Subway Lit series.

A Slovene translation of *Ma' Rebecca* was first published in Arzenal Magazine in 2007, with the English version appearing in MTLS No. 4.

Man Rating was first published in 2011, in Sentinel Magazine no. 7.

Bullfight, Gluttony, The Ghost of Sani Abacha, B.O., A History of Human Servitude, The Las' Foolscap, The Colour of It, The Provocation of Jay Galamba, Cousin Kashim, A Taste for Leftovers, Marital Accounts, High Fidelity, Going Straight, Confessions of the General's Marabout, Diary of an Honest Girl, The Butcher's Revenge, and *The Accidental Man* are published here for the first time.

Other Books by Chuma Nwokolo

Memories of Stone (poems)

One More Tale for the Road

Diaries of a Dead African

for my children,
Zitam, Nkech, Lota and Gozim ,
with more love than words can express

Contents

Contents

Preface

Every blooded Nigerian remembers the day General Sani Abacha died. It was June 1998 and I was leaving chambers in Lagos when the news broke. I remember the spontaneous party that poured onto the streets – horns, loud music, dancing... and the spectacle of perfect strangers in public embraces. It was wilder than the day Nigeria won the junior World Cup, and eerie as well – all that public joy unleashed by the death of a head of state.

Abacha had been plotting coups since the '60s but it was his 1993 coup that finally made him top dog. He did not invent any new sin but he certainly added his own spin – and he remains in the running for Nigeria's Most Unpopular Head of State award. So he died and Nigerians broke onto streets like prisoners out of jail... indeed, within months democracy was underway, military rule was history... Sani was dead... but his ghost died hard. The ghost of decades of military occupation took some resting, especially in corridors of power.

Yet, these tales are told by a storyteller, not a stymied politician. They do not concern Sani Abacha as a person, and only four of them might rate as 'political' stories... What haunts this book is not Sani's ghost so much as the miasma of a 'post-traumatic stress syndrome' that hangs over the post-autocratic streets of Waterside, of Ikerre Oti... of Accra even... wherever new thresholds of worship arrive at the cult of self, wherever flesh hankers after flesh, from regular beds to dining tables groaning with the roasted flesh of whales.

Today, across the world, people are waking up in new 'democracies' having buried the spectre of their old autocracies... from Tunisia, through Egypt to Libya... this book is presented with a prayer that the ghosts of dead regimes remain in their crypts.

Chuma Nwokolo
Asaba, October, 2011

THE REDEMPTION OF PATI MUGODO

I visited Toni Mugodo and his new live-in lover, Pati, on Friday, intending to make my own little caustic observation on his new relationship and leave it at that. That is my style really, just one or two telling comments, nothing heavy-handed that anyone can take offence over. After all, I am just a pastor. Ikerre-Oti may be a village, but this is also the twenty-first century and I do know my place. It is probably one caustic observation too much that earned Father Jose his empty church on Cowry Road.

Frankly this was not a trip I had been looking forward to, but it was already a week since Constance Mugodo flashed me and burned up my thousand naira recharge card weeping on the phone. Their twelve-year-old marriage was in mortal danger; concerning this, there was no question. And if there was a time for all good men to make their feelings known, it was now, before Mugodo did something silly and game-changing – like giving the new girl a ring, a baby, or both. Although she didn't put it quite so pointedly, as she wept she hinted – rather crudely – that since I couldn't pray a baby into her womb despite the half-dozen expensive vigils I had hosted on that account, the least I could do to justify my pastoral credentials was to confront the wench of a home-breaker.

I did have my reservations as I made my visit that evening, for Mugodo wasn't a man that abided The Work of God courteously. It seemed to me a foolhardy undertaking, this attempt to move a man from the woman he *wished* to live with, to one he *ought* to live with; especially when he had made his wishes so clear by leaving his Lagos house for Constance, and hurling her bags through the windows of his Ikerre-Oti house (in the sight of scandalised neighbours) when she followed him there. It seems only fair to admit that, as I pressed the bell that Friday around the end of June, I didn't exactly have a sleek succession of caustic comments on the tip of my tongue.

A small woman opened the door. It was a hot day in Ikerre-Oti, and it grew even hotter as I stepped into the modest, air-conditioned bungalow for which Mugodo had given up his expensive Lagos mansion by the lagoon.

It was hard to decide who was the more beautiful, between this home-breaker and Constance, but only because true beauty was a thing of the heart rather than the physical body, and my pastoral eyes do not look upon women in the superficial manner of other men... yet, if one were to look at women with the eyes of other men it would be hard to disagree with Constance's teary opinion that her husband had clearly been bewitched by an occult enchantress.

This strange woman had nothing to weigh against Constance. She had inch-long hair, full eyebrows, and no protuberant feature; there was nothing there to snag the eye of a roving man (and Toni Mugodo had roving eyes). She was just this wisp of a woman, hardly an inch over five feet, and her only riveting feature was, perhaps, the engaging smile which seemed tailor-made for her face. Constance had far more going for her in the way of statuesque beauty, having clinched a vulgar beauty crown in her youth – which happy season could not be terribly more than fifteen years ago.

The woman in front of me was still in her youth, and as comfortable as I was not. She wore a glittering ring on the critical finger, which threw me off my stride. My heart fell on Constance's behalf. I shook her hand, but she hung on to mine, leading me by the hand into a chair. At a more propitious time I will write some more about this overlong handshake, in the meantime, she was saying, 'You look like you need a drink,'

'No, I'm fine.'

'And a meal,'

'No, really, I am fine.'

She excused herself politely. I looked around the room. It had been many months since I last visited Toni and Constance here and I did not recognise the place. Constance's garish photographs were gone, of course, from the walls. In their place was just the one photograph of the new woman sitting demurely on Toni Mugodo's lap. They were both smiling widely, with Mugodo's grin a clear inch wider than that of the girl-woman in his lap. My ulcers burned unaccountably. My own Hannah had never sat on my lap for a photograph (which was a good thing; were she ever to do so, I could not have smiled so for the camera). The chairs of the new dispensation were comfortable, but they were so low that I was almost sitting on the ground. The aroma in the air had clearly come in an expensive aerosol can, although I wasn't sure I liked it that much. This was definitely the lair of another woman... and that other woman seemed to be spending quite a while away. I glanced at my watch. The chairs were so low that having sat down, I was reluctant to get to my feet.

I heard a ping that sounded suspiciously like the *all done!* of a microwave oven. I frowned as she returned with a steaming plate of stewed catfish on a bed of rice. This was all heralded by an aroma of luxuriant sumptuousness, in the midst of which I caught a whiff of something coconuty and quite agreeable. I swallowed. I had not eaten coconut rice in... twelve years? A cold beer sweated beadily beside the food. I hadn't drunk alcohol in much longer, but the beer was of course completely out of the question. Concerning the food however, it was indeed a pity that I happened to be on a fast, and that I had an unflinching policy never, *ever*, to eat while on Reconciliation Duty. Besides, there were always going to be moral questions about eating a woman's food and then advising her lover to throw her out.

So I waved my hand in a firm, pastoral, No. Her smile widened, if that was at all possible, 'In my own village, she said, as I tried hard not to stare at her mid-section, 'hospitality is not *offered*, it is *pressed*.' Her stomach looked as though someone had pressed

15

on her a couple of large dinners that she really didn't need. My heart fell even lower, on Constance's behalf.

'An excellent Christian virtue,' I agreed, 'but today, I must insist-'

Swiftly, she uncorked the bottle of beer, which sighed a belch of lager into my nostrils; I knew the nostalgia of forbidden things, and realised (*by God!*) that there were suddenly more things at stake here than the sanctity of Constance's marriage, '-and in my village,' she laughed, 'it is the height of rudeness to reject the hospitality of a hostess.'

I laughed right back. As a pastor, I had a fail-safe way of rejecting hospitality without causing offence. Nobody ever wants to be the cause of a pastor's fall from grace, 'Unfortunately,' I said, fingering my white collar, 'I'm on a fast-'

'-Aha, you have to end it now, won't you?'

'I do?'

'Well it's pointless continuing, now that you've told me. You'll have to start it all over again... It is scriptural, isn't it? The Bible says that when you win the glory of man, you lose the glory of God... or something like that...'

After that deft bastardisation of scripture, she hurried back into her kitchen (and by this pronoun I do not mean, of course, to concede that the kitchen was now *hers*; I only mean that she *possessed* it as utterly as a woman could possess a kitchen – without being a maid). She fetched a thimble of what smelt like curry sauce, and a napkin. Then a side dish of... banana fritters? Everything went onto a trolley which she positioned, with a delicacy of exactitude, precisely in front of me. I must also confess that up till this point – and this was some fifteen minutes into my visit – I had not had the opportunity to formally introduce myself, how much more to ask after Mugodo. Indeed, my language, up to this point had very little of the caustic in it.

'And what do your fellow villagers do,' I asked, genially, 'if they are too full to eat, and they don't want to be rude to a hostess?'

'They stay in their own houses,' she smiled, slipping out again.

I am of course a pastor with fifteen years' experience. I raised my eyes upwards (from where my help cometh) and left them there: I did not look temptation in the eye. Yet, the food was hot, releasing such a stupefying aroma into the air that the aerosol sickliness was quite overwhelmed. I was drinking more saliva than was my wont. This was ridiculous; and I knew I had to pull myself together.

I visualised Constance's teary face and reached for my stiffest and most formal attitude. The only means of saving this visit was to create professional distance between me and the Subject of the Adulterous Liaison, which was not compatible with the acceptance of irresistibly presented meals from a home-breaking hostess. This was not true hospitality; she had every reason to court her lover's visitors – particularly one that arrived in a clerical collar. When she entered with ices in a small glass, I steeled myself and rose, offering a polite handshake, 'The Reverend Moses Ekpo,' I said formally. My voice was the gravely one I used for my Jezebel sermons.

She set down the glass and we exchanged another, more formal, handshake – which ended promptly on this occasion. Her hand was cold from the iced drink, and limp from my pastoral put-down. Her smile was quite gone. 'The *irreverent* Pati,' she said. There was mischief in the voice and I looked at her carefully. She sat down abruptly. I sat down too, this time, away from both food and woman, but she rose and rolled the trolley up to me, the ices of my water tinkling invitingly (and by this pronoun I do not mean of course to suggest that I had mentally succumbed to her blandishments). She smiled, spreading her small, expressive hands over what I must confess was now a minor feast, 'my *dishonourable* hospitality,' and then she curtseyed; despite her flippancy it was difficult to handle such vulnerableness. Her voice was very supplicant… indeed, never did a fallen angel approach the throne of mercy with more supplicant words, 'you will at least drink a glass of water and bless me?'

This was the point at which I drank; which was also the point at which I knew that Constance's cause was quite hopeless, for the distance between the glass of water and the first, delicate, fritter of banana was but a half-inch. Concerning the fast, she had a point, of course; and it was there in Mathew chapter 6:

17

*When you fast, do not look sombre as the hypocrites do,
for they disfigure their faces to show men they are fasting.
I tell you the truth, they have received their reward in full.
But when you fast, put oil on your head and wash your
face, so that it will not be obvious to men that you are
fasting, but only to your Father, who is unseen; and your
Father, **who sees what is done in secret,** will reward
you.*

Since I was not going to get the credit for this particular fast
it seemed logical to get the benefit of the meal, before it went
cold. So I put that first fritter into my mouth and chewed. O,
how simple are the greatest pleasures of this sinful world! (I was
well into the meal before I remembered that Satan also quoted
scripture when he tried to derail Jesus' fast in the wilderness,
but... Satan had come with the *suggestion* of a meal. This was
a feast. And then again, I was no Jesus.) Still, I ate with Christian restraint, soberly contemplating the terms of the blessing I
would have to render to the home-breaker when I was done; did
I dare bless the child growing in the womb? I had to be careful
not to bless her in terms incompatible with Constance's conjugal
entitlements...

Yet, there she was: sitting, not on the chair beside me, but on the
arm of the chair in which I sat. And let me clarify: it was not a
sexual gesture, this sitting on the arm of the chair in which I sat;
neither was her proximity suggestive in the least. It was simply
witchery of the most motherly kind. What it said was: *I am interested in the next spoon you are going to put into that mouth, in the
next word you are going to say.* It was like that continuation of our
first handshake that evening, that leading of me by the hand into
a chair. That also was not sexual, being more of a superfluously
tactile solicitousness.

'So where is Mugodo?' I asked,

'Aha! So he was the one you came to see after all!' that laugh
again, 'I shouldn't have cooked for you!'

'It is not that at all,'

'Oh really?' Constance's caustic and satirical voice echoed in my head.

'Beg your pardon,' I asked, disconcerted.

'I said, "Oh, really?"' she replied.

I paused as I put the first spoonful of fish into my mouth. That lucky bastard, Mugodo. The fish was unbelievably flavoured. Hannah cooked all my meals at the rectory and the crustiness of her fish left me vulnerable, oh so wide-open, for this olfactory, gustatory experience. The fragment of fish dissolved on my tongue. I felt a twinge in my throat as salivary glands convulsed, flooding my mouth with fluid. I trembled in catfish heaven, lost in a rapture than I only occasionally found, halfway through devotional services on the mornings that my gifted chorister, Grace Okitipa, was at her phonic best. I shut my eyes, tight; most pastors are alike in this actually, in the closing of the eyes as they enter into transcendental experiences… but additionally, I was trying not to weep over catfish.

'What's the matter?' anxiously.

'No, nothing.'

'It's a bone!' the alarm in her voice, the hand on my shoulder.

'No, I'm fine,' I took away her hand politely, but it was a mistake, that closing of my eyes. I now felt the prick of moisture in my eyes, which she was sure to spot if I opened them now. I kept them shut.

'Here, drink,' a glass in my hand.

I gulped… 'beer!' I rose precipitately, spilling the rest of it down my black suit. Eyes wide-open now, I grabbed the glass of water and drank it down.

'You don't like it?'

'I don't drink beer!' I spluttered, 'I'm a pastor for God's sake! I haven't drunk alcohol in fifteen years!'

'But Jesus turned water into w-'

'And Satan preached to Christ as well!' I snapped angrily – and I was truly furious now! Probably more furious than I have been in all the years of my ordination! I cannot recall how many times that year alone I have turned down a glass of whiskey, a tot of gin, with the modest, *Thanks, but I haven't had a sip of alcohol in the fifteen years of my ministry.* Now I would always have to add: *...apart of course from that glass of beer Mugodo's lover slipped me, which doesn't really count because my eyes were closed and she was sitting on the arm of my chair...*

I raged, 'I am not going to enter into a theological debate with you!' I set down the glass of water, and the glass of beer.

Now, I have replayed this final scene in my mind hundreds of times. I did not plan what happened next. It was probably the shame of it all. At any rate, my indignant words had launched me on a certain trajectory of outrage, and much as I longed to sink back into the comfort of the chair, the catfish and the Christian conversation, I found myself stomping for the door.

'But, Reverend Moses-'

Her voice was conciliatory enough, but the momentum of my outrage swept through her, 'Do tell Mugodo that I called,' in my gravely voice, and before I knew what I was doing, I was standing outside the slammed door, feeling a little like a man that fled a restaurant without paying, halfway though an expensive meal: I hadn't blessed the woman.

Many a night I have started up from sleep with the clap of that door ringing in my ears, haunted by the forlornness of that final *But, Reverend Moses*, squirming at the idiocy of my pompous *Do tell Mugodo*, and chagrined at my betrayal of poor Constance; for in the dead of night it was the home-breaker's unborn baby for whom I prayed, not for the wife's empty womb. Yet, it is the thought of that slab of barely-tasted catfish, forever enshrined in my bereft Cathedral of Taste that gives me cause to groan (and brings the sleepy slab of Hannah's arm across in her motherly embrace).

BULLFIGHT

When they started calling him "Treeman" he stopped climbing the boughs of the flame of the forest that grew in front of his late Granpappy Fred's house. He had been used to hanging there like a lanky sloth for hours on end, motionless for the most part, barely responding to waving villagers who knew better than to try to talk him down from his arboreal retreat. It was too late though, for the name stuck – as well as that sense of *altitude* in his company, a sense that he spoke from some great height, far removed from the banality of human concerns. Treeman invariably got the worse of every transaction and shared the intransigence of timber at the approach of a chainsaw. Overall, he seemed a mentally-challenged coward who lacked the basic instincts for life in a competitive society like Waterside.

All that changed when Dr. George won the logging concession for Badforest. Dr. George was medical director of Equi Hospital, Waterside's only private hospital. He was not really a Watersider, but he had lived there so long that Enemo, the first baby he had delivered at his hospital, was now pregnant with her third daughter. Unfortunately, none of Enemo's girls had been born at Equi hospital. – His fees were reasonable enough, by Warri standards, but in the context of Waterside, they were extortionate. The benches at the hit-and-miss health centre near the market groaned from the weight of Waterside's sick, but Dr. George's reception remained empty and quiet.

He would have closed down but for his streak of enterprise. He developed his practice into a regional centre of excellence and for a season his fame as an abortionist drew traffic from places as far-flung as Ibusa and Oleh. Unfortunately, that income source was soon thwarted by a Christian revival that saw penitent mothers turning from abortion clinics to church. And when the pregnancies grew to term, rather than Dr. George's obstetric interventions, they turned to the nearest health centre.

He would have closed down too, had he not Received the Call of the People. For another season he turned to politics, becoming councillor for Uregbe-Waterside District Council. Soon he was supplementing his medical income with a substantial political one – which arrived mostly under the table. The four years were soon up and he was replaced in the council by Ma'Comfy. That was when he set up his timber company. For the first few months until he got his logging concession it was a briefcase company; indeed when his first chainsaws arrived in Waterside the delivery agent spent most morning looking for 'Equi Timber Ventures'.

'Is only Equi Hospital I know,' ventured Chief Butema eventually, when the exasperated dispatcher ended up at the palace, 'Maybe you should try there.'

These days, Equi Timber Ventures occupied its own large premises on Equi Street where half-a-dozen tractors, tippers and bulldozers waited impatiently for the first of June when the logging concession would go live. 'Equi', as every Watersider now knew, was of course the name of Dr. George's beloved mother, whose 80 x 80 inch portrait dwarfed the photographs of the governor and the head of state in the hospital reception. His penchant for naming everything after his mother was beginning to get on everyone's nerves, especially when he changed the name of his fifteen-year-old house to Equi Cottage.

Tonye, the short-fused scrap merchant, was still chafing at the memory of it: 'What am saying,' he explained to Treeman, who had called to sign him up for the Save Badforest Campaign, 'is that all his Equi-this and Equi-that is winching the rest of us; yesterday Mama was asking why I can't just call my business "Ibuloma Yard". So I ask her why? Something that I have been calling "Tonye and Sons" for more than thirty years now – and she said that "Tonye and Sons" was a good prayer, but that now that I have borned six daughters and MamaGogo has finished borning, I should kuku show my own mother some respect like Dr. George! Can you imagine that kain thing?'

'No,' said Treeman, whose conversational skills were not prodigious.

Tonye studied the petition again. He thought he was holding it right side up, but he could not be sure. He'd had a couple of years of schooling but that was literally a lifetime ago. He nodded approvingly. 'Is very good, keep it up.' So, saying, he handed it back, tut-tutting at the black smudges he had left inadvertently on the paper.

'Please now,' said Treeman, offering a pen, 'sign it for me,'

Tonye studied the guileless eyes of the twenty-six-year-old. Nobody had asked him to read – or sign – anything in the forty-eight years since he ran out of class after a flogging by his English teacher back in the early sixties. Yet, there was no hint of mischief in the young man's eyes. It was possible that he had spent so many years up his tree that he did not know what was going on down here any more. He shrugged, deciding against the instinctive punch, 'Let me not dirty the paper for you;' he said caustically, 'just sign it for me, eh? Keep it up.'

By midnight, with stoical doggedness, Treeman had signed up most of Waterside. He'd had no luck with Chenge, Dr. George, and the nurses at Equi Hospital, but he'd had the lack of imagination to approach the near-senile Equi, who had served him akara and pap and signed happily. He however met his match in the cantankerous Imam at the uncompleted mosque, who offered to sign the petition if Treeman would convert to Islam.

Most of his signatories did not share his passion for the trees, which were not called *Bad*forest for nothing. The place had such an impenetrable history of iniquity that grown men grew incontinent with terror just to hear it. It was a primary forest that had not been harvested for centuries and the crown of its forty-metre iroko and sapele trees could be seen from as far away as Bushemina. Half the villagers of Waterside supported the felling of Badforest (so long as they did not have to wield the chainsaw), the other half were indifferent to its fate; but everyone had signed

Treeman's petition: he did not have an enemy in the world, it was the first enterprise in living memory he had ever embarked upon and it was unthinkable not to support him. – Especially as he only needed them to sign a piece of paper. Despite their apprehensions, Treeman had not even hinted at a donation.

And they all knew very well that at the end of the day, an ordinary piece of paper could not get between a bulldozer and its timber.

***

On the first of June, at 6 a.m., Treeman took his pieces of paper – all ninety pages of them – and stood on Cemetery Road, which led down to Badforest. Although the petition had been successful, the *Save Badforest Campaign* was such a non-event that neither community nor press were on hand for the protest advertised in the petition itself.

At about 7 a.m., Paulinus, the driver-mechanic of the lead bulldozer, turned the corner on Cemetery Road and rumbled past the burial ground and river on the right, towards Badforest. Neither Paulinus nor the three other woodsmen in the bulldozer's cabin were from Waterside, there being no Watersiders brave enough to undertake the actual logging. When they first saw Treeman in the middle of the road, they misunderstood his purpose. Then as the bulldozer approached, the youth raised his petition above his head. The men on the bulldozer laughed incredulously, but the machine did slow to a crawl and halt before Treeman.

By this time the four other vehicles of the logging company had formed an untidy queue on the dirt road. Dr. George had come along, with his video camera, to record the historic felling of Badforest's first tree. Chenge, who planned a Badforest Residential Estate, was there as well in his four-wheel-drive.

'Okay, Treeman,' said Dr. George irritably, waving his licence, 'the joke is over now. You have your paper, I have my own paper. My *government* paper. Give my boys chance, let them go and do their work!'

'No,' said Treeman, who did not have much by way of the gift of rhetoric.

Chenge looked at his watch; he was due in Warri by noon. 'Just drive forward,' he shouted to the bulldozer, 'he will run away!'

'Maybe we should send for Sergeant Onoja,' suggested Dr. George, with undue anxiety, but Treeman's quiet nonchalance in the face of the yellow menace fired a primordial rage in the heart of the bulldozer.

From his dinosaurian height, Paulinus looked down on mere mortals. He was not just the king of the road, he *ripped up* roads before him. And he dragged even towering irokos to their death by sawmill – and their humble reincarnation as tables and firewood. If Treeman approached life from an arboreal high, the driver occupied his own mechanical one, and he sneered, 'Lef am for me, Oga!'

He revved the diesel engine and the monster shuddered and strained forward, pawing at the ground as clouds of dust and exhaust fumes darkened the skies. He trod on decelerator and brake and the roar of indignant machinery filled the morning air. Paulinus was an old hand at bulldozers and that whole array of prehensile construction and logging equipment. He had worked from Shendam to Abuja, from Kafanchan to Minna. He had driven for Cappa in the seventies and Julius Berger in the eighties. Although he had dissipated the nineties running a brothel at Ore, it was now the noughties and despite his potbelly, he was redeemed and back in the saddle of a diesel monster equipped with a clam grapple log loader at the one end and a massive dozer at the other. With him at the control, the hydraulic limbs of the Caterpillar were usually sinuous rather than jerky. Yet, he yanked at the right joystick, raising the blade of the bulldozer up so fast that it locked into place with a jarring *CLANG!* Caked mud descended in a dusty vortex. Dr. George shielded his afro from the fine dust as sleepy villagers began to gather, procured by the roar of machinery.

Treeman did not flinch.

So Paulinus went a little bit mad. Leaping from lever to lever he shot the crane of the log loader to its full, groaning, extension and swung its grapple to and fro like the grotesque testicle of a Caterpillar in midlife crisis. With his dozer blade cranked right up, Paulinus stood on his brake, leaned on the left joystick, and, above the sound of the engine, yelled his final challenge, 'You dey go, abi you no dey go?'

The youth stood firm. A single leaf from his petition slipped from his trembling fingers and sailed away towards Badforest. It represented some fifty signatures, a whole wedge of the previous morning's enterprise, but Treeman did not budge. He was no Che Guevara, but he was planted to the spot by the sick knowledge that he was the last hope of the majestic trees, which completely overwhelmed his own sense of self-preservation.

Paulinus dropped into his seat and eased off the brake pedal. The bulldozer surged towards Treeman. The villagers flinched. Paulinus, timing the manoeuvre down to a fine second, stamped on the brake, so that when his oily boot slipped off, there was nothing to stop the bulldozer from running down the youth and roaring another two dozen feet towards Badforest. Then the engine died fitfully and Paulinus jumped down from his cab on suddenly tottery feet.

The two dozen or so people who had seen the bulldozer crush Treeman had screamed so loudly that their collective roar had drowned out the bulldozer momentarily. Many lost their voices in that scream of horror, a few were still keening as they fled for their homes, convinced now that the stand of irokos had not been called "Badforest" for nothing. As the rest gathered around the body of Treeman, it was in utter silence, deferring to Dr. George who hastily bent over the felled man. Treeman looked more complete than a body had a right to look, which had just been gored by a bulldozer. There was blood everywhere, a gash in his forehead, and a cheekbone that looked like a pulsing fist. Yet he was alive.

'Ambulance!' screamed Dr. George in amazement, realizing that – thanks to the height of the bulldozer's mainframe – Treeman had been knocked down and 'run over' without being *crushed*. He screamed again, 'bring the ambulance!' The bulldozer driver was the first off the mark, and despite his fifty-odd years, his greasy boots and the nervous energy that caused him to slip and fall several times during the sprint, he was the first to arrive at the hospital. Yet, after a moment of sober reflection, he jumped out of the ambulance and fled his job on his motorbike, leaving behind an overdue month's wages.

Which was how Dr. George's hospital acquired its first intensive care unit patient in the three years since Daud lost his fight with cancer. Treeman did not do much fighting himself, he just lay comatose as Dr. George wrestled with his own conscience. Treeman was not exactly a hopeless case, but the x-rays confirmed the fractured skull. Dr. George could abort a roomful of half-term mothers, blind-folded, but brain surgery was well beyond his expertise. He was friendly with a neurosurgeon in Warri, but their friendship did not affect call-out fees. Dr. George knew that it would probably cost him an iroko and a half to cure Treeman and before too long he was resenting the height of the bulldozer's mainframe.

So for two days, Dr. George pottered anxiously around the bed of the unconscious campaigner, administering palliative drips with anti-inflammatory steroids and antibiotics. The stranded bulldozer sat on Cemetery Road, its very inactivity an outward sign of corporate penitence. Yet, Treeman had not a single enemy in the entire Waterside, and his recent campaign had provided every villager with a private anecdote of a recent interaction. They were quickly established then, those two poles of village pilgrimage: the hospital bed, around which they surged, ignoring the visiting regulations of the ICU, and the spot where he was mowed down, where his dried blood was still visible on the dirt track. The children had scoured the cemetery, tracking down most of the pages of the now historic petition, which was now plastered securely to the south wall of the village hall.

That was where Ma'Comfy first saw the list of names when she returned from her trip to Sapele. 'What is this one again?' she asked Bara the mechanic, even though she knew very well what it was. The regular clump of glum gossips, which had become a feature of the village hall since the felling of Treeman, parted grudgingly to let the short restaurateur through.

'Is Treeman's list,' explained the mechanic, 'you see my name there?' he loved to do this, for his name was sixty names ahead

of Chief Butema's. They seemed to have a new 'hierarchy of ho-
liness' thing going, related to the promptitude with which they
had signed on to support the fallen Treeman.

'That's my name there,' said Tonye, 'come and see all the questions the poor boy was asking about bulldozers–,'

'Where's your name?' asked Aguom mischievously.

'There,' said Tonye, pointing vaguely with his chin at the sheet
defaced by his greasy fingers. Then, jiggling his bunch of keys,
he stepped backwards with some alacrity and another mournful
villager stepped into his place.

'*Shoo?*' marvelled Ma'Comfy, 'So Treeman get supporters like
this?'

'Is the whole Waterside that sign for him,' explained Aguom.

'Yet is only him that face the bulldozer!' said Ma'Comfy, drawing down a pall of silence on the boisterous crowd. She sighed,
'that's a real man, I'm telling you!'

***

By the third day after the accident, judging that sufficient respect
had been paid to all concerned, discreet arrangements were
made for another bulldozer driver and a fresh logging crew to
assemble at dawn at the stranded Caterpillar on Cemetery Road.
That morning, Dr. George and his (increasing less-) silent partner Chenge arrived to find a stand-off: some three dozen villagers massed between bulldozer and Badforest. Dr. George gaped:
Aguom, Bada, Tonye... he knew them all individually, but they
were ranged in a corporate sullenness he didn't recognize.

'What's this now? Aguom, Bada? What's all this?'

Dressed in Treeman's inarticulacy, the fidgeting mob stared
back sullenly. The entire protest scene was new to Waterside.
This was not a place of choice for the early hours, sandwiched
between cemetery and the spiritual repository of every demon
in Waterside cosmology. They were not treepeople like Granpappy Fred's grandson. They did not have the deep pockets of
an indignant Ma'Comfy who had rescued Treeman from Dr.
George and sent him by ambulance to a surgeon in Benin. They

were regular folk shamed to take a stand by the courage of a coward. Yet, suddenly it made sense for everyone to leave well alone. Badforest had endured for centuries; whatever foul spirits sheltered in the branches of those irokos were welcome to stay there one more generation. If they were evicted from Badforest, where else would they go but Waterside? One boy was already fighting for his life. He was enough.

Chenge, forced into activity by the doctor's increasing timidity, snatched the logging licence from him and marched up to the group of villagers. 'You know what this is?' he demanded, waving the page that had cost tens of thousands of naira in under-table payments, 'This is a licence from Forestry Department! *A licence from Forestry!*'

'Which licence?' asked Aguom, snatching and ripping up the red-sealed document. The wind snatched and bore the pieces towards Badforest. Chenge blew his top, releasing choice expletives that grew bolder and ruder with every step he took away from the sculpted Aguom. He got behind and harried the motley crew of loggers, but they had come to earn a day's wage, not a lynching. As they shifted somnolently from foot to foot, Dr. George hissed and turned on his heels.

'No shaking!' shouted Chenge, shaking with rage. He jumped in front of his partner. His voice was shrill with tension, for the bulldozer was tethered to Waterside on the short leash of his short-fused overdraft, 'Look at those irokos! *Look at them!* Am talking thousands of dollars a log! *No shaking!*'

'I'm not shaking,' replied Dr. George, 'I am just going to the police post to bring Sergeant Onoja.'

'Yes?' grated Onoja, swaying cantankerously under his placard in the rear of the demonstrators, 'this is me here. Wha's the matter?'

SEER & SONS

On that last evening when Felmat's house was finished, when the clan gathered for the feast in the *phul*, and the music and smell of roasting duiker had drawn every last clansmen up to the yard of the newest house in Boromio, a grey stranger came also. He appeared suddenly at the gate, complete as a coin, and although it was clear that the aroma of the roast had brought him, he stood there swaying slightly, and cried: 'I have need of a wife!'

Now, Boromio was as good a place as any to go mad in, and although they laughed, those villagers that heard that cry, they also knew that the desert fever commanded many a passing insanity that could be cured by food, so they put a horn of wine and a dripping hunk of duiker in his hand. He took a sip of the wine and no more, but the meat he ate until it was gone, drinking also as many horns of precious water as were put into his hand.

There was only one Boromio, a forty-year-old village founded by a Kapla clan that tired of travelling. For the first thirty years it was shirked by nomadic Kaplans who considered them outcasts. But in the last few years of the drought, three Kaplan caravans had pitched in Boromio, breaking camp one week afterwards for the long trek north, leaving, now and again, a new family to 'stay awhile', who could live for some weeks in their tent before joining up with another caravan.

***

Felmat was one such. His wife had lost all of her three previous children in the nomadic weeks after childbirth. She had been pregnant again, and he had left the last Kaplan caravan to 'stay awhile'. He lived in his camelskin tent, on the outskirts of a village built of burnt brick. The baby had arrived, a lusty girl child whose breakfast pangs still woke nearby villagers three months on. Then he had brought a goat to the central *phul* to ask the clansmen's help in building a house.

They had told him it would take seven days but it had been done in five – they had reckoned without the excitement of the villagers, for this was the first time a travelling Kaplan would decamp to their sedentary cousins. And it was well-finished too, the central room was as big as any in Boromio, a second room adjoined the first, and the low wall of the *phul* ran round the two, wide enough to hold the gathered clan.

With the completion of his house, Felmat was expansive and generous, carrying around a platter of meat and a gourd of wine, forcing helpings on his guests, with judicious emphasis on those who had worked the hardest.

The music faded early: the best drummers had been laying bricks all day and within an hour their arms had nothing more to offer. Done cooking, the women gathered around the duiker fire, clapping pre-pubescent girls into a frenzy of competitive dance. Done eating, the grey man rose. He was startlingly lean, and his voluminous robe could not hide the hollows behind his clavicles. 'I have need for a wife – and sons,' he said, to no one in particular. Although clearly sighted, he spoke in the vague direction of people, in the way of blind folk. The dancers melted into the circle of still clappers. The silence that greeted this second declaration was more hostile than the first. This was a madness that survived the slaking of thirst, the feeding of the ovens of the gut.

'Is it not rather late in the day to seek a bride,' asked Paralo with gentle sarcasm.

'Even the market for chickens has closed,' grumbled Mareke, 'and he's looking for a wife!' Mareke had the most violent hands in the village and Chasa, her husband, could tell tales of what else they got up to – when they were not plucking and decapitating chickens in her market stall.

'She must be a widow with grown sons,' explained the grey man meticulously, as though they had not spoken. 'They must want a trade. We must be married by your custom. We must set forth at dawn.'

The clansmen stirred uneasily.

Felmat had the most to lose from the souring of the evening and he stepped between stranger and villagers with his platter of venison. He knew there was another form of insanity that came from a horn, which could only be slaked by sleep. The stranger had only taken a sip of wine... but perhaps he had arrived drunk. 'There's a village not too far from here with such a widow,' he lied, turning a conspiratorial wink to the villagers behind him. 'Sleep now, tomorrow I will point it out to you.'

Felmat indicated a row of slumbering teens overcome by their day of work and their night of feasting. The grey man looked at them longingly. Then he shook his head. 'Higher ground;' he said, 'this is no good, it will rain tonight.'

When he left, even the most reticent laughed. Rain indeed! There was not a wisp of cloud in the skies and it had not rained in Boromio for twenty months. The Boro Stream was a parched bed of mud; all the water in the village had travelled an hour on donkey-vats all the way from the spring at Tonton.

***

It began to rain on the stroke of midnight. They knew the minute it started, for the villagers slept on roofs and in the open courtyards to escape the heat. Startled cries went up across the village. Within minutes it was clear that this was no errant patch of pregnant cloud. Soon it was sheeting down. They worked like soldier ants, turning up every available vessel to catch the rain. Within twenty minutes every empty pot and drum and jar in Boromio was full and the mothers had no reason to keep the children from stripping naked and cavorting in the streets.

By dawn, even the children were cowed. Most of the mortar from Felmat's new walls had been washed away and one wall had failed, causing the roof to list dangerously. He and his young family had taken cover in Minakro's house across the street.

The celebration in the village turned to dismay as they watched chicken coops float away and runnels from overflowing vats join the concourse of the streets flowing into the Boro Stream.

'The stranger!' cried Felmat, snapping his fingers. He jumped up without another word and broke out of the house. Minakro hesitated and joined him. They ran west up the dirt track, now a furious streamlet, that led up the Rumpama Range. The outcrop of hills were just outside Boromio and by 4 p.m. on the average day Boromio was usually in the shadow of the hills. They were panting by the time they made the shelter of the caves.

They saw his fire as soon as they entered. He had retreated deep into the belly of the hill and a reedy snore rattled from his bony chest. He had wrapped himself in gray sackcloth and his travelling clothes were neatly folded into a pillow for his head. He lay on the narrow bed of his travelling bundle. The only property that was not secured by his sleeping body was the fire. It burned steadily, three feet from him, a curious, smokeless flame that rose from half-a-dozen thin, bamboo-like sticks. Felmat and Minakro exchanged knowing glances. Felmat sank to his haunches and touched the sleeper's foot respectfully. He slept on, so Felmat slapped it firmly.

The stranger came awake immediately. He looked around him, taking in the two clansmen and the pools of water at their feet. With an oath he rolled to his knees. He was naked but for a loincloth. He drew up his bundle to the fire and pulled a raffia pouch from it. He sprinkled a powder over the fire with a perfunctory mutter and rose, padding slowly to the entrance of the cave. Felmat and Minakro watched the fire splutter angrily and go out in a cloud of acrid smoke. They turned to the entrance of the cave. There was a distant rumble then and a crack of lightning momentarily framed the stranger's gaunt body against the lighted entrance.

They felt the fury of the rains ebb almost instantaneously. By the time the stranger padded back to his makeshift bed, the backdrop of buffeting rain was now a polite patter.

'It was the meat,' said the stranger, rubbing his belly ruefully, 'I do oversleep when I overeat.' Still muttering, he took his bamboo sticks, which did not look like they had been burning all night, and stowed them in his bundle. He looked towards the men, but not at them, and in that split-second the assurance of a man that ordered the heavenlies shifted and they saw inflected a certain desperation, the votive passion of a seer who, nearing his end, saw no heir to a lifetime of wisdom. Then he drew the sackcloth back over his head.

**

He also overindulged his sleep. By the time he came down that day, it was evening. There was very little resentment in the flooded village for the man that repaid the gift of a horn of water with a brimming stream, instead they watched him from a distance as he walked down the street, surrounded by children, until he finally got to the gate of Felmat's house where a small clump of men were busy restoring the failed wall. They stopped working as a man and turned to the stranger.

'I have need for a wife,' he said earnestly, 'she must be a widow with grown-up sons, and they must need a trade.'

Nobody laughed; indeed at that moment – in that thirsty country – there was not a man that did not wish his mother a widow.

GLUTTONY

Nobody knew exactly when the whale arrived on the river beach but Pastor Dego was halfway through his regular four-hour-service when the news filtered into his church that Sunday morning. By then the carcass had suffered the attentions of five or six neighbouring villages for several hours and the prospect of missing out on this manna from the seas, which had so providentially swum all the way upriver to beach near their village, thinned the hundred-strong congregation until the pastor was preaching to a die-hard core of the faithful. Then his own wife slipped away, and there was such a run on his congregation that Dego was forced to close the service. Only then did he hear the news and join the pilgrimage to the riverside for his first sight of a flesh-and-blood whale. He walked slowly: he was big-boned, possessed of a sizeable paunch, and easily the heaviest member of his church.

It lay on its belly, the whale, and even then it lay higher than the height of a man. A sad, black eye the size of a small sea stared at the pastor as half-a-dozen impromptu butchers hacked at the breach they had made in the left flank of the beast. He felt holy and connected. He wondered if his congregation would remember that only the week before he had preached on the subject of Jonah and the whale! 'Your ancestor swallowed a man of God like me,' he whispered to the dead animal, 'but nobody is going to save you from our bellies today like God saved Jonah!'

He shut his eyes and before that sea monster, he suddenly felt a touch of divinity quite unlike anything in his previous experience. He usually started his sermons with the formula *Yesterday, the Lord said to me...* when all he truthfully meant was *Here's what*

I think today... but at that moment he truly heard a voice telling him to continue his sermon right there by the riverside by preaching to his errant parishioners to make one pilgrimage to the whale and no more... to take meat for one day and no more... but over the excited hubbub, he could hear machetes hacking at whalebone and he feared what would happen if he put himself between his people and the meat of their desire. So he opened his eyes and made the sign of the cross to ward off the deceptive voices of marine spirits.

He saw his wife approaching, staggering under the weight of an overloaded pail of meat. He looked around, alarmed. The Carriage of Meat in Public Places was too undignified an undertaking for a pastor's wife. Where were her housemaids, the young giggle of girls that so delighted in parading themselves, scantily-clad, at the critical moments of his communion with God...? Then he saw them behind her, just as laden. 'Thank God you're here!' the wife shrieked excitedly, dropping the pail before him. He had to grab at a massive chunk – to stop it from slipping to the dust – and a vaguely rancid odour rose to his nostrils, 'You were praying and praying and praying,' she scolded, 'but God had already answered our prayers!'

Then she turned and hurried back to the queue of buckets, and the man of God found himself staggering home at the head of the trio of maids.

Recently, many Watersiders had become involuntary vegetarians. The oil spills from the wells had thinned the fish and the poor custom had disenchanted the butcher who used to bring the weekly cow to the slaughter slab at main market. The appearance of the whale changed everything. Every fridge was emptied of their sweet potatoes and pawpaws and requisitioned to the storage of whale flesh. Bintu returned her beer to their crates and converted the freezer in her buka into a bloody cold-room. In no time at all every fridge and freezer in the village was crammed and they were fetching out pots and pans. Emergency barbecue ranges were set up in every yard. Firewood stacks were broken up, smoking kilns and charcoal grills fired up as columns of smoke began to rise from hundreds of yards in the village. The stream of heavy basins from the whale continued unrelentingly.

By noon the sun was furious and it was clear that the whale would not remain approachable much longer. Emergency butchers attacked its second flank. Households sat down to their third meal of the day, to make space for the newly-fried, smoked and salted slabs of meat. The pastor's wife carried a steaming steak into the Bible Room in search of her husband. That worthy was detained on his dining trolley by a plate that refused to, quite, empty. He was disciplined enough to stand up from a meal once he was full, and he was almost full. He wondered how many of his congregation would remember that the subject of that morning's ill-fated sermon had been gluttony. It was a subject that he had resisted for several Sundays in a row, despite the many omens that kept insinuating themselves into his subconscious, because he felt odd preaching against gluttony to a congregation that mostly looked like they were on a perpetual fast. – Especially with him being plus-sized from his mother's womb. He chewed slowly. 'You want more?' asked his wife, ripping at a chunk of meat herself. He knew that another mouthful would about fill him up, so he shook his head, but his wife (who did not pay much attention to his sermons either) put the fresh helping on his plate anyway, it being as good a place as any to store it. Through the window, he saw the maids scamper away with their empty pails.

He fought increasingly strong waves of drowsiness. But for the appearance of the whale – and his second lunch – he should have been on his pastoral visits around the village. Just then, his bed seemed a more attractive proposition. He began to rise and froze halfway, realising from the pain in his guts that he had miscalculated the robustness of his appetite. He decided that the best course of action was to walk off the food. Waterside was a small community and within fifteen minutes he was visiting with the normally fractious couple on Cemetery Road. They did not seem in need of pastoral care that afternoon. There was jollity and amity in the air and before the greetings were fully exchanged, the wife set before him a plate of stewed meat whose provenance he did not need to guess.

'My sister!' he protested, 'I'm full!' but she ladled on the chilli sauce over his objections, in the best African tradition, before returning to a Blackberry which had been pinging rudely for her attention. The brother sat at the other end of the room, applying himself diligently to his own plate, and what a plate it was – piled high with a generosity that would (in normal times) betoken marital bliss. The entire living room was suffused with the aroma of fried tomatoes... and as he considered the meal the pastor saw how his wife's cooking was such a criminal waste of a good appetite. The luscious stew before him was the perfect accompaniment to the whale meat. He speared a sliver of meat, impaling with it an onion ring and a mushroom button, hating the way his tongue escaped his lips with a will of its own, sinuously mimicking the motions of his fork. He chewed, slowly, noticing that the rancid after-taste was totally drowned in the delectable flavours.

An hour later, he felt able to leave the table but he made no pretence to any more pastoral visits. Instead he set off, carefully, for home and bed. An increasingly painful cramp forced him to detour through the chemist, where he found a long, unhappy queue of villagers waiting outside a 'Gone to Lunch' notice. It was quite unseemly to be seen on what was so clearly a queue of the gluttonous for antacids and laxatives and he was tempted to return more discreetly under the cover of night, but the cramp was now so fierce that it took all his willpower to retain the erect posture that preserved the dignity of his white collar. He joined the queue as Agidi doubled over and vomited a slurry of beer and barely-chewed morsels of meat into the gutter. There was a chorus of 'sorrys', to which the pastor contributed grudgingly: the drinking of beers on Sundays being one of his Eight Deadly Sins. Orisi broke away from the queue with swift, mincing steps and rapped on the door of chemist's residence next door. The chubby, good-natured chemist let him use the toilet – and seeing the desperate queue before his shop, decided to reopen early. He took his interrupted lunch in a plastic bowl and walked across to the shop.

On the queue, Bintu began to retch. This second incident recalled the story of Jonah and the whale to the pastor's mind. He realised that he may have – inadvertently – thrown down a gauntlet

46

that God had picked it up. He was suddenly very scared. What if – like the manna of yore – all their stored meat turned out to be poisonous? What if the whole village was going to vomit up the whale in a punitive rewriting of the Jonah story? He began to pray then, for forgiveness for his effrontery, for his cowardice, and for the weakness of his fellow Watersiders.

By the time it was his turn to share his symptoms in the chemist's private confessional, the shop had run out of laxatives. A messenger on motorbike was dispatched to a Bushemina pharmacy thirty minutes away and the pastor decided to wait. Five minutes of small-talk passed and the chemist's fidgeting grew more and more spastic until he gave up on the strictures of propriety and opened his bowl, liberating a stupefying aroma of kitchens into the antiseptic air of the drug store. Inviting the pastor to join, he resumed his whale meat lunch with a gusto that Dego thought curious, considering the possibility of food poisoning that must surely have crossed the mind of any medical professional seeing the number of casualties seeking medication after the same meal. When Dego shared his fears, the chemist glanced around confidentially and showed the pastor an empty bottle of laxative. 'We fat people know the secret,' he whispered, 'I will enjoy the meat, but it won't stay inside! If I don't bring it up I will bring it down!' He laughed and pushed the bowl across the small table, 'Eat, it's still hot. My messenger will soon bring your own medicine.'

Dego was painfully full, but it was also true that his mouth was still filling up with saliva. The problem was that the chemist had had the brainwave to barbecue the whale with garlicked suya sauce. The pastor was curious about the taste of whale suya generously garlanded by slices of red peppers and coated with crunchy groundnut paste... plus... was that a hint of *utazi* in the air? Adding utazi to suya sauce was pure genius! Yet, his curiosity was throttled by the physical pain twisting like a dagger in his guts, and the rolling waves of nausea that threatened to spray vomitus over the antimalarials on the desk counter. He also took exception to being lumped in a weight category with the obese chemist. 'Fat' was not a word he associated with himself. So he shook his head firmly. The chemist shrugged, burped, and excusing himself, waddled to the loo.

Pastor Dego shut his eyes and began to pray. He massaged his painful stomach, using it as a point of contact with every constipated gut in Waterside. He took captive the Prince of Gluttony, cast him down in the name of Jesus, and bound him in chains of Self Restraint. He prayed against the lust that entered in through the eye gate – and the greedy conduit of the nose. He shackled Desire to Righteousness. He neutralised the magnetism of piri-piri chicken, suyaed whale and the particularly diabolical combination of moin-moin and soaked gari. Errant visions were now running amok in his mind and he rebuked the deliciously satanic okporoko fish that swam the red seas of banga soup. He came against the principalities of marine spirits who had sent the snare of the whale to break up his service and ensnare his parish. He prayed against the slavering serpent of the tongue. He manacled the Pied Piper of Alcohol. He railed against mouths that hungered beyond the needs of sustenance. He cursed guts that distended like elastic bags... guts should be finite and firm, should fill up like steel petrol tanks, and spill over, and say *no more!* He prayed and... *God...* he prayed!

Then he opened his eyes and the plate was still there. He sighed. He had really hoped for a miracle. He reached for the suyaed whale, thinking, despairingly, that he was lost.

THE GHOST OF SANI ABACHA

*I*s *this it?'* I asked the French Ambassador and he gaped at me through half-inch-thick glasses. He was clearly about to say something diplomatic and quite beside the point so I turned away from him and walked off, looking for someone without that *Gimme-Contract* glaze to the eyes. That was how I saw you. You stuck out in that party of ministers and hangers-on, with your necktie gathering your oversized collar behind its knot like a noose securing a sack of beans. You looked quite the objective journalist. Not that put out by my billowing bedspread. Hungry all right, but not the brown envelope type of reporter. There was something reticent about the cunning in your eyes. You seemed the type that won't print everything you overhear today in to-morrow's edition – perhaps because you were saving the real-ly salacious stuff for your book. But I really don't give a damn when – or what – you print, you understand? If I can just get a straight answer to my bloody question: *'Is this it?'*

Take away five years and I'm standing in this cursed hall, a waiter. You won't believe it, would you? To see me now – or to read my CV. That was the PR company, airbrushing out the bits that didn't sit well with the profile of senate president. Take five years and three days away and I was getting the slap that changed my life. I can still feel its sting all right, on this right cheek. Never saw a southpaw slapper before. Never saw one since, either. She was easily the most beautiful woman in this hall that night, and she had just received a bribe that she was keen to salt away in her suite up on the twenty-first floor. I was the waiter serving her table and she had me carry the bag.

It wasn't one of those outsized *Ghana-mus'-go* bags. The bribe was in dollars you see, so the bag, though the weight of a rural health centre (or six days' ministerial shopping at Harrods) was just a little bigger than an overnight bag. I hauled it and followed her towards the elevator. It was sixty metres away from the table where her American briber from the oil company simpered into his goblet of rosé. I had seen the flash of currency when she inspected the bag, as I sauced her peppered breast of chicken. I could have retired on that bag on my shoulder, but I was not tempted in the least. She was the wife of the minister for oil and steel, you see, and had arrived in a convoy of black limousines. Her black-suited protectors were just a scream away. Her husband may have been as scrawny and as wattled as a cockerel, but her security detail was no impotent joke. All I hoped for was a tip.

Yet, that would not have been enough to save my life.

She slapped me in the elevator. The temptation of the money had been easy to overcome. Her body was a different thing altogether. Was it the stun of her perfume? Or the bewilderment provoked by her beauty? Was it the hunger in my stomach coalescing with a madness in my groin? Or was it the way she stood with her back to me – and the curious muscles with which she began to tremble her mounds between the eleventh and the sixteenth floors? That was curious, will you not admit? Any other minister's wife forced to stand with a minion in an elevator would stand shoulder-to-shoulder. She would not turn fully away, leaving her backside to the unprotected glare of a waiter. And emphatically, she would not agitate them so. So I grabbed at them.

It was just a brief grab, you understand. I was not altogether mad; not then. And the way I figured it, I was owing Dabo Shogunle a few thousand naira that I could not pay, so I was dead already. Every three or so weeks a Dabo debtor was found in the gutters of Animashaun Street. There was nothing the police could do about it. (Some of the dead were policemen anyway.) I did not see that the black-suits downstairs could punish much worse than Dabo's boys. So I figured: grab her arse and die and go to Heaven. That was win-win in my book. So I grabbed her briefly, and she turned around, and slapped me hard.

And then she turned her backside back to me again.

That was the puzzling thing, you understand. The turning of her backside back to me again between the sixteenth floor where she dispensed the slap and the twenty-first where the door sighed open and the more conditioned air chilled the sudden sweat beading my face. She stepped out and walked, eventfully, down the corridor without a word to me. So I had five seconds to decide, as the doors tensed: whether to leave her bag on the floor outside the elevator and try to escape with my life, or whether to… then the doors began to close and I jumped through, and followed her down the corridor.

That was how I changed my life. Had the doors given me another moment to think it through, I would have made the more rational decision, and possibly ended up in jail. As it was, that same night, I was bedding the wife of the minister for oil and steel. I was her toy-boy for quite a few years. And every now and again she still gives me a call, (although I am far too busy these days, and far friendlier with her husband, to *fully* resume our old shenanigans). I had more *balls* than her husband; that was what she said to me, that first night. More *balls* than the minister for *steel*. How do you like that?

That was the night I first asked myself this question. As I rolled off her, as I stood in that falling elevator, with shrunken balls and pockets swollen with more American dollars in tips than any bag-carrying waiter dared dream, I asked myself,

'Is this it?'

There was a rank odour under the expensive perfume anyway. And she gabbled and slobbered in the grip of orgiastic joys. And if I entered Heaven at all, it was on the turntable of a revolving door. So I maybe went to Heaven, but I was in and out in three seconds flat, and here I was back in waiter's livery descending to my table-ten-to-twenty beat, where the American briber was waiting, bleary with rosé.

'Is this all there is to it?'

Her money was enough to pay off Shogunle, anyway. I resigned of course. They all said I was mad, but I resigned immediately.

I'd sexed the wife of the minister for oil and steel, so I couldn't wait tables any more. Over the next week I ate every dish on the hotel's menu. As a waiter, I had served them all, on an empty stomach, from duck to rump of lamb, from buttered salmon to lobster, swallowing frustrated gobbets of saliva as I drank down aromas and served the food to the diamond-ringed fingers of the rich. Now I resigned and returned night after night, dressing my raging appetite in a polyester suit, washing down double portions of the restaurant's dishes with goblets of wine. And after every dish, as I stared queasily at the plates of shattered bones and greasy cutlery (like the broken mangroves and slicked wastelands of the oil delta) I wondered,

Is this really it?

I think I think too much. I should never have read philosophy in school. All that Kantian junk and Hobbesian hobblings acquired by mimeograph from libraries full of empty shelves. Forty years ago, a clutch of indifferent GCEs would have secured me a respectable berth in the managerial cadre of the Civil Service; but that's life for you – I had come out with a B.A. Philosophy and had been lucky to find a waiter's apron. And I was days away from a gutter on Animashaun Street before I was lucky enough to grab the butt of the right minister's wife.

I was a few dollars away from broke as well, when she sent her car for me again. I sent the stunned driver away. She probably thought, *What balls!* again. (Although it was actually my moral scrupling with the last levees of the matrimonial taboo. That; and the smell I couldn't get out of my nostrils. Still, she must have thought, *What balls!*)

So she came herself, and… well, it was not just the perfume and the dollars; you understand? She had the kind of face you had to look away from, to continue to say No to. I did not look away. Yet, as I came, again and again, in that twenty-first floor hotel room, that revolving door into Heaven spun faster and faster, until the exercise barely relieved the fetor of my life. And I realised that the true Heaven on earth was located on the twenty-*fifth* floor, in the presidential suite where I had occasionally served the late General Sani Abacha.

Let me tell you about the presidential suite. If I finally get to Heaven and it is not like the presidential suite, I am coming straight back down. You cannot walk fast in those rooms. Your eyes are caught by a hundred and twelve luxurious things. The air itself is heavy with luxury and you are wading through the most sumptuous atmosphere, like a man wades through water... In my waiter days, when I knelt to set down the champagne buckets with which the damsels bathed the general (each rare champagne, the weight of a hundred thousand meningitis vaccines), once my knees touched that carpet, they did not want to rise again. Now, can you imagine *lying* on those beds?

But you can only imagine it, of course. In this country, money can only take you so far. After that, you need *power*. The general, Sani Abacha died here, you know, I saw this for myself. You should not believe the official line about him dying at home in Aso Rock. You see, it was passé for a dictator-president to die in a hotel room, however grand, so we bundled him up in a Persian rug, stashed him in the boot of a Peugeot 504 (to throw you journalists off the scent), and smuggled him back into his bed in the presidential residence. Since then, you cannot book this suite unless you are a foreign head of state – or a *very*, very senior member of government. And every time I dropped down the elevator, I remembered how the true Heaven on earth can only be found on that twenty-fifth floor, in that presidential suite. Slowly, that became my obsession: to *enter* that Heaven.

You see how simple it was? That seed of my ambition? I had never before thought myself a politician. But one night I was sitting there in the aftermath, smiling through cigarette smoke and thinking, *what a smell!* She was businesslike as usual, post-sex; bridling at the thought of habitually laying a layabout. 'So what do you want to do with yourself?' she asked.

'I was thinking of politics,' I replied.

It was not hers to give, but her husband was minister for oil and steel, and probably the second biggest shot in the party. The diabolic incongruities of matrimony were adumbrated in this farce: that in due course he leaned, in my behalf, on the party candidate for the House of Representatives in Agamba East, who withdrew for family reasons. I took over his nomination. It was a one-issue campaign: they wanted a water reservoir. I promised it. I won.

Of course every other candidate had promised it as well, but my own election was a matter of course – I was the candidate of the government party, which usually won every election. Even if I grew horns and a goatee, and bleated through my campaign speeches – like most of my fellow party candidates – my election was guaranteed.

I proved a natural, too. I went further and faster than those that had been at this all their lives. I think it was the way I said the first thing that came to my mind. I did not have a Sycophancy Filter, and they had never seen that sort of thing before: a politician that said the first thing that came to his mind. Yet, the contractors feared my lip and I was always the first to be *settled*. But because I talked the talk, my constituency loved me – at first.

That first year was great. We were the most productive Assembly in recent memory, passing three Acts within the first few weeks of session. (Our first Act was an anti-corruption law to insulate us from temptation: we doubled our wages, becoming the best paid legislators in the world.) After that we somewhat ran out of steam – till *Ghana-mus'-go* bags began to arrive in our chalets. Energised, we pushed through the Privatisation Act that transferred a few national universities to the private sector. I bought a Grand Cherokee, which I drove discreetly in the small hours. It was a fine car, but... (look, a conscience is a terrible thing. Could never forget those years of studying mimeographs on Nkrumah's philosophy in empty university libraries... so) I drove around in my Grand-*one-million-library-books*-Cherokee, asking myself,

'Is this it?'

I slugged away at the job, and the currency bags continued to arrive. There was a whooping cough epidemic, children dying in thousands from fake vaccines. I got myself appointed to the Probe Committee (a coup, considering the competition). We approved federal budgets, retaining our share of the appropriation at the legislators' quarters. I built my Abuja mansion. The swimming pool was to die for – though I never swam it. Felt like I was swimming in Agamba's water reservoir, it did. There's also an alabaster cupid in my garden, a placatory water feature gifted by the vaccine supplier whom I had drilled mercilessly on the Whooping Cough Committee. By day, the pissing of that white statue was all there was to hear in my quiet garden, but at night my house became a Babel, with all that coughing and whooping from the statue in the garden. Back then, it was a relief to get a call from the wife of the minister.

Unfortunately, by the time the general elections came around again Agamba was still lacking a water reservoir. Of course, the government party had no problem "re-electing" unpopular candidates, but I was a man of principle. Besides, I didn't like being stoned at rallies. And, in any case, I had not started this journey just to end up in a mansion where I couldn't even get a good night's sleep. I had to focus on the Heaven on the twenty-fifth floor – and an ordinary Rep could not presume to book the presidential suite.

I had to find another constituency and move upstairs into the Senate, and land myself the chairmanship of a big committee. Our minister had retained his portfolio, and his wife, her attraction to me. Yet, I was now wining and dining with her husband, and... well, I am a man of conscience, but she brushed aside my compunctions contemptuously. 'Just leave that matter! Do you know how a professor of history like him became minister for *oil and steel?*' I thought it was more polite to shake my head, 'I see! Do you know why he is still minister even though a whole *Nigeria* has been importing *petrol* forever? Look, this is a government by *kongo*. The day I stop sharing my own is the day he starts looking for another job!'

So, one night, through cigar smoke, I discussed my political future. I had just reached the minimum age for the Senate. In due course, I became the youngest senator in the Federal Republic. I was still in the middle of the electoral euphoria, when the bonus prize dropped into my lap. I did not even have to lobby for it. It was the outworking of an inexorable political horse-trading formula made in Heaven to take me there. I am not much of a mathematician, but it works somewhat like this:

$$Power \mp negotiation = \{6\ GZ\ (Z1 + P)\ (Z2 + VP)$$
$$(Z3 + S)\ (Z4 + DS)\ (Z5 + SP)\ (Z6 + DSP)\} / Nigeria$$

In plain English, the major political offices were allotted on the basis of Nigeria's six geo-political zones. Zone one had provided the president, zone two the vice president, zone three the speaker, and so forth... therefore my zone six was entitled to produce the senate president.

There are five other states in my zone, all of which had previously produced a principal officer. It was my state's turn at the trough. Now, there were only two senators from my state and the senior senator (a pregnant professor of economics on her third term in the House) was so clearly the right choice that she went prematurely into labour at the excitement of her prospective selection. Her supporters were in an uproar in the floor of the senate, but she was having her baby abroad (for the citizenship, you understand) and the other senators couldn't wait, so they gave it to me.

This victory party was a week in the planning, but the very first thing I booked was my presidential suite. I gave hard thought to the issue of Heaven on earth and contacted the agency that supplied Sani Abacha's foreign prostitutes. They had a glossy brochure, but three days passed and I could not even settle on a short-list of a dozen girls, so I left the choice to them. I wanted Orientals, Europeans, Latinas – the works... but I drew the line at Indian girls. I am superstitious that way. They had been the death of Sani Abacha, and my own session in Heaven was not going to send me to an early grave.

I am the guest of honour, but I took my time to come downstairs. This is the meaning of power: the ability to keep hundreds of very important people waiting on your whim. The dead general was a dab hand at it. Who could ever forget the traditional ruler who came prospecting for a contract and ended up pounding yam for the general? It was the thought of these waiting minions that excited me most, as I rode those foreign prostitutes. Once again, the thoughts of windowless, teacherless classrooms, waterless taps and powerless electric cables attempted to torment me; but in this room, in this Heaven, I am suddenly possessed by a begoggled demon, I am ridden by Abacha, and suddenly, it is Nigeria herself, the spoils of a war of military conquest, waiting for my thrust. Yes, the sumptuousness of this hotel is an ache in the wound. Yes, this oasis of plenty, rolled out like a mat in four directions, will electrify factories, water abattoirs, clothe pupils... so what? Jungles have lions and jungles have deer, and I would rather be senate president than slave.

The foreign prostitutes were worth their flight expenses. I climbed from climax to climax until, at last, I was past the seventh Heaven. Then I rose from the last of those ravished imperialists. I, illiterate soldier, begoggled idiot, have done what the Awolowos and the Azikiwes could not do. I have conquered them all from America to rampant Spain, from France to broken Britain. They lay vanquished upon my carpets, on my beds, on my couches. And I am standing, still, not like Abacha who was waterlooed between Viagra and quisling India.

And this is the thing about the presidential suite: the bedspreads here are even more luxurious than my lace agbada. I toga myself like a Roman emperor and descend to my victory party. This is my moment. After five years of agonising, despite the wailing banshees of the babies on my conscience, I'd far rather be senate president than waiter. That leaves just one question agitating my mind. Waiter, give me that champagne flute. And you, that salmon cracker. Damn. There goes my toga. Now I look as ridiculous as a potbelly on a general. But, here's the question I have for you, hungry journalist,

'Is this it then? Is this what it is all about?'

BILLY GOAT

Sometimes he wondered if he really knew Sara after all. In his little village of Sandia, Gwarimpa was getting all the wrong signals from his wife of six months. She was no longer as responsive to the playful palm he laid on her shoulder of the evening. It took that much more to say what he wanted... and even then she managed not to understand. In that young house of his matrimony, much now displeased Gwarimpa, not least of all the pungent smell of the billy goat they were fattening in the yard as a gift for his mother-in-law's sixtieth birthday.

That day he returned a day early from his monthly field trip to the Langa Valley to find his bed better-dressed than it had ever been before. A succulent beef stew whose aroma put all the previous meals of his marriage to shame simmered on the stove. A heady incense also hung in the bedroom air, staying the rank smell of billy goat from the perimeters of that romantic space. Of his wife he found no trace. He enquired of her from a little neighbour; she had dashed to the chemist across the square on a little errand.

Gwarimpa sat on his bed to wait, knowing that silent dread that was the curse of spouses who returned home inconveniently. He did not wait too long before Harki rode up, approaching by the low road rather than the more public high, propping his bicycle up against the mud wall, and knocking gingerly. Getting no response, he entered confidently only to stand flummoxed at the sight of Gwarimpa in full glower.

'You're welcome,' grated Gwarimpa, whose hands were sweaty and cold, whose voice was croaky and hoarse.

'As you are, welcome,' replied Harki, not very coherently, sporting a grey vest that showed off his magnificent biceps, biceps that seemed to wilt visibly as he took a step backwards.

'Sit down,' said Gwarimpa sarcastically.

'Oh, I won't be staying, long, at all, I was just passing by, bye…' and he was gone. Gone so fast he forgot his bike on the wall, a bike that Sara, walking in the moment he left, could hardly have missed.

She entered singing, '*Darl-ing, darl-ing*,' in a song that harked back to their days of courtship, a song that broke abruptly when she saw her husband.

'You're welcome,' grated Gwarimpa.

'Da- darling? You're back? You're back!'

'So I am I suddenly your "*darl-ing*", again? When I left yesterday, it was *Gwari* this, *Gwari* that…'

'Don't be silly Gwari, you are always my darling.'

'And why is this house looking so clean? And smelling so nice? And why is the meat in the pot smelling so sweet? And what is Harki's bicycle doing outside the house? And what was it that you went to the chemist to buy?'

At the last query, a delicate arm tensed on the purse in the armpit but Sara laughed with an irritation that came naturally to spouses in her situation. 'You should hear how silly you sound, Gwari? Why is the house so clean! And smelling so nice! Any man would come home and buy his wife a gift for this but no, not you.' With that she flounced out to the yard.

He sat for a moment, reflecting on the Silliness Quotient of his words. Yet, the handlebar that poked adulterously through the window into the room and the Guilt Quotient of Harki's shifty eyes intruded on his emollient reflections and he stalked after her into the yard – which was how he saw her fling something from her purse towards the overflowing bin, a package too small for his eyes to conclusively identify at that distance, but which looked suspiciously like a packet of condoms. He sprinted wordlessly for it. She cried, 'Gwarimpa!' and locked him into an embrace.

'Let me go, you harlot!'

'Me? You call me a harlot? For what!'

'Let me go, and I'll show you what for!'

But the billy goat rooting in the vicinity of the bin had also been attracted by the bright colours of the thing. With the unbelievable avarice native to his kind, he ate first, leaving regrets for later, which regrets he had in plenty in the way of the thumps and kicks and curses that followed on the eating of the indifferent snack.

'My mother's goat! Why are you kicking my mother's goat?'

'He's not yet her goat,' he panted, returning to the kitchen. By the time he emerged with the gutting knife, between the screams of wife and the bleats of desperate goat, a brood of neighbours had been procured. They saw the knife and cluck-clucked regretfully from a safe circle of appeasement.

'He wants to kill me!' she screeched, casting a wider net for a more courageous circle of neighbours. 'He's killing me over a packet of chewing gum!'

'I'm killing my own goat,' he told her – and potential mediators, 'and when I find the evidence I am looking for, your mother can have you instead of a greedy goat.'

She then began to wail, and in the ensuing melee, a sufficiently bold neighbour separated Gwarimpa from his knife. Spooked by the furore, the goat tried to bolt but the frustrated husband seized his horns and didn't let go – until the mother-in-law arrived. She was a successful trader, a short, matronly type who was partial to fiery goat-meat-stew. 'My son,' she remonstrated, 'this is not like you, what seems to be the matter?'

'Ask your daughter!'

'He wants to kill the goat we bought for your birthday!'

'I will buy you another,' he said, 'this one has eaten evidence, which I will produce from his stomach.'

'Evidence of what, my son?'

'Of harlotry, Mama.'

At the vile word his mother-in-law gasped and staggered into the crowd. A chair was produced in the nick of time and she fell heavily into it. When she had collected her faculties she expressed a great fascination for the prodigious height and particular colouration of the billy goat.

'I will give you his skin, and his meat,' promised Gwarimpa.

'My freezer is full,' she replied, 'I want his kids, that's what I want. I've been looking for this type to breed, this goat will father...'

'...am I hearing the voice of a mother here, or the voice of a mother-in-law?'

She rose to her full, indignant height, raising her trading voice to make up the deficit. 'Look into my eyes!'

Which he did, resentfully.

'I am a woman of the world,' she charged angrily, 'I have bought and sold lace from Malumfashi to Biu. There is no scam that dupes and 419ners have not tried on me. None has succeeded. Do you trust me?'

'Yes,' he lied grudgingly.

'I am not a child! You see this slipper on my foot? That's the cane I used to raise my daughter – and she's not yet too big for me – If there's any truth in what you say. I said: do you trust me?'

'Yes,' he grudged, less hypocritically.

'Then leave this to me. I'll get to the root of it,' she paused, and continued less angrily, 'look, Sara is not my daughter more than you are my son, you hear? Go and ask about me. If there is any truth in that "har-" word, I will find it.'

'Mama, there's no truth in it, I swear...'

'Shut up, Sara!' rebuked her mother angrily, 'this is between me and my son,' a warmth spread in the guts of the son as she turned to him. 'What is this evidence that is supposed to be inside my goat's stomach?'

'Condoms,' said Gwarimpa poisonously.

'*Condoms?*' she marvelled, 'inside a goat?'

'Imagine that nonsense!' cried Sara, 'What am I...'

'Shut up, Sara!' swore her mother, and at that moment it was hard to believe that the husband was not in fact more her son than the wife her daughter. She turned to Gwarimpa. She sighed, 'My son, what makes you think there are condoms inside my goat?'

He wondered whether to remind her that it was not yet, in fact, *her* goat; but – between *mother and son* – such quibbling over pronouns seemed excessively pedantic. So he tamely narrated the suspicious circumstances he encountered on his return.

'Where is this bicycle?' she asked severely.

He pointed a finger, a finger that faltered as it indicated, unavailingly, a largish region of wall. Someone had clearly taken advantage of the earlier confusion to remove the bicycle. 'It has gone...' he said, lamely.

'God knows I didn't see any bicycle,' sniffed his wife.

'Shut up, Sara,' said her mother, less severely. They then went on a tour of the house. The heady perfume had since dissipated, the stew was burnt, and although the bed was still impeccably made, Gwarimpa sensed the ebb of legitimacy from his case. 'You realise how silly all this is looking,' the mother said quietly.

'There are condoms in that goat,' he insisted stubbornly, 'and I will prove it!' and with that he drew a machete from a pail of implements and headed back to the yard.

'I am a woman of experience,' she reminded him, 'bring my goat to my house, I will get to the root of this once and for all.'

***

They adjourned to her house, losing the disappointed neighbours in the process. Hours passed. The mother, the couple, and the billy goat reassembled at a privy in the bottom of the yard where the goat was fed choice lettuce doused in purgative. A seeming age passed before the spluttering started from the rear of the animal, producing copious dung, and a pong of such fetor that only the inhuman steel of jealousy riveted the husband to the spot. The wife fled to the comfort of a bed in her mother's house, on which she sobbed, bemoaning the inconstancy of a husband's trust. The mother-in-law sat on the stool of her self-less vocation, in that privy in the garden, seemingly untroubled by the stench, as she palpated pans and pans of runny dung before dumping them down the pit latrine. Over her shoulder, Gwarimpa watched beadily, until she shook her head sorrowfully and sighed. 'Lack of trust, my son, is a terrible thing.'

He grunted stubbornly and kept up the watch.

After twenty crowded minutes in a small stall designed – and ventilated – for the brief exertions of one person, the sitting woman was drenched in sweat. She asked for a drink of water which the man was powerfully tempted to refuse, but the conditioning of obedience was a difficult thing to override. Besides he could not deny the extreme privations she was enduring on his behalf. He hurried to the house, barely arriving there when a victorious shout issued from the garden shed. He ran back without the water, his wife at his heels.

The mother-in-law was standing at the door of the latrine, pan in hand. Her face was severe, although the target of the severity, whether unfaithful wife or untrusting husband, was unclear. 'I have found it.'

'Is it...?' began Sara in a small voice, which disappeared in a sniff.

'What is it, Mama?' he demanded, 'It's condom, not so?'

She remained silent.

'What is it?' urged Sara, anxiously, 'Look at it with the eyes of a mother.'

Finally, the older woman broke her crusty silence. 'A packet of chewing gum!' she said coldly, 'you owe your wife an apology, Gwarimpa.'

'Let me see!' he demanded, incredulously.

Her jaw dropped slowly, succumbing to the gravity of a venerable Sandia taboo. She stepped up to him, malodorously magnificent in fury, pan held high with ambiguous intent. 'You want to reduce me to your level?' her voice dripped with a disgust more odious than the stuff all over her hands and clothes. '*You don't trust me? You think I will lie? For what?* It is not enough for you to drag me through this… this… this… goat shit!'

'It's not that.'

'Then what is it, exactly?'

He could not say what it was, exactly.

'I will show you the chewing gum packet,' she said, 'but you must never call me "Mama" again! I won't be a "Mama-for-nothing!"'

He gripped the whorled horn of the billy goat, trying to hold on to the sight of the bike on the wall, the guilt in Harki's eyes, the scent of the perfumed bedroom air – all those legitimate bastions of his rage, bastions which were now as slippery as eels in a greased pan. He said something in a hollow voice, but there was a hot, liquid din in his inner ears, and when he had repeated it, he was still unsure what it was he had said exactly. She paused, as though assessing the sincerity of his words; moments passed during which it was uncertain whether she would show the contents of the pan and take away her motherhood of him, then she poured the pan of shit ceremonially down the latrine.

'I told him!' Sara wept, twining in the agony of his public slander of her reputation, and her private vindication of it; but her mother lived in a Sandia suburb and there were no horrified neighbours to lament her abused innocence. 'I told him!'

'Sara.' That single word from a tired mother, and the daughter turned and flounced for the house.

Gwarimpa let out his breath slowly. His stomach heaved, ploughed by the purgative of self-loathing. He wished he had killed the goat on his terms, even if he had found nothing; he would far rather have been smeared with that blood than this shit. He did not know what to do now, but he could not do nothing forever, so he put one foot in front of the other. The mother-in-law released her hard-won goat to graze, which goat did not need the slap on the rump to bolt from the scene of his humiliation. Gwarimpa stopped a dozen paces away and turned to the woman. Her face was drawn, perhaps from her stench, perhaps from the exertions of the tumultuous hours. '*And if you looked at it with the eyes of a mother-in-law,*' he asked softly, '*what would you have seen?*'

She issued a long-suffering sigh, and he realised that it was not so much that he did not really know his Sara, as that he had not known, at all, this loam from which she sprang; she said now, 'How many times must I tell you? I am not your mother-in-law, I'm your mother.'

ORANGE CRUSH

I still remember the taste of the Maitama orange, oddly enough. Nine years have passed since I ate it on a bus stop bench on seventeenth August, 1999. I also remember the lonely night that led me there. And the fruit seller that hawked barefoot, her slippers slung like strange ornaments around her neck. I had bought a single fruit, out of boredom, and a habit for oranges, and we barely talked as she peeled and quartered it, the way I always ate my oranges. Her fingers were lithe and quick, going like clever mechanical things, and her carving of my fruit was performance art. It must have been a good day for her, for she waved away my money, and then she left.

The stop was lonely once again. I ate the first quarter as she walked away, balancing the tray of fruit upon her head. A passing cyclist warned that there'd be no more buses along that night, and I ate the rest as I walked the fifteen minutes home, where I found a torch with which I retraced my steps, with a pounding heart.

(I am, by the way, a connoisseur of oranges, having savoured them from Kumaganum to Kaltungo. In Dadiya is an orchard of thin-skinned oranges that juiced quite well. The Numan crop in '84 was a memorable one – and the road into Shendam has fragrant groves on either side. In season, it is a sin to drive through without a tasting break... but every connoisseur dreams of the perfect fruit that will put every prior memory of excellent fruits in the shade… I retraced my steps with a pounding heart.)

I found three pips on the journey back, and there at the bus stop I found all eight pips from the first quarter. Two were neatly cut in half by the hawker's blade. Nine precious seeds, from which

I would later raise ten seedlings… and yet a decade was a long time to wait to taste, again, the most sublime orange of my life. The following evening I found a bike on which I haunted Maitama, pausing at the bus stop every now and then, from where I rode slow whorls around the neighbourhood. Yet, of the previous night's tray of oranges I found no trace; of that barefoot hawker, or the receding sight of her back, straightened into a graceful arabesque for balancing trays, I found no glimpse.

Ten precious, vegetative seedlings; guaranteed to replicate the Maitama orange. I raised them from pot to larger pot, nursing them – like the pets and children I did not have. Too soon it was time to let them out into the world. When they were three years old, I replanted them in the garden plot in my home village. It was the permanent home address, immune to my itinerant postings by the ministry. I bedded the plants in heavy loam, fifty yards from the foundations of my retirement bungalow, and built a shield of wire mesh around them. I found a herd boy to water them during that drought of '03, while I worked at the grain silos at my new post in Abak.

There is a balance of sugar and citric acid, of romance and bite, to the taste of the *Citrus sinensis*. Somewhere within the range of a hawker's barefoot trek from Maitama was a tree – or orchard – that had got it right. I have eaten one, two hundred thousand oranges before and since that night in August 1999 without finding another. And so I waited.

My seedlings grew, sprouting that spray of violently green leaves that tempted goats. Perhaps it was a similar mutation to the one that created the navel orange in that Brazilian monastery in 1820. I did not know. What I knew was that orangey heaven ingrained in my tongue on that Maitama night, the memory of which still filled my mouth — again and again — with springs of anticipation. I pruned and waited.

The next year a canny goat broke in, tangling his horns in the wire mesh for a feast of tender shoots. It was a tragedy that fell just short of catastrophe: when I visited home that Christmas, two ravaged plants were left. I built a wooden fence around those then, and watered them, composting and fertilising them as I savoured cuts from the curried goat. I waited.

My seedlings grew into saplings. The one was healthy, but the other never quite shook off the gnawing trauma of the goat's attack. I raked up and built watering basins around their trunks, fashioning, with my indulgent herd-boy-caretaker, a slow hose for the dry months. Then the sickly sapling succumbed to a rash of mealy bugs and died.

Years passed. My one surviving sapling grew into a tree. As it grew, the walls of my retirement bungalow rose as well, as my career at the agriculture ministry dribbled to an end. My tree grew a small canopy as I roofed my bungalow, and I built a chair in her shade. This was a reincarnation of the Maitama bus stop bench, on which I would re-enact a feast perfectly replicated from the flawless genetic memory locked within a seed. It was not long to wait, now.

For me, the taste of oranges is wired into my sense of ease. Pineapples can't cut it. Mangoes are an affront to my tongue… No other fruit comes close to that flooding ecstasy of orange's juice, nothing else approximates that crushing yieldedness of an orange's tumid flesh. And here was the perfect tree. I was soon to retire. Soon to spend the rest of my life as I spend my vacations: in her shade, paying out the fraying tether of life. In those nether years, I will eat her fruit, but she is yet the juvenile. So I sit in my chair in her shade and eat, adulterously, oranges from other trees, and wait.

Years passed. She grew a profusion of leaves. Soon, the aroma of blossoms spread, beckoning pollen from afar. Shed petals eddy in drifts around the legs of my chair, along the ripples from the surface roots of the iroko at the end of the garden. The first tiny bumps of fruit appear, dying that first year without growing beyond an inch or so across. I wait, and wait.

The waiting ends today. I have been three years away from my home village. My orange tree is an impressive presence now. I arrived home to find her greenery speckled gold with ripened fruit. Dusk has fallen as I hold the first fruit on the chair of my long patience. It is heavy for its size, clearly gravid with juice. I cut. Her flesh is soft, but firm. A delicate fragrance flirts with the nostrils, even before the taste buds engage (I am, as you know, a connoisseur). I have greyed somewhat, but the heart of the animal is ever red; even though I have been pensioned off, the tooth, the claws of desire drip a fiery red. I close my eyes and ravish the pulp, the juice of the encore of my long-lost Maitama orange, a decade deferred.

I swallow in awe.

Yet, I am the implacable connoisseur of sweet citrus. I can tell the age of the roots from the tang of her juice, her provenance from her savour. My taste buds are a church onto themselves. They do not kowtow to sentiments. They judge unerringly.

I open my eyes slowly. It is sweet – like hundreds and hundreds of oranges in my past – but it is *not* the Maitama orange. I eat all four quarters delicately, with the same mechanicalness with which I have eaten two, three hundred thousand oranges throughout my life. It will be better as the season waxes, I know this; as the fruit matures on the boughs. Besides, next season's fruit will be more flavoursome, richer... yet even as I console myself, I know the truth now. For though the heart of the animal is cannier than his tongue, it was clear that I knew my fruits far better than I knew myself. I had waited nine years, only to discover that I had fallen for the hawker, not her oranges.

B.O.

The professor was completing his field research into the local fetishes in the Delta region. He had spent six months in Waterside and had filled up dozens of tapes and notebooks; but because he held his interviews at Bintu's Buka there was always one more interviewee with something interesting to say. When his grant ran out he was unable to afford the fish soup and beer that lubricated his interviews, and the stream of villagers that had kept his project running finally petered out.

That bereft evening, he sat at his usual table in the corner, three feet away from that propitious hatch through which all food arrived. An earphone that snaked from a recording machine was plugged into his right ear and he transcribed his recordings steadily into his laptop, pausing the recorder from time to time to sip his tepid beer. This phase of his work was better done from his air-conditioned office at the university, still he remained in Waterside, telling himself that any problems with his research could more easily be corrected this way...

Yet, he did not fool himself.

From her corner behind the till, Bintu stared balefully. She was a thirty-eight-year-old divorcee who ordinarily did not take nonsense from anyone. Yet, the professor had been her most loyal customer for the better part of six months, faithful to her egusi, through stingy beef and stale pork. Eventually she seemed to make up her mind and rose. She walk-danced slowly across to the only customer left in her restaurant. 'You smell,' she told him without heat.

'Beg your pardon?'

'Are you surprise? A whole professor like you! I said you smell; but there's something I can do for you – if you will 'gree o. I know you book people!'

It was not often that Kisuje was rendered speechless, for he was a professor of anthropology, experienced in the rendition of the most insubstantial thought in reams of dense, cataleptic prose. It was not an uneventful speechlessness, though: he swallowed, drank his beer and relieved his ear of its phone as he tried to think behind, beneath and above this unprovoked act of pre-meditated heartlessness. He coughed eventually, 'I hardly know what to say to you.'

Then he snapped his laptop shut, rolling up its cables briskly.

She was not a beautiful woman, although it was also true that from her waist downwards he had never seen her match, any-where in the world. Had she noticed his lingering glances as she eddied to and fro? Was that it? Was his lingering over his meals that transparent then? He lived in the guest house on Arisa Road, but took all his meals here, held all his meetings here. Half his grant had gone steadily through her till, those past six months. Now that he was dry, down to the occasional dragged-out beer and meatless meals, did she think to drive him away then?

She pulled out a chair and sat, as he pushed back his chair and rose. He was now really angry, wishing he had put a choice abuse into his first response. It was too late to let fly the vitu-peration that had arrived belatedly, tripping now on his tongue. It would sound too much like an afterthought.

'I'm not driving you, o-' she began,

'I am not the one driving away your customers, if that's what you're thinking,' he said, heart pounding, 'It is your rotten soup.'

'Shame,' laughed Bintu, 'because I tell you that your body is smelling, you tell me that my soup is rotten. What kind of pro-fessor are you?'

'It's true,' he said angrily, 'for the last two days…'

'That's because of the freezer that spoiled. And you! You can't even tell me that my soup is not so nice unless I tell you your body is smelling? Get away from here. *Yeye* professor!'

She rose and walk-danced back to her place behind the till. He had secretly thrilled for the many vexes in the life of a restaurateur, which provoked so many of those violently kinetic walks, but was naturally beyond titillation, now that he was the umbrage that provoked it. He felt small, but could hardly have apologised to a woman who had just used him so ill. He walked away instead.

***

Yet, he could not return to the solace of his bed in Arisa Guest House. The freezer at Del Monte was working and he bought a can of Castel which he could not drink. After twenty minutes, he bought another one and took it back to Bintu's Buka. He could not apologise, he decided, but he could give her a beer colder than anything in her miserable freezer.

When he arrived, Okoti was eating. If it could be called that. He mined salt at the local works and when he stopped by for his usual dinners on his way home his appetite was usually too keen for petty niceties like mastication. 'Proessor!' he hailed briefly through a large mound of cassava shavings, as Kisuje walked past.

He did not like the sneer on her face as he put the can of Castel down before her. She ignored the peace offering, counting her lean takings for the day with a studious concentration that crinkled her nose. He focused on the twist of mist that rose from the can in the hot and humid interior of the restaurant. He took a swig from his own beer. She was breathing more stertorously than usual, and he remembered his alleged body odour. He turned to go.

That was when she put the plate of fried meat on the table between them. 'I don't wan-' he began,

'Is free of charge,' she replied. The sneer was less snide, somewhat.

'Is that?' heckled Okoti from the sidelines, 'what about my own share now?'

Okoti had paid for his food and left before they spoke again. When the last piece of meat was inches from his mouth she had snatched and eaten it, with a playfulness that he had not suspected all those months, dissolving into a paroxysm of laughter – at his shocked expression – and laughing until tears stood in her eyes and the bray ricocheted through the village. As he watched her crude abandon, he could not for the life of him imagine a woman farther from his live-in partner, the beautiful, intelligent Chantelle waiting for him in Lagos.

***

That night he lay naked in her bed as her herbs boiled. She had thrown off her top as the evening wore on, but it was a hot house and her brassiered bosom was not a sexual gesture, he did not think. Not with the brusqueness with which she had ordered him to strip, or the smothered giggle that had attended her casual glance thereafter. Her bosom had been heaving with repressed mirth as she had spread a mackintosh on the bed, and he was feeling more shrunken than usual as he lay there, wondering what – *in the name of God* – had come over him. Despite the heat of the small house, the coolness of the rubber on his skin and the outlandishness of his situation goosepimpled him through and through.

He told himself he was there for the sake of his science: how many times had he seen that pained, distracted expression in the eyes of an interviewee? His interviews usually started with such promise, and then ended with unexpected brusqueness. How much better his life would be if this odour problem was solved for good?

As her herbs boiled, the most offensive odour he had ever perceived permeated the house. It was so strong he found it hard to breath. It seemed illogical that the traditional cure for body odour could be a deep skin massage with a herb that smelled fouler than skunk. Yet the three feet that separated him from the chair on which his clothes were draped seemed like three miles. The gouged lino seemed like broken glass. Finally, he confessed the truth to himself: he did not have the willpower to get off that bed, even if there was a good chance of being decapitated.

Was this what they called the mid-life crisis?

When she entered the room with towel and bowl, the smell was strong enough to make him gag. He shut his eyes and waited. He flinched at the heat of the wet towel but gradually relaxed and began to... *enjoy* it. Her hands were strong and manly. She turned him over as though he were an emaciated side of mutton on her kitchen counter. As she kneaded the herbal tincture into his skin he seemed to lose his sense of smell, to gain a heightened euphoria. A distant part of his mind wondered if the herbs were hallucinogenic. Gradually, he lost his shrunken aspect, rising steadily, shamefacedly, until he was nodding headily, flushed with blood.

'*Yeye* thief,' she chuckled, slapping him aside playfully as she bore away the bowl of her toilets.

***

He had no way of knowing if her treatment worked. He never picked up his body odour himself. Back in Lagos, Chantelle had wordlessly kept him supplied with roll-ons and sprays, which he used reflexively. When they ran out in Waterside he had not thought to restock them. And he did not know how to go up to people who had never previously told him that he stank, to ask if he still smelt quite as bad as he did the week before. Yet, she had boasted of the five-day treatment that she had learnt from her grandmother, it was free-of-charge, and he had not need-ed much persuasion to spend that hour, for those consecutive nights, naked in her bed.

And yet, on the last night, as he struggled to pull on his clothes, which did not fit quite as snugly as they had an hour earlier, he knew the first pangs of humiliation. She had slapped his tentative hands away as usual and the numerous sites of the not-so-play-ful swats throbbed relentlessly. He pulled on his shoes grouch-ily and blundered to the bedroom door. He pulled it open and was halfway to the main door of her bungalow when he noticed that she was spooning helpings of banga into two plates on her elephant stool. It was a rare beast sighting: a Bintu-cooked meal for two. He stood helplessly in the middle of the room.

'Come and sit, now,' she said mockingly, 'let me quench the hunger that I know I can quench.'

He complied meekly, grudging eventually, 'This is better than your buka food.'

'Of course, now,' she laughed, 'What I cook for my husband must be sweeter than what I cook for the whole market,' He tensed instinctively, but it was impossible to chew her *kpomo* without relaxing, and he supposed he had misheard; or at any rate, that she was speaking figuratively, "husband" being a loose enough metaphor to fit a dinner guest. When he was done, she took away the plates, firmly rejecting his offers to help. She served a half of a grapefruit whose flesh looked like blood, which tasted like crossed orange and grapefruit.

As he ate his fill, he realised that he had been leading with the *sex*, while she was foiling with the *relationship*. Once again, he felt a mild flush of shame. Then he wondered how far down *this* road he could go, with his return to Chantelle overdue by a fortnight at least. As he followed this thought, he felt rather more guilty about the special banga meal for two, wondering if there was a way he could pay for it.

He was picking his teeth when she hit him with it. It came from the blues. One moment she was walk-dancing with a stack of plates for a shelf, the next she was there in front of him, with not an ameliorating grin in prospect. Indeed there was a little irritation in her voice – almost as though she thought: *fine, dick-head! since you won't* **propose**, *let's* **presume it**, *and move on to more important matters!* She was at her most serious, and she looked him right in the eye and dropped it on him: 'Look, let me say my own: I can't leave Waterside. You know that, not so?'

'What?'

'Because you men always want your wife to follow you, not so?'

'Em...'

'But me, I can't leave Waterside o. I've gone to Lagos before-before, and me I just didn't like it at all at all. This is my village, my business, my everything.'

'…yes, of course.'

'So me I don't mind to be village wife, o: when you finish carrying my bride-price, is here I will be waiting for you. I just want you to know, tha's all;' then she laughed uproariously, 'see his face! Like person wey see ghost!'

That same evening he packed his bags and settled his account with the blind hotelier at Arisa. He did not have enough ready cash to pay his bike rentals, so he went to the home of the bank clerk with his account book, where he signed and left his slip with a small 'dash', making an informal withdrawal which would be formalised on the morrow. Such were the benefits of the small town or big village... benefits that utterly palled as he marvelled at the enormity of the matrimonial trap he had just escaped.

Before dawn, without seeing her again, he was gone. It had taken the reverse proposal to snap him out of the rut that six months in Waterside had sucked him into. He had gone native in the most dangerous, insidious manner. It was that wretched culmination of things: a disreputable research project that was tearing his professional life into shreds, a professional life that was going to pieces anyway, an empty relationship that was eight years old that month. Too old to walk away from, too empty to formalise in marriage...

He travelled on an empty stomach and all the way on the seven-hour drive to Lagos he could not stop trembling. He had heard of stories of women like this. Enchantresses. They usually worked as cooks and restaurateurs, and when they found a man they wanted, all they had to do was slip the appropriate charm into his food. He groaned and leaned forward. *She had cooked all his meals for the past six months!* It was no wonder he had not wanted to return home when his project was done.

'You well so?' asked the conductor solicitously, 'if you wan' shit, we fit stop for the nex-'

'I'm fine,' he snapped.

Yet, he had not only eaten her food. He had actually spread himself naked on the slab of her bed! *She could have decapitated him at will!* Some Samson! Some Delilah! He remembered her kneading her herbs into his skin and felt her several slap points smart again, burning from shame this time. Only God knew the nature of the odorous herbs she had rubbed into every part of his anatomy. He groaned. He was hopelessly lost. Yet he was leaving wasn't he? Her charms could not have worked. Could they? Perhaps it was the *M* word that broke the spell. Despite the delectable *kpomo* of the night before, she wasn't as good a witch as she thought she was. He was fleeing... At the thought of the *kpomo,* his empty stomach rumbled greedily and he saw that the conductor was staring dubiously at him. 'Driver, be like say we go stop o, make this man no go shit for inside moto-'

'Don't stop anywhere!' he shouted, 'Go straight to Lagos!'

***

'Well, that's a surprise,' Chantelle said, turning down the volume on the TV's remote as he stepped through their door in their staff quarters in Lagos. The abruptness of his return did not seem to discomfit her. There was no strange car in the drive, no scrambling to the bathroom to pick up things. She just sat there in the easy chair in which he'd met her, swinging her reading glasses by a flexible arm, waiting until he came over, then extending her long neck for the kiss. 'There's some cottage pie in the fridge. Rather burnt I'm afraid.'

'That's fine, dear. You weren't expecting me, after all. I just...'

The phone rang, and she had to speak to her dean. It was a long call.

She *is* beautiful, he thought. What had got into him? He took a shower while he waited for her to finish her call, bathing long and hard, scrubbing away the memory of Bintu's hands, soaping away the contours of her kneading... unexpectedly, she came into the bathroom with a towel. 'Some dry cotton...' she began, 'oh-oh;' her eyebrow rose a notch.

'Thanks,' he said, a little embarrassed.

Stepping out, he kissed her again, but she was perfunctory, not responsive. It did not seem like six months. As he walked past, he noticed that her dressing table was clean. A small finger of alarm began to grow, to worm its way into his complacency. 'Is everything all right? Chantelle?'

She met his eyes coolly. 'Never better. And you, Kisuje?'

The full name pushed him a metre away from her. It was usually 'Kisu'. He sat down to dinner truculently. *Her dressing table was clean.* Usually, her dressing table was anything but. This evening everything was neatly packed away. Something was afoot. Suddenly he knew this with a reverse certainty that collapsed the placidity with which she accepted his maybe-weekly telephone calls into the logical affair. She came to the point as he put the first spoon of burnt pie in his mouth. 'I've been asked to direct our new Africa Centre in Dakar.'

'You're serious?' her face registered the inappropriateness of his comments and he scrambled, 'Chantelle! I'm so happy for you.'

'Thank you,' stiffly.

He chewed a salad leaf mechanically, unable to resist involuntary comparisons with his last supper in Waterside. *Director, Africa Centre.* It was a promotion that rocketed her six years ahead of expectation to what was potentially the pinnacle of an academic career. It was unthinkable to ask her not to accept it, just so they could share a bed every night. They would have to get used to a long-term long distance relationship. It sobered him. A six-month project in the bush was one thing. This… They ate in silence. There was little to add. He knew the blow-by-blow details of the two-year campaign, which he had privately thought impossible, which had now come to fruition. The only question was the several hundred miles between Lagos and Dakar.

'It's over Kisuje.'

His mouth dropped slowly open, and an excruciating wound bruised open in his heart. He had never expected anything so final. He stared at her, realising suddenly that it was pride, not ordinary love, that he felt for her. Pride that so lovely a being was his – not his to own and control of course, not Chantelle. Yet, he could absolutely appropriate segments of her, the exclusivity of their domesticity for instance, of their dinner table, their cocktail promenades, of the cloning occasions of couplehood… and despite the fact that the night before, he was stretched out naked under Bintu's kneading fingers, that pride was enough, by far, to stab him through with a pain he had not thought himself capable of feeling, those six months in Waterside.

'It's another man isn't it?' he was embarrassed by his ugly voice, by his unscientific and illogical words but he could not help himself, 'Is your dean going…'

'I don't need this childishness,' she said without heat. She rose and took her plate out into the porch, where she shared the remnants of her burnt pie with the neighbour's shameless dog.

***

An hour passed and his anger was adrift in despair. He put aside childish things. She was sleeping. The dog, having licked the plate clean, drowsed under the chair. He stood in the door and watched her for the twenty minutes until she woke, thinking on their eight years, on the fact that Chantelle, for all her feminist sophistication, would never have propositioned like Bintu. Or perhaps it was merely that she did not want him enough… Suddenly the chasm of Dakar appeared under him, swallowing everything his life had been for the last decade… he stood there in the doorway of the house they had shared for all of their years together, wondering if he ought to propose, if that would keep her, if keeping her would actually make him happy.

She rose and walked up to him, bearing her plate. She sniffed speculatively. 'You smell nice.'

He started, grinning helplessly. 'I ran out of roll-ons and sprays…'

'You still smell nice.'

'Thanks,' he put an arm around her waist. 'Friends?'

She studied his eyes briefly, he saw a truce there, but not surrender. She nodded, taking his arm from her waist, passing through into the house, 'but not lovers.'

***

Two days later, when her things started disappearing into the cardboard boxes, he broke down and proposed. They were sitting on the living room floor, wrapping up the glass chessmen, which he had bought for her with his last thirty euros of a Paris trip. 'Will you marry me?' he asked softly, laying his black king down before her white queen in a cheesy gesture.

She looked genuinely startled. 'You'll marry me just keep the chess set?'

'I'm serious, Chantelle.'

She laughed quietly. 'No you're not. You're looking at my legs, not my face.'

He looked up at her face. He was not smiling and she sobered up too. 'Listen Kisu, I'm glad you're being mature about this, but we don't need this, not now.'

'We've done eight years. Eight *good* years.'

'I lived with my parents sixteen years, and I still left them.'

'I'm not your father, Chantelle. I'm your-'

'Okay, okay, let's think beyond a wedding. So we get married tomorrow, what next?'

'We'll work it out. That's what families do.'

'How? I won't give up my Dakar job, Kisu. Never. And you don't speak French. You could never teach there.'

'Couples live apart as well... I could start a business... I am only twelve years shy of retirement anyway-'

'Let's be serious Kisu. And I don't believe in telephone marriages... okay, maybe for six months, but no more. Life is too short-' she broke off.

He was staring intensely at her, trying to convey the telepathic weight of his desperation. She sniffed ambiguously. She'd been catarrhal that morning, so he was unsure just what the sniffling portended, but he also sensed a capitulation in her mien. He was 'Kisu' again. With quiet fear, he took the leap and made the final sacrifice. It was the ultimate commitment she had been wanting, all the years of the relationship, with the pointed references to her "ticking body clock", 'I want to have children now, Chantelle. Not next year, *Now*.'

'That makes two of us, Kisu, but I'm sure now,' she swallowed and looked away, 'I don't want to have *your* children. I'm really sorry,' she hesitated, then added, putting a hand on his to soften the blow of the words, 'and, Kisy dear,'

'What?'

She met his eyes. She had the air of one that gave a goodbye gift – of honesty perhaps, 'You have to start using the roll-ons again.'

After that, they packed her things rather faster, with less nostalgia for glass chessmen and things.

A HISTORY OF HUMAN SERVITUDE

John Jeff could not drive and had never owned a tyre in his life. After thirty-one years' service as a steward in an Ikoyi mansion, he had retired without a pension, gratuity or final salary, so many had wondered how he ended up with his new 7-series BMW. Most evenings he sat in his limousine, listening to Celestine Ukwu CDs on the car's matchless stereo. It was parked under a dongoyaro whose branches sheltered his humble Waterside house. Idle villagers would sit on his bench, share his *kokori*, dance to his music, and then go away to spread the malicious rumours that his car was the payoff for a "419" scam, It was, of course, nothing like that. This is the brief story of his limousine.

My uncle, John Jeff, was no ordinary steward; he was the sort of 'steward' who did everything. Of course he shopped and cooked and pounded interminable mortars of yam – that went without saying, but he also mopped and scrubbed floors, polished windows, mowed grass and bathed the master's invalid father twice daily until his death at age ninety-seven. – And when his employers went abroad for their annual vacations he was loaned to neighbours as gardener, security man or whatever menial position was required to ensure that he did not laze about. He had been slapped and kicked in the line of duty – and on one unfortunate occasion, horse-whipped by a borrowed soldier on account of some money which turned out to have been 'taken' by the master's teenage son. Still, as John himself constantly pointed out, he was no ordinary houseboy: he wore a starched, green uniform, was employed by a big Lagos corporation, and was entitled to a pension after thirty years of service.

Ordinarily, John was a man of unmitigated spinelessness in his place of employment. He had lost his surname more than twenty years earlier when an irritated expatriate replaced the Okorodudu on his chit with the moniker, 'Jeff'. My father, the elder Okorodudu, did not speak to his brother for years after this slight to their ancestral pride. My worst childhood memory was of an early visit to the boys' quarters of the Ikoyi mansion where John Jeff lived. It was night and we were sharing a meal of yam pottage on the lino floor when the door snapped open without the formality of a knock; a short, angry woman stood there, stout torso wrapped in blue-striped housecoat. She was shaking in an apoplectic fit, which had clearly overcome her in the middle of a bath, for her half-washed face was missing a painted eyebrow. She wore a scowl that froze my blood, '*John!*' she screeched, '*did you or did you not empty the laundry basket?*'

'I empty her, Ma'am,' said my uncle. He had sprung to his feet, although his waist was locked in the subservient bow that made him appear shorter than his very short mistress. He spoke excellent English – until he came within earshot of his employers, when he seemed incapable of the flawless sentence.

'*So what are these?*' yelled the woman, flinging half-a-dozen garments on the floor. Some knotted panties uncurled their pale stains six inches from the rest of our dinner. I drew the aluminium plate away. Unfortunately, that action was enough to draw her attention. She stepped fully into the room. I was hypnotized by her browless eye, and her voice was the low snarl of a canine approaching cornered prey. 'And who are *you* looking at like that?' she asked menacingly, 'have you no home-training?'

'Sorry Ma'am,' said my uncle, yanking me unceremoniously to my feet by my ear. That assault was so utterly out of the blues, so completely out of character, that I stood there without protest. (Not that there was much else a ten-year-old boy could have done in the circumstances.) 'Bomboy, say "sorry"!' he ordered, and I must have still been in shock at the pain radiating from my ear, because I did. 'Greet!' he ordered, which I did as well. She stood there another moment, weighing apology and greetings for sincerity, before returning wordlessly to her ablutions in the main house. Without meeting my eyes, my uncle gathered up the clothes and left for the laundry beside the kitchen. I was gone before he returned, abandoning our half-eaten meal and walking the three miles to my father's menial quarters in South West Ikoyi.

That was my uncle then: a man with a very simple philosophy, a very measured response to every indignity: 'I can't fight every battle,' he would say, 'I have to keep my eyes on the pension. It is only seventeen more years.'

Well, the years passed and although I was never able to eat yam pottage again, we eventually mended fences (and if there was anything I still held against him, it was the way he occasionally relapsed into the atrocious nickname they had for me as a child.) Strange and interesting things seemed to happen around John Jeff – once he had a glass of *kokori* inside him. When I was younger, to make me laugh he would spit kerosene in the air and set it ablaze. As a teen, he shared adult confidences that would have shocked his employers. For instance, his only child had been conceived upstairs in the master's bed while he was on tour with his wife. It was the best possible start in life that he could give his otherwise hapless spawn; and it helped that his wife was, at the time, a maid in the mansion.

The closer he came to his pension, the more desperate his circumstances grew. His salary had not improved in the last two decades of his employment. For many years he had coped only because his wife and daughter mostly lived off a garden plot beside his village house in Waterside. At first he used to visit them every Christmas, but in the last decade, he had only managed the trip twice. Yet, few natives of Waterside were as useful to the youth of the village as my uncle. – Over the years, some thirty young men and women had got their first jobs in Lagos through him. The maids, guards and drivers who worked at the mansion never kept their jobs for long (six months being the typical duration). After every sacking, or walkout, the master would swear never to hire another menial. Yet Uncle John knew the psychological moment that a prospective driver or maid who knocked on the door of the Ikoyi mansion would get a warm welcome. The one condition he gave his protégées was that his relationship with them be kept a secret from the master.

Uncle John was three years short of his pension when the master took issue with an over-salted omelette (which he flung at him from across the dining room). John Jeff was summarily sacked, and he only managed to hang on to his job by throwing himself prostrate on the ground – and staying there through kicks and insults for the twenty hours it took his master to relent.

Although he got his job back, that experience cost John Jeff the assurance of his pension. A few months earlier, his salary had stopped arriving in the usual crisp cheque mailed in a white official envelope from the company's personnel department. These days he was paid directly by his master in used currency stuffed down a brown manila envelope. The usual chit that broke down his salary and calculated his pension entitlement was no more. All that came together into a black unease that soured John Jeff's natural good humour.

All this concerned me more than usual because my father had just retired to Waterside and I was sharing Uncle John's room for a few days while looking for new living quarters. I had seen the new lines etched on my uncle's face as he worried about his pension. I had parked the cab I drove for a living in its owner's garage. It had been a good day, there was money in my pocket, and our evening's *kokori* was on me. I sat across the bench from Uncle John, on the veranda of the four-room boys' quarters. It was quiet: the maid had turned in for the night, the gateman was at his post, and Rufaso, the driver, had taken the madam out to a party. Although we could not have known it then, that was the last night of John Jeff's stewardship. I opened up the paper bag and pulled out the half-pint of *kokori*. John Jeff took the first sip and began to sing a mournful Waterside song.

It was going to be a long night.

When Rufaso trudged in, we knew instantly it was trouble. He did not disappoint. The stammer that he successfully mastered came back as he described how the madam had nearly slapped him deaf from her rear seat. She had kicked him out of her car, right in the middle of the highway. There was a commiserative silence when he was done.

'Dododoes that mean I'm fired?'

'Usually,' said John Jeff.

'Dodoes she have a right to do that?'

My uncle cracked his knuckles. 'What did you yourself do? Tell me the truth.'

Rufaso hesitated, 'It was the horrible beans I ate this morning... plus the air conditioner was on, too...'

'Air conditioner? Beans?'

'She said I fafafarted,' he explained shortly; 'but it was an accident, true. And come and see how she was slapping and popopunching me like an animal – and me driving so fast! Is because of God that I didn't crash!'

John Jeff stared suspiciously. He had himself been slapped and punched and kicked hundreds of times in his career; it only cemented the master-steward relationship. 'What else did you do? Tell me the whole truth.'

Rufaso shrugged, 'I told her that my fafafart did not smell as bad as her own.'

Uncle John's jaw dropped, 'You told her that?'

'That's when she told me to stop the car and kicked me out.'

Uncle John scratched his head gloomily. Rufaso had not quite spent three weeks on the job. He would be the third Waterside youth in a row who would not even collect a salary. If he didn't know any better, he would have made something of the pattern, 'This is not good at all,' he sighed.

'Can you beg them for me?' asked Rufaso, kneading a cheek that seemed two sizes larger than the other, 'at least you know them very well...'

Uncle John reflected long and hard, probably on the twenty hours he'd spent on his own face, begging for his own job, 'That's a big problem,' he said uncertainly.

'What about the three weeks I've worked already? Will they pay me for that one at least?'

Uncle John scratched his stubble, not looking at anything in particular. It suddenly occurred to me that Rufaso was far better off fighting his own corner. John Jeff was more slave than servant. In thirty years he had not stood up for himself. He was unlikely to start that night on behalf of anyone. 'That's a very big problem,' Uncle John confessed.

'Is not fair;' grumbled Rufaso bitterly, 'cococome and see how her own fart smells!'

He was packed and gone within the hour, leaving with a blessing from John Jeff and a handout from me – which I could ill afford. The evening took a grimmer turn as we waited for the return of the madam, who usually took out her employee-frustrations on her longest-serving staff. It was close to 11pm and my uncle was gently drunk, 'I wish I had the guts to fart in their face,' he said resentfully.

I grinned at the very thought, 'Remember your pension,' I laughed.

He hesitated and pulled out a much-folded letter from a pocket sewn into the inside of his vest. It was wetly warm to my touch. As I opened up the letter from Chanka Chagril Corporation's personnel department, I smelled the rank sweat of fear:

> *...as a result of the global economic downturn, the company had suffered crippling financial losses and is having to retrench...*

> *...Sadly, the company's pension fund has been liquidated by the global crisis; however you are welcome to retain the company's properties in your **legitimate** possession to assist you in your future plans...*

I glanced at him in some confusion, 'What company property?'

He gestured at the threadbare khaki jacket hanging from a nail on the wall. His voice was unsteady, 'I'm finished, Bomboy, I have no company job, no pension, nothing...' his voice broke finally. 'I am just an ordinary houseboy...' his head was bowed but I could see the dull wet spots growing on his green shorts. I was too flummoxed for words; I had no comfort to offer. *The Pension* had been his great religion. He had endured the foulest indignities for the sake of it. To end up now with nothing was like a bishop rising from death to find a communist collective in place of the gates to Heaven and Hell, '...I should have farted in their face and walked out more than twenty years ago,' he whispered.

'You have nothing to worry about,' I lied, 'the company may have sacked you but you've been working for the same rich family for three decades! There's no way you'll retire empty-handed.'

He looked at me quietly, scratching his chin, the same chin that had lain twenty hours on the master's rug. He said nothing.

That was the moment that his BMW drove into the Ikoyi mansion; of course at this moment it still belonged to the master. Normally, it would pull up on the carport in the front of the house, or into the garage of six or seven other luxury cars; this night, it sped over the rear lawn to screech to a stop on the hard court in front of the boys' quarters. We heard a door open and slam and two unsteady heels click towards the main house. They paused as she yelled, 'JOHN! WASH THE CAR!'

'Yes, Ma'am,' he called back, rising and bowing reflexively, even though the woman was well out of sight, 'I washing it tomor-'

'*Do it now!*' she shouted, 'But bring me a brandy and coke first!' the sound of her heels faded towards the house.

I continued to stare at my uncle. Under my gaze, he slowly straightened at the waist. There was a ruefulness in his eyes that I had never seen before, for this midnight rudeness and over-time service would be neither remunerated by month end nor justified by the expectation of a pension. He donned khaki jacket and buttoned it over his vest. He was ready. 'I'll get her drink,' he said shamefacedly.

'And I'll wash the car for you,' I offered. I could see the shock in his face: I had never before indulged any act of servitude connected with his job. Yet, I had just received his tragic news and was anxious to do anything to comfort him. I filled a pail with water and fell to the task. Only hours earlier, I had been washing the Datsun that I drove for a living and the contrast between the two cars was vexing. My Datsun was visibly riveted from the earthly remains of half-a-dozen scrapped cars while the BMW was seemingly cast from a single dream of glass and aluminium. In the light of the courtyard, it seemed unnecessary to wash this spotless, scratchless car... until I got to the front bumper, which had a small dent in the lower profile, tinged with a distinct smear of red. I was squatting there, lost in thought, when John Jeff returned from the main house at a trot.

He went straight to the maid's door and knocked her up. There was a whispered consultation and she slipped on her slippers and flitted over to the mansion. He sat down on our bench and hugged himself, shaking his legs. 'What's happening?' I asked.

'The madam is crying.'

'Where?'

'Inside the master bedroom,' he said shortly, and shut his eyes. That was clear enough, as hints went. I kept my own counsel.

We sat there drinking *kokori* for thirty minutes before the maid returned. Ayla, another John Jeff recruit from Waterside, had caught my eye earlier and was the real reason why I opted to sleep on a mat in my uncle's room instead of half-a-dozen more comfortable places across Lagos. Unfortunately, in the few days I had spent in the BQ so far, we hadn't exchanged five words. My uncle was married and there was a thirty-year-gap between them but – perhaps because I hadn't made much progress in her direction – I was not too happy to seen them huddling together.

'What's going on?' I asked, when Ayla had withdrawn to her room and John Jeff was back on our bench.

He poured himself another glass. He was going to have a headache in the morning. 'Hit and run,' he said.

'How did Ayla know?'

'If you stand in the guest room wardrobe, you can hear everything they're saying inside their master bedroom. Madam sacked Rufaso on the way to her party. She drank pieces there. On her way back, she jammed one child near Oworonshoki. '

So I told him about the bloodstain and the dent. I took him out to the car, but rather than look at the blood, he walked slowly around the car, running his hand lightly over the immaculate bodywork almost as though he were romancing another maid in his master's employ. When he came round to where I stood before the dent, his wet eyes met mine, 'This is my pension,' he said quietly.

I knew he was drunk, so I said nothing. Then he added through gritted teeth, 'Please, get me the head of a lamb; a fresh head with blood and everything. Hurry!'

'You know what time it is? All the butchers are...'

He ran his fingers over the BMW badge, 'This car fits you more than that Datsun taxi, eh, Bomboy?' he murmured quietly,

I glanced at Ayla's door and dropped my voice, 'Uncle, about this "Bomboy" thing...'

'...you can drive it for me at the Warri Airport,' he continued, as though I had not spoken, 'three hires a day is a pension for me and a salary for you, not so?' he glanced at Ayla's door and added discreetly, 'even for two married men.'

He was not so drunk then. I took my savings from the tobacco pouch and within an hour I returned with what he wanted. He hacked briefly in the kitchen and wrapped the newly-bloodied head in a white napkin which was soaked through with blood in a moment, then he had me carry it into the main house behind him. It was the first time I saw him enter that house without the servile stoop. He seemed quite the actor at the end of a long run of appearances, entering the stage, out of character, for a final bow.

'What do you want at this time, John?' rasped the master when he finally came downstairs. A ghastly-looking madam, eyes puffy-red, paused a dozen steps down the staircase. The master seemed to notice me, 'And who is that?'

It was an aristocratic gift, this ability to *look at* but not *notice*. I had been in and out of his compound for the past seventeen years but he was still unable to recognise me.

'Sorry Sir,' said my uncle without much sorrow in his voice, 'but what I am do with the head of the little girl? I finding it under the bumper.'

Uncle John was still in character then, as far as his grammar went. There was the silence of broken lives and reversed roles, of whiskey hangovers and nights where murderous stares killed quicker than careless tongues and drunken bumpers, then the master barked, 'what head of what little girl?'

My uncle turned and took the blood-soaked burden from me reverently. He made the sign of the cross and began to unwrap the napkin with such confident deliberation that I thought he had somehow swapped the lamb's head for that of a child, but it slipped from his hand and thudded, sickeningly, rolling a foot and leaving blotches of red across the white Persian rug. The madam gasped and fled upstairs. The master screamed, '*Are you mad? Get that thing out of here! Now!*'

'Yes sir.' He picked up the lamb's head, which was still securely wrapped, and turned for the door, then he paused, 'To where, Sir?'

The master became hysterical, 'To my nose! – No, to my bum! *IMBECILE!* Get it out of here!'

So we took it to the BQ and made a late night stew of lamb's head and couscous. I could so very easily have done it myself, but while Uncle John was away at the gatehouse I took a deep breath and knocked on Ayla's door again. It took her a while to get to the door, and I pretty much used Uncle John's formula. She just glared at me, 'Do you know what time it is?'

Behind me, I head the cracking of knuckles. I stared at Ayla. Her features were usually a plump and sainted genialness. It was astonishing to watch that face transmute into refrigeration equipment, 'Please?' I added, the mutton weighing heavier in my hand. A seeming age passed and she relented.

She was bossy in the kitchen, but much more personable as we sat in Uncle John's room to devour the very-early-morning re-past. The early hour and the illicit liquor combined with a stomach engorged with lamb, and I soon had to take a glass of kokori from the nerveless hand of a snoring Uncle John. I thought that a perfect scenario to get to know Ayla better... but I started to my feet and she was gone. It was almost dawn and I had half-chewed meat in my mouth. The barrage that roused me was still hammering at the door but Uncle John was already opening it.

'Where's that thing?' his master demanded without preamble. His eyes were bloodshot and baleful.

'What thing sir?' asked Uncle John, still struggling to recover his wits from the ethereal grip of *kokori* spirits.

'That *thing*! The *thing* you brought yesterday night!'

'Oho, *that* thing,' and my uncle primed his torch and led us to the outside dustbin where we searched futilely for the very mutton that was digesting inside us. The longer we spent there, the more distraught the master grew. On the stroke of 6 a.m., Ayla left through the gate with a Bible and a pious scarf, on her way to morning mass. I returned her polite greetings; the master did not.

'You're mad,' the master cursed, 'how can you put it in the dustbin! What kind of steward are you!'

It was growing lighter, with growing potential for neighbours to catch the preposterous sight of the master rooting in a garbage bin.

Kwetu the gateman stood uncertainly by his kiosk. He had tried to help his master in his unseemly task, but had been stopped by a growl. Now, the master turned abruptly to him, 'Did you see a dog at this dustbin last night? Or a pussycat?'

'No sir,' he said, positively. 'Na only police jeep wey come here.'

We held our collective breath, '*Police jeep*?' the master repeated.

'Yes sir, one military police jeep like that, with twelve police.'

'Twelve? In one jeep?'

John Jeff coughed and pounded his chest violently,

'Either six or twelve,' prevaricated Kwetu, 'na night, I no too sure. Anyway, dem dey find the car wey kill one brigadier him pikin like that.'

'They didn't come in?'

'Me, I no 'gree open gate sir.'

'Good man. Did they search the bin?'

'Yes, but-'

The master turned abruptly and hurried across the lawn. We followed him apprehensively, I had never seen a man that fat walk quite as fast and I realized that if he had a heart attack at that precise moment it would also kill Uncle John. The steward patted Kwetu on the shoulder as we went. The gateman's performance had been brilliant, if a little over-zealous. He had been at the mansion three years and it was his first real opportunity to thank Uncle John for a position with more longevity than the jobs of drivers and maids.

'Let me go prison instead of you and madam,' panted my uncle who was still breathless despite the ten minute wait for the master to finish from the toilet.

There was a look of affection, almost, on the master's face, but his voice did not give anything away, 'What are you talking about?'

'For thirty years,' lied John Jeff shamelessly, 'you have been like papa to me. I will go prison for you! Is me that drove the car!'

'You can't even drive!'

He shrugged. I realized with some shock that Uncle John was standing erect. He was still addressing the master deferentially, but he was addressing his face, rather than his feet, 'I'm learner; that's why am killing the poor girl,' he said, 'I will say I buy the car from you only last week and this morning I carry it and go...'

'You're a bloody steward,' he snorted, 'how can you pay for a brand new BMW 7 series?'

Uncle John shrugged again. 'We can say that I use my gratuity – my thirty years' service gratuity...'

That gave the master pause. A sneer passed over his heavy features.

Uncle John shuddered on cue and took a step backwards. He signed and grumbled, half to himself, 'But am too old for prison... me that has wife in village... to become another man's prison wife...'

'It's not like that,' I began.

'Is thirty years for hit-and-run, not so?' said Uncle John to me, I don't want to die in prison,' he looked at his master anxiously, 'maybe you can buy good lawyer... and bribe the DPO... and the judge... and the witnesses–'

'Go and pack your things,' snapped the master abruptly, 'let me think about this.' Then he closed the door on our faces.

It was depressing how quickly it took to pack up the possessions he had accumulated in three decades of employment. In fifteen minutes we filled a portmanteau and two jute bags. For the first time, he did not wear his threadbare uniform: He folded them both neatly on top of the thin mattress, the twelve-year-old set (which he wore Mondays through Wednesdays), and the sixteen-year-old set (which he wore Thursdays through to Sundays).

I endured fifteen minutes of Uncle John's anxious knuckle-cracking, then Ayla returned from her church. I mouthed a greeting, but she was apparently a one-greeting-per-day sort of girl. She was hurrying to resume her duties in the main house when the master came in with the bill of sale. It had taken him twenty minutes to weigh up his options and draw up the papers, but he kept hemming and hawing, and it took him twice as long again to finally part with the keys and documents. I will never forget the master's bereft eyes, although I am no longer sure what loss afflicted him more, the new car, or the punching bag of a steward who had not stolen a retributive spoon in three decades, who had been so meek and submissive as to be unsackable, enduring for three decades what others could not brook for three weeks.

I didn't like the idea of leaving Ayla behind, or Kwetu for that matter. Yet, Uncle John was determined to avoid any suspicion of a conspiracy, so Ayla stayed on at the Ikoyi mansion another fortnight. The day she collected her November wages, she got herself sacked on schedule by watching one of the master's stockpile of porn videos at the wrong time; although the madam bit off more than she could chew when she tried to slap her...

I picked her up at Obalende bus stop in Uncle John's car, and we laughed all the way to Waterside.

Kwetu refused to give up his Lagos job, but four months afterwards, he lost it anyway. He had been drinking and he boasted to the new maid – who had no Waterside affiliations – of the day he made a fool of the master. The new maid, trying to strengthen her shaky tenancy in the BQ, told on him and he was fired right away. He fled to Waterside in a panic, but Uncle John is not much concerned, and – now that I have had a good think about it – neither am I. People like the master can afford to lose money, but not face. He has many more limos in his garage, but he cannot afford to have this story as widely known in Ikoyi as it is in Waterside.

These days, I run a limo service at the Warri Airport. It is a comfortable living for my uncle and I, although much of my own income is invested in Ayla's Waterside supermarket. (I will probably have to marry her soon, to secure my investments...) Most evenings, John Okorodudu holds court under his dongoyaro tree. He is happy to tell and retell the story of his pension car, indeed, he hardly does anything else.

Yet, the rumours of '419' scams die hard.

THE LAS' FOOLSCAP

My dear Timi and Ogogo,

Many many months have passed since I last talk to you, or write to you. (God knows is not my plan, how things have spoil in this our small family.) Since then, many confusions they are that have entered my head, but still yet one thing that I know (which *I know* that I know) is that I still love your mama, even though is this my very hands that kill her dead.

My dear childrens, maybe by now you have torn this letter, maybe not. I will still be writing it should in case you have not. And should in case you're saying in your mind, 'let me just read this next sentence, see what the evil *agbero* is going to say', let me say this very quickly now: is that same spirit of anger that you can use to tear this letter that the alkali said I used to kill your mama, just because I saw her drinking birth control medicine, remember? – Of which no normal husband should vex like that because of one common pill. So go on and tear this letter, if it must be that your generation won't learn from my generation's sin, go on and tear me dead as well, because the only life that I have remaining now is this very foolscap that you're holding in your very hands. The rest of me is already gone – you heard the alkali's judgement yourself, not so? By the time you're reading this letter, I must be dead, like your mama, like my Rashi (of course because of this Sharia trial that I chose with my own hand, is not a rope that will hang me dead; is by stoning that they will kill me at the old market.)

Is very funny about this their reformed Sharia, how they can sentence somebody to die, yet the dead person's childrens can stop the death sentence just by saying: I FORGIVE YOU, and then the convict will go to jail and pay the childrens millions upon millions of naira compensation... is very funny, true. (– Of course I know that you can never say those three small words in one hundred, million years, so that's not the reason why am writing this letter, true). So go on and tear me dead if you like, just don't be telling the radio people how am evil *agbero* and et-cetera, because the same murdering spirit that the alkali thinks I have is the same spirit in you as well.

But if by now you haven't torn this letter then my God (and yours too) will definitely bless you as you hold yourself. (Is very difficult, true, to keep on writing this, when I don't even know whether am in pieces inside a dustbin or talking to my daughter and my son). People are saying now that I killed your mama because of the rumour of the nonsense between she and that her boss, Mister Wey. That was the story the papers have been print-ing since the day they arrested me. All that is nonsense, true.

I know what you're thinking now. You're thinking: why didn't I talk when it was time to talk, when I was standing in the dock, dumb like a Christmas goat waiting for the knife. What you have to remember is: what was the point of opening all my mouth? When nothing I can say was going to bring my Rashi back? I was like a Christmas goat true-true, because nothing it can say can take away the butcher's knife. My talking would only give those newspapers more gossip to write about our family. I had already killed her dead, what was the point of killing the small dignity left remaining in our family? Let it be that in the eyes of the world am a big demon, and that Rashi was an angel, so that at least people can look at you and pity you as angel's chil-drens. But with you I won't hide anything. We are family, so I won't hide anything at all (– and am not saying this just for you to come to where they're stoning me and shout 'I FORGIVE YOU!' so that they can save me under this their crazy Sharia law. I know that you can never do that in one thousand years. And anyway, by the time you get this letter, I will be dead for many hours, because I will tell the Reverend Father to give you this letter only when am dead. Am only writing this because the reason why I killed my Rashi is a big, big story I cannot take with me to Heaven's gate.)

You can see how small my writing is becoming now? Is because am coming to the end of my only foolscap. I begged and begged the yellow warder in my block for paper and he looked at me as if the thing he drop inside latrine has opened mouth to talk to him. They will come for me in the morning to stone me dead, so if I don't get more paper just know that things are not what they seem and that your father is not black and black the devil they have painted me. So bye bye, maybe for ever and after. Is your father, 'Yeni, saying bye bye, maybe for ever and after. Amen.

***

Haleluya, I got the paper. My next-cell-neighbour, Kilango *told* the warder to give me paper and true-true he gave me two more foolscaps. So I can say everything, if I say it straight and to the point. The problem is that stories never go straight and to the point. I don't know what is between the warder and Kilango, true, but is powerful, whatever it is. Powerful like the thing I have on that Mister Wey. I hope he is taking care of you as me and him agreed. If he is, you don't need to thank him. Is not because of the love that he loves you that he gives you money. Is because of the fear that he fears me. That is the deal I made with him, that concerning what I know about him, I will close my mouth, *kitikpam*, like coffin, until I die. After all, is for a father to provide for his childrens, not so? Because is good for me to give Angel Gabriel one more good thing that he can argue for my case at Heaven's gate. – And if that Mister Wey isn't giving you money yet, (because I know how difficult it is for money to leave the gumming hands of rich people) just call him and tell him that I messaged you a secret for his wife and you will see what will happen. Don't say am teaching you blackmail o, after all if a mother hen leaves *cluck-cluck* what else will she use to raise her childrens, eh?

So to come back to what I was saying before-before. I didn't kill your mama because of the nonsense she was doing with Mister Wey (of which you can't believe that is me that permit her) no.

Only someone that didn't know how it was between your mama and me can accuse me like that. Of course nobody knows how it was between your mama and me, except the two both of us who are dead now. And no one will ever know – unless you finish reading this letter, so don't just vex now and tear me dead. Just hold yourself – because I know how Ogogo can like to vex – just hold yourself and keep reading. You see, if common jealousy can make me kill Rashi, you won't be walking all over the place today, giving interview to newspaper and TV and crying tragedy like I heard you crying on the radio this very yesterday. They won't even have born you even! Are you sitting down? Sit down very well, because is not my sperm that born the two both of you.

I know this is coming like the wound of catapult to you. Even, you may now begin to think of tearing me at this junction, but let me ask you, if you tear me dead now, won't you wonder, maybe in another thirty or forty years when all your vex of today has die (because every vex has expiry date)... when your own childrens are asking you questions – won't you wonder if not my sperm, whose? Won't you wonder what it was that I had to say? So therefore, just hold yourself, eh? Just hold yourself very well.

So, to come back to what I was saying before before, is not my sperm that born you, true. I know you're thinking, *No wonder! Thank God for that!* but wait, because the story doesn't finish there. Am talking about twenty years ago when we first marry, me and your mama. Three long years have come and gone and no childrens; so we went for the test, the two both of us. The doctor vexed and said that your mama's womb was fine, but as for me, why did I put tap water inside the semen bottle? So I said no that it was semen I put and he rolled his eyes. So I asked him what medicine I could drink and he vexed again and said there was medicine to *increase* a man's sperms, but was he God? to be making sperm for men who were bringing tap water instead of semen? So he said that if we wanted noise in the house we can buy dog or pussy cat, but as for that other thing, we can be doing it for exercise, not to born childrens.

We couldn't discuss the doctor's test, me and your mama, for two whole weeks. That time was for crying, (she was crying all the time and me I was crying when I lock the toilet door). But after two weeks I faced the matter like a man. After all, there are some husband and wife who born many childrens – and bury all of them as well, so what is it? So we can't have childrens, so? Does nothing else remain for us in this wide world? So I faced the matter squarely like a man. I told your mama that it was fine with me, that I will do my business and she will do her nursing and that it was me and her together... that's how I story-storied on and on like that for three hours, I swear to God. You know what she answered me? You can't imagine what she answered me: she said that she will kill herself! That she will wait until my family have come for Christmas (so that they can hold me) before jumping in front of a Zungeru truck. I said to her, *what?* And she said to me that it was out of love for me that she was doing it, because it was better for me to be a widower than for me to be the husband of mental case – because if the childrens of her own womb did not suck the very breasts of her own body, then the only room that can contain her in this wide world was the ward of a asylum.

I begged and begged and begged your mama, until me myself was near to taking card in asylum too; but when your mama makes up her mind, is like a bank has closed his door – you have try to change her mind yourself, not so? What was there again for me to do? I even said to her that we can adopt childrens, but she just laugh one little crazy laugh like that, which made me never to say 'ado...' in her presence again. Everybody was asking me,

What's wrong with Rashidah?

Did somebody die?

Why is she thinning like this now?

and I knew that it was not that somebody died, but that somebody was about to die. Already what separated us from Christmas was just three common weeks. – And if you see how our marriage was sweet at that time! We didn't yet know what the world was talking about! Have I said that it was only three years we were married at this time? So I was begging and begging and begging your mama, and you know what Rashi was doing? She was giving her clothes to her sisters. She was dashing her shoes away, then she resigned from her nurse job at the Health Centre! And throughout all this, I just tried to be a man. I said to her, *stop this nonsense,* I just said to her, *Rashi, stop this nonsense now-now!*

You know what finished me finally? One night she brought out her wedding gown and began to iron it. I said to her, *Rashi, what's the matter now?* and she said she wanted to lie in state in this her wedding dress, but that if the Zungeru truck's tyre should climb her face and she's not fine again, then I must promise to nail the coffin *kitikpam* and let nobody see her. You know what I did? Me myself I began to cry! I cried and cried and cried. Like a baby, true! I was crying as if to say that my wife was dead already! I swear to God! I knelt down and begged her that since her womb was working well and it was just me that was bringing tap water, that she should... go outside. Yes! I said that nonsense with my own very mouth! But what was there again for me to do? I said to her that me myself will bring somebody for her to do the nonsense with. She cried *No, no, no, no, no!* and *Over my dead body!* that's what she cried; but it was also that very same night that she woke me up at 11.30 and said *okay.* That's the thing. 11.30 at night on second July, 1989. That's the very same night I died. The stick of my life just did *kpikim* and broke. I didn't close my eyes till morning. That's the very night that something deep inside me, where the manness in every man lives, that thing just quenched and died. The man that they stoned this morning was a dead man.

I know what you're thinking: you're thinking, yes he can say anything now, just because Mama is not around to say the truth. But don't believe me, just go, the two both of you, and sit in front of a mirror with my picture (that is, if you haven't burn all my pictures already). Timi, where did you get that nose. Check my own nose, check my father and my mother's, they're still alive. Check your mama and your mama's mother and your mama's father. You knew them well before they died, not so? From where did you get that kind of nose? It was from the nonsense man I pointed out to your mama. And you, Ogogo, your cowry eyes, where have you seen cowry eyes in the two families? Is not there; is from the third family. And in case you don't believe your eyes' evidence, you can try your ears' evidence also. The doctor that born the two both of you is the same doctor that test my semen. He's still alive, 249 Ahmed Avenue. Doctor Weikpe. When we first took Timi's pregnancy to him, his eyes became big like your mama's six months' stomach. So we lied that it was the prayers of a miracle church and he nodded big nods that banged his chin against his chest, and shouted *Praise the Lord*, though he couldn't look at me, but he said nothing more, after all this is Nigeria. So if you like, go to Doctor Weikpe and ask him; if he pretends he has forgotten, he's lying because although it was twenty years ago if you see how big his eyes were that evening. Ask him about the day he kept shouting *Praise the Lord* and banging his chin on his chest and his hand on the table until the junior doctor ran in from the other consulting room and saw the miracle and started shouting *Haleluya*, although he was dodging my eyes also, and he said nothing after that as well because after all this is Nigeria.

Still you may be asking yourself why am saying this now, why am telling you something that I should have taken to the grave like any man that calls himself *papa* – not because is my sperm that fathered you, but because is my chest that was your napkin, because is me that woke up to feed you all those early mornings that your mama did night duty, because is me that you called *Papa*, which – let me tell you now – is the most powerful word in this wide world, because is a word that – say it long enough – it can turn a man who is just a bystander... look, *just say it long enough* and it turns a bastard into a father, true. And that is what I am to you, a father... no. Am not telling the full truth! *No...!* I can't be telling my childrens half-true-half-lie now when my killers are already gathering the stones that will send me to Heaven's gate! Why should I cover my sins at this very junction when one small lie can be the very thing to fall the scale and close Heaven's gate and push my soul into hellfire? I will tell the truth and let the devil be ashamed. I will tell the truth, even if it makes you curse my stoned corpse. The truth is this: many times I tried to kill you. *Yes!* (Look... this father-thing is not easy.) When you were babies, when I carry you – try I as like – I always see the nose, I always see the cowry eyes, I always see the two nonsense men that fathered you. – And what I think is this: ...accidents are accidents not so? ...what if you fall from the cot... what if blanket suffocates you... after all Rashi has now suckled her own childrens, not so? It will be sad but is no more an asylum case or a case for the Zungeru truck...

Until one day... I swear to God, there was one day that all my double-mind ended, that day that Timi marched broken bottle – I know you can't remember now! You were just four years old, you can't remember, but check your left foot and see, the scar will still be there till today! It was one hot day like that, and the blood, ah, the blood, it was everywhere, and your mama was there, but Timi ran, they were calling her to come, but Timi ran, pouring blood on the ground, on the walls, on the carpet, Timi left your mama and ran to the room where I was, crying! If you saw her crying: *Papa, Papa, am dead!* and I held her wound, and the blood was on my hands, it was everywhere, and I thought, so this is the famous blood? So what's the difference with my own blood? And she was crying, *Papa, Papa, Papa, am dead!* and it was that last '*Papa!*' that entered the seed of my soul, because she didn't go to her mama, she didn't go to the nonsense man that fathered her, it was me, *Papa*, that she brought her wound and her blood to make it well. And I held her to my body, no, I held her to my soul, and you too, Ogogo, I hugged the two both of you to the seed of my soul. And I said to her – she can't re-member now! – but I said to her, No, Timi, you're not dead, Papa is here, you're alive, *Papa* is here.

That, my childrens, was the day I fathered you. Before that day I could have dropped you by accident. From that very day, I became like Jesus Christ to you, I could have died for you, I'm telling you – the way I killed my manhood so that your mama's breasts can feed the childrens of her own womb. I swear to God! You're laughing now, not so? Have you forgotten how I first got into police trouble? Was is not because I beat that wicked teacher that flogged Ogogo until the poor boy fainted? Did I not beat him until he was quarter to dead? Did I not spend six months in jail for that? What about that time that Timi went for extra lesson and was missing for three good hours, and people were saying somebody saw her school bag at mile six, that ritual killers had caught her, did I not enter that thick Mile Six Forest all by myself, armed with only machete – which as anybody knows is suicide pure and simple? How many ordinary fathers would have done that? Tell me that? If it was Mister Wey that his daughter was taken by ritual killers, will he not take his six mobile phones and be pressing 999 till kingdom come? So don't just tear this letter now, you hear me so? Don't just say *Thank God he's not my blood!* and tear me dead and throw me inside dustbin the way government is going to throw away my corpse this evening for dogs to eat, because am your Papa. And if I could do what I did, give my wife's flesh to two nonsense men whose names six thousand angels and demons will never get me to write on paper even though they are stamp in my mind for ever, even for the bribe of entering Heaven... (although maybe I should tell you who they are... now that you have no more any mama or papa...) but if I could do what I did twenty years ago, and yet live with her despite that she's Moslem and am Christian – if you like, go and ask our neighbours then, how we were living, fifteen, twenty years ago, before all this nonsense with Mister Wey happened, if I could do all that, and yet live with her, just so that she did not kill herself on that Christmas of 1989, is that not love? So tell me then why this same hand that is writing this letter can kill Rashi just because I saw her drinking contraceptive. Yes there's a good reason that even Rashi herself understands. Is the reason why am writing this letter to you, so just hold your vex now. Just hold yourself very well.

You can see how my handwritg. is becoming small again. Is still 3 o'clk in the morning, still 3 hrs b4 they'll take me out to stone me dead, but is nearing the end of the 2nd foolscp now. Is long since I been tryg to say these things to you, but the greatest tragedy is how my paper has now finished b4 my time. There is no time to tell you how Rashi wanted anoda child. 'Look at this wicked economy,' I said to her, 'is 2 childrens not enough?' But she cried and cried: that she wants one fine child at least. That how can beautiful woman like her be borning childrens with nose like jerrycan and eyes like traffic light... until I said, 'ok, let me look-' but she said no, that she has already seen the person with the perfect genes to born a fine baby... and just like that Mister Wey began to come. For five years he was coming and coming but the fine baby refused to come... my time is still re-maing small but my paper has almost finished. Still, I will finish this story in Heaven, I promise... unless the Rev made mistake, and gave you this letter too early. Check your watch, If is not yet 6 a.m., then am still alive, and you can still take taxi to the old mkt before they begin to stone me, and shout I 4GIVE U – (not bcos of the money that I will pay you, or becos you have 4given this old *agbero*, which of course you can never do, even in 100 yrs, not so? Not with that angry spirit still burning eh? But just for me to finish this family history, becos what I have write so far is not even quarter of what I have to write) – but of course you can never say those 3 small words, I.F.U. – even on a wkend of Sundays – so let's just 'gree to finish this story in Heaven, eh? Though is difficult to make a Heavn appointmt, when you and Rashi's Hvn is even different from my...

MA' REBECCA

Her given name is Idia, although everyone calls her Ma'Rebecca now, after her daughter. I passed her low fence on my way to farm. Ever since the fire in her kitchen, she has been cooking on a brazier in her backyard. Rebecca was there as well, hanging up washings on a line. I waved, but they didn't see me. Despite my shouted greetings, they didn't see me. And I can't blame them. I know that type of embarrassment very well: that invisible wall you can wear everywhere you go – so that people can gape and gossip about you all day and you won't even see them.

Ikerre-Oti village is not a good place to make mistakes. Idia's own is more than twenty years old, but ten-year-old Ikerre children know it better than their catechism. She's a widow, twice over. Her first marriage was three years old when her husband choked on a fishbone at a cousin's I-Survived-Cancer party. Poor woman. I remember how that party ended as if it were yesterday. These very hands were in the tug-of-war that pulled her from the mortuary.

Idia was only thirty-one in those days, and people really pitied her. No gossip could stick to her. (- And it wasn't as if Ikerre's bitter old women weren't trying.) But people really pitied her in those days.

It may not be fair, and it may not be right; but young and beautiful widows are easier to pity; and Idia was young and beautiful in those days. She continued to receive condolence visits, months and months after her bereavement. Of course, most of the visits were being paid by one visitor, an absent-minded theatre nurse who often went home from work still wearing his surgical mask. Idia herself didn't like the embarrassing visits, which she finally ended by marrying the nurse.

That marriage caused quite a few gray-speckled eyebrows to rise slowly in Ikerre-Oti. The village is that sort of place. People carefully counted the days between the dying of Husband One and the marrying of Husband Two, getting only twenty-two months, two weeks and three days. That simple arithmetic caused a number of respectable Ikerre eyes to roll slowly in their sockets. It was not a *very* bad thing; and yet, it was not a *very* good thing, either.

Had she taken advice from Ikerre's old women, she would have discreetly entertained her condolence visitor another year, at least, before accepting his presumptuous ring. Yet, she was a beautiful, thirty-three-year-old widow in those days and it was hard for any gossip to stick to her. So she married the nurse and the Ikerre heavens did not fall. Four years passed, and if there was any whispering at all (and to tell the truth, Ikerre-Oti was that sort of place) it was how two husbands and seven years of marriage had produced neither pregnancy nor child.

Then Husband Two died.

Once someone catches the eye of Ill-Luck the big problem is how to escape his future attentions. See her burnt-out kitchen for instance. People have been buying second-hand bits from Ekun for years and years without problems; but only last week Ma'Rebecca buys a second-hand electric kettle that burns her kitchen down. Anyway, the theatre nurse caught jaundice and died.

This time, the struggle to keep Idia from jumping into the well continued for seven days and nights. *Serpents and scorpions!* That widow *cried!* – And only an Ikerre indigene could have understood why her grief was deep like a well: she had buried two husbands therefore a third one could never come from Ikerre-Oti; never mind that she was still beautiful and in her thirties. It was one of those silly superstitions. Catechist had talked and talked; Reverend had preached and preached, but it is easier to pluck all the hairs from the hairy chests of the Ikerre male than to pluck that fear from his heart. Even bachelors who dated three-time divorcees without qualms began to stutter in the presence of a twice-widowed.

And she was only thirty-seven. People really pitied her in those days.

Once again, Idia found herself receiving condolence visitors. This time though, within two weeks her visitors were very thin on the ground. Then the news broke, like the ripe seedpod of a flame of the forest: Idia was pregnant! It was the sort of gossip that propped mouths open. Think about it: that the absent-minded nurse could have planted such a valuable seed in the very nick of time! Of course it would be hard, raising a child as a confirmed widow; but this was Ikerre-Oti. It was a hundred and one times better than being a childless, twice-over widow. Plus, it would bring the ultimate crown of Ikerre womanhood: the replacement of her given name with a wombname. Idia would be *Mama-somebody!*

Four weeks passed, the burial rites ended, and she packed her things to leave for Lagos.

Veterans of Ikerre-Oti's Health Centre nodded wisely: this child was too precious to trust to our hit-and-miss Health Centre, one of whose midwives had sneezed during my son's circumcision and castrated him. So she packed her bags and left Ikerre-Oti.

April and May passed. A letter came for our chief, another came for the nurse's cousin: things were hard but God was good. She had found a job and a good doctor to care for The Pregnancy. June, July and August passed. Three telegrams came, one after the other: she was bleeding! She was rushed to hospital! – And, praise God, The Pregnancy was fine. Ikerre's churches began to pray for Idia's pregnancy along with Sunday collections. September and October passed. She wrote a letter to the nurse's mother: the doctor thought it would be a girl, could she send a name? The mother wrote back: Rebecca. Then, November's telegram arrived: Rebecca was born. It was like the day Nigeria won the junior World Cup. Ikerre-Oti cheered like lunatics on an asylum's open day. Drivers honked their horns on the streets.

Then four more years came and went and all she sent were photographs.

Ikerre's bitter old women didn't need that much time. Four years in a row? What kind of job had she found in Lagos that gave no annual vacations? Was Rebecca hers alone? Didn't the child have a grandmother? Shouldn't the poor old woman carry her only grandchild before she went to meet her ancestors? Indeed – come to think of it – *was there truly a Rebecca in the first place?* Did The Pregnancy survive that June bleeding? Was 'Rebecca' anything more than pictures cut out of a magazine?

Lagos was four hundred kilometres from Ikerre-Oti, but an Ikerre rumour was a diabolical instrument of long-distance torture. Almost five years after her departure, Ma'Rebecca returned to Ikerre-Oti. *Stupid, stupid, stupid.* She was forty-two, but you could still tell that she once was beautiful. People got a measure of the hardship of Lagos' city life just by looking at Ma'Rebecca's face. 'Haven't you seen Ma'Rebecca?' was how mothers used to douse their teenagers' dreams to move to Lagos. Those were the days when Ikerre gossip really began to stick to Ma'Rebecca, because although Rebecca was a beautiful child, she was as dark as the nurse had been fair. – And she did look small for a four-year old; who was to tell how old exactly the child was? – And the dispatch with which Ma'Rebecca had fled the village following her husband's funeral... was that just the fear of the Health Centre, wasn't it more likely that she wasn't pregnant after all? – And that 'doctor' she had so gleefully announced by telegram, was it a doctor to deliver a baby, or one with whom to make an urgent one?

Much later, I wondered why the widow returned to Ikerre at all: if Lagos had kept her for five years, it could have kept her forever. Ikerre's rumour mill had ground stronger women to dust. The sight of Rebecca ended some rumours, but it fuelled far more vicious ones, for as the young girl grew she failed to develop any resemblance to her late father.

Nonsense and tenpence! This world is a terrible place.

Three years passed before the CID traced Ma'Rebecca. That very day the police car arrived in Ikerre was made in Heaven for gossips. What sweeter words can a wolfer-of-meals hear than, 'eat quickly, it's time to go'? The plain-clothes detective didn't talk much. Had he had come alone, he could have quietly taken away Ma'Rebecca and her child, leaving Ikerre-Oti with a big mystery on which they could have speculated till Kingdom Come. Unfortunately, he didn't come alone. He came with an unhinged woman who fell on Ma'Rebecca with such single-minded fury that she did not care that she had lost the wrapper around her waist. She would have strangled Ma'Rebecca, half-naked as she was, but for the dozen or so villagers on hand. 'What's the matter? What's the matter?' They asked her, swathing her with her recovered garment, but she had only one question for Ma'Rebecca: 'how can you claim to love a child, and *steal* her from her mother?' The astounded villagers turned to Ma'Rebecca, waiting for her furious denunciation, but she meekly crept into the police car for the next phase of her life.

It was as tragic as that.

But not as simple. There was one thing no one could explain, no matter how many times her tale was retold: why she returned to Ikerre after her jail sentence was done? Returned to a village whose natives, with supercilious exactitude, had now reverted to calling her 'Idia'. Were there no more villages in Nigeria? Could she not have found one of those face-me-I-face-you rooms in Lagos, into which to crawl and hide her shame forever? Me, I couldn't understand that one: how she could be homesick for a village whose relentless expectations had ruined her.

Maybe Rebecca was trying to explain it when she fled her real parents in Lagos to return to Ikerre-Oti, to the home of the child-thief. By then it was impossible to look at Ma'Rebecca and tell that she had once been beautiful (– unless you spoke with her, or saw her speaking with Rebecca). Rebecca was twelve when she first returned to Ikerre, and Idia took her straight to the police station, from where she was returned, kicking and weeping, to her real parents. Back in Lagos, Rebecca was policed between home and school, but within six months she was back in Ikerre. Nobody could understand that either: that a girl who knew the facts, how a heartless thief had stolen her from her real parents, could be to that thief what Rebecca was to Ma'Rebecca. So they

125

carried on like that, bearing off a screaming girl to Lagos three or four times a year, until she turned sixteen, when her parents gave up the battle and disowned her for good.

Ikerre-Oti folk are ordinary villagers. They will gape at everything they can't understand; and our biggest mystery is the bond between Rebecca and her old woman. 'Haven't you seen Rebecca?' is how Ikerre mothers chastise their rebellious teenagers, unconscious of the irony that a stolen child should be a model for real children to live up to. It is a complex bond, that thing between Rebecca and Idia, who the wide-eyed villagers have taken to calling 'Ma'Rebecca', once again.

A ROMAN JOB OFFER

I had been trying to sleep for an hour or so when I heard a scratching at my front door. It wasn't quite a knock, but it definitely wasn't a pussycat either. So I opened the door. Young Bona was standing there, still in the green overalls he wore at the fridge repair shop where he was serving the final year of his apprenticeship. I looked back at my clock – it was almost midnight. The street behind him, which led towards the Village Square, was as empty as a cemetery. 'I hope no problem,' I said to him.

'No problem, Sir,' he told me.

He was the only person who called me "Sir" in Ikerre village. It made me uncomfortable. And it was nearly midnight, anyway. He could say "no problem" a hundred times but, *nonsense and tenpence!* I wasn't a child. People don't go visiting at midnight unless a crisis was keeping them awake. My own problems had already extinguished my sleep; adding another man's woes to the elephant on my head-pan was an expressway to the Benin Asylum.

Yet, this was Bona. He was an age-mate of my first son, Abel; but where Abel had already done three years in prison, Bona had never put a foot wrong in his life. He lived with his young wife of twelve months in a one-room-apartment behind the post office. He did have a personality flaw though: a shyness so crippling that it approached disability. There he was now, wringing his hands at my doorway. And I realized that when a person like Bona scraped together the gumption to knock on my door, it was wickedness to turn him away. Reluctantly, I let him in.

He sat down opposite me. I folded my arms, looked at his mouth and waited. This was not the time for silly small-talk. Slowly, he cracked the knuckles of his eight fingers, one after the other. He paused. I watched his mouth patiently. He cracked the knuckles of his thumbs. I put my feet in my slippers, looked up at his mouth and waited.

'I'm sorry I'm coming late like this, Sir,' he said eventually. Then he started on his fingers again.

I saw that this thing wasn't going to work. I sighed: 'Bona, it is twelve midnight, Ikerre people will think I'm starting a wizards' coven in my house. What's the problem?'

'It's about my wife, Iqua.'

I nodded quietly; inwardly, I began to boil. I gripped my thighs but my legs were shaking furiously all the same. Yet, it wasn't anger winding me up; it was shame. Didn't he have ears, this idiot gaping earnestly at me? Couldn't he hear the silence in my house? Ma'Abel's snores were notorious in the whole of Ikerre-Oti, did he think she had been suddenly healed? Was he so stupid that even momentous items of gossip – like Ma'Abel's desertion – escaped him completely? Why did he come to me for matrimonial advice, when my wife was at that very moment sleeping in a vulcaniser's bed? 'I'm in no mood to settle quarrels,' I warned.

'We're not quarrelling, Sir. It's just that she's leaving with the agent at six o'clock tomorrow morning...'

'What agent is that? Where's she going?'

'She's going to Rome with the Recruitment Agent from Benin.'

A bucket of cold water poured over my shame and my legs stopped shaking. I see. I said. I looked at my slippers. I slipped my feet from them. I arranged them carefully, side by side. The right slipper was slightly longer than the left. Just like Iqua; she was slightly taller than Bona. She was slightly shyer as well, which was incredible, coming to think of it... Such a slight whisper of a woman... I looked up – but my eyes slipped over his shining, earnest face and hit the hole in the corner of the ceiling. I had punched it many years ago to let the TV aerial wire through. Now it was a rats' highway; their dirty feet had marked a distinct brown lane on the yellow paint between the window sill and the ceiling. I forced my eyes down to Bona's face. He was looking at me with that attention you only find on faces waiting for an oracle to speak. For God's sake, what does this idiot want from me?

'What do you want from me?' I asked him.

'Your advice, Sir,' he said; his voice was very, very solemn. 'You know that of all the people in this village, it is your advice I respect most. Should I let her go, or not?'

I put my feet inside my slippers once again. I rose; I found a dry kolanut lobe which I shared with my nocturnal guest. I scratched my head as we chewed the bitter fruit. I scraped at the farmer's grime under my fingernails. I sighed many times as the minutes passed. Where could I start to tell such an innocent about the facts of life? The farthest I had ever travelled from Ikerre-Oti was Kano, but in my better years I never missed an issue of the Daily Times; and I tried not to let the same conman take me twice.

I knew a few people who had been hired by the Recruitment Agent. He stopped at Ikerre-Oti once or twice a year. He stayed at the Goodnight Inn on Katai Road and trawled the streets for talent: people strong and hard-working enough to be trained as 'housekeepers' and 'chambermaids' for foreign hotels. He interviewed both men and women of all ages – although the successful ones were invariably young, attractive, and female. In the past he had found very few recruits in Ikerre-Oti. But Bose had gone along with him the year before. For forty years, Bose's mother had fried akara on a brazier at the junction of Nkisi Street and Katai Road. Yet, within two months of Bose leaving Ikerre-Oti, her mother had retired from the fast-food business. All she did these days was collect weekly Western Union messages from her daughter in Italy.

I had known that the Recruitment Agent would get a warmer reception this year, ever since I saw Bose's storey building growing near the stream. It was nearing completion after only nine months. What I had never suspected was that Iqua of all people would be in the running. 'I thought she was doing well at the seamstress''. I murmured.

'The Recruitment Agent said she could be earning a hundred and fifty times more, Uncle Jumai, *one hundred and fifty times more*. They will do the visa, they will do the plane ticket, they will do *everything*: Iqua can be sending back Western Union within three weeks!'

I scraped at my finger nails. I asked him: 'Did he tell you the *kind* of job she will be doing?'

'Yes sir, and we really don't mind it. We're not proud people, Uncle Jumai, it is better we swallow our pride and do the menial things that people are looking down on, and get a better tomorrow. Look at the house that Bose is building! Within nine months...'

'Leave the house that Bose is building! Let us talk about the *job* that Bose is doing!'

Bona shrugged: 'Just eight hours a day – and they pay overtime. – and they have housing allowance! Her whole salary...'

'Let's leave her salary for now! Let's talk about the job! You know that people will talk, you know that people will laugh...'

Bona shrugged again. After a long time he managed to say, 'They've been laughing at me all my life anyway. Let them laugh a little longer, Uncle Jumai, let them talk. After all, nobody is laughing at Bose anymore.'

I took a deep breath. 'Don't you know that... forget all this nonsense about "chambermaids" and "housekeepers"... your Iqua won't be mopping hotel floors. She will be working on the beds... and she won't be wearing hotel uniforms... in fact, she won't be wearing anything at all!'

In the silence, what sounded like a grandfather rat strolled across the length of my ceiling. When it had made itself comfortable in the other side, Bona shifted in his chair. He seemed to be embarrassed on my account. That's the funny thing about shy people.

They are embarrassed for themselves, and when rats disgrace you, they will also be embarrassed for you as well... Then he said, 'We're not children, Uncle Jumai, everybody knows that Bose can't build a house in one year from a housegirl's salary.'

That was when I realised that his embarrassment had nothing to do with the rats in my ceiling. I tried to speak, but he cracked the knuckles of four fingers at once and shrugged bravely, 'After all, it doesn't have a meter.'

There was a small click as my clock struck 1 a.m.. I saw that this nonsense had to end immediately. I pushed my feet into my slippers, 'What advice did you want from me?' I asked him.

'Do you think she will forget me? My friends at the workshop are saying that she will. They are saying that women get there and forget their husbands immediately. That they marry Europeans and...'

My legs began to shake again. Was I now the Ikerre-Oti expert on the Desertion of Wives? Were Ikerre people using Bona as bait to twit me? I stood up furiously, the angry words jumping to my mouth... then I saw his face... and I realised that this stupidity came from deep, deep within his very soul. My anger tripped over into a very deep pity. 'You don't need to worry about that. I told him gently. Iqua will never forget you.'

He stood up as well, smiling with relief, 'You really think so?'

I nodded as I held my front door open for him. The shy idiot stepped outside and paused on my threshold. He took a deep breath and said, proving that while shyness was a curable condition, there was no hope for idiocy: 'This your compound is very large Uncle Jumai, will you want to sell part of it?'

If I punched him now, Ikerre people will ask what the quiet Bona could ever have said to warrant such a treatment at 1 o'clock in the morning. So I held myself and said quietly, 'Try the Igwe's palace, I think he mentioned to me that he will sell at the right price.' Then I shut the door on his face and went to bed. An hour later I was still staring sleeplessly into the darkness. I was the disoriented chorister who had sneezed in the pew and found himself singing from a different page of the hymnal, out of sync with the rest of the choir. How had I become the innocent, relative to Bona of all people?

In the ceiling the grandfather rat roused his family. A multitude of tiny feet scurried to and fro and I felt a tenant in my own house.

THE COLOUR OF IT

D id you bring her letter?'

Aka nods, sinking onto the bed by my wheelchair. She is friendly but cool, her floral gown is a sober blue-green. Her mood is the grass-green of the lawn that slopes away from my window towards the cliff. We haven't spoken since the will was read, and only infrequently since the illness and the burial... 'And I haven't opened it yet, as you asked. What is this about, Pa?'

I shake my head, 'I'd rather not say, Aka.' I look away, 'Can you... will you give it to me, no questions asked?'

She looks steadily at me. There is a new distance between us that dates from my divorce. 'This is Mama's last letter to me. How can you ask for it? Pa, what is this about, really?'

The silence lengthens. Gulls circle and cry, calling me down, down the long narrow ledge, to their haunts on the beach. It is a beach I loved to visit, but the path down the cliff is narrow, treacherous, with a sheer drop to the right, where I broke my back. I never go any more...

'Pa?'

I take a deep breath. 'Can you take me down to the beach. We have to... talk.'

***

Colours are life. To drink in the red of tomato, the green of okra, the yellow of maize... all before the first bite. The teal knife that

137

caught her umbilical cord also cut it. The burgundy bloodiness of it stained me, stayed with me all her life... but no more of this, for now.

For now I sit on my final island of the present as my radius of memory shrinks; lost already are the islands of work, of old friendships... Other islands fade as I brood upon them: Ruma. Fifty years of marriage and a rose-red eruption blends with yellow apology and steel-blue divorce to yield the russet harvest of terminal cervical cancer. Ruma Island sinks slowly. Dementia will drink in every intimate day, every passionate conversation, every fillip of love etched on the rock of that island... I focus away from Ruma, every memory is shaded in aseptic ochres... everything except the brilliant cinematograph of Aka's birth... but no more of this – for now.

For now she sits, my magistrate daughter, in shocked silence on a beach bench, down the cliff from my retirement home, soaking up the orangey blue sun rays and my quiet words... The walk down the path holding back my heavy wheelchair from hurtling down the steep cliff path, has tired her. Yet, it is the sentence I blurted out – to get it over quickly – that drains her.

This moment calls for indignant rage, furious tears, for curses, even – but it does not come. I have broken my truth on her, and the blues have seeped from her blue-green dress, leaving an insidious slime-green. 'It's... time you knew the truth...' I mumble again.

The cobalt sky is maddeningly reticent. It has been threatening for days. It is low and overcast, but it will not burst conveniently to end this scene. My nightmare stretches out, every racking pause of it.

The release I crave doesn't come with confession. I want her to scream at me, to call me some of the names I have called myself in the prickly hell of my conscience during the decades of my penance. Once I watched her work, my magistrate daughter. She was sentencing a... a paedophile I think it was... it was her *cause celebre*. My heart had pounded at the righteousness of her angry judgement, and I never felt prouder of her than there under the sound of her indignation.

Today, her judgement is silent. She lies back on the bench, digesting every word of my sentence, mining their lacerating pain. My hands are trembling. My voice is worse. She irradiates quiet. Her calm breezes over my pebbled despair.

A crow caws. Aka sits up. Her regular breathing is the rhythmic murmur of sea. I cannot hold her gaze. I try, but my eyes slip from her mossy stare, latching onto her lips, which curl; I slip once more. I am staring at the scatter of slate grey pebbles on the sand. They are speckled ultramarine blue, a rich, lustrous sheen of...

'Say it's not true... Pa.'

I study my nails instead.

'If it's true, you'll look me in the eye.'

I raise my eyes to hers.

'Say it's not true,' she says softly, 'and I'll forget everything. I promise. I don't want any details. We'll put this... this statement of yours down to your dementia-'

'No!' I bite my lips. I shake my head, 'I'm not demented, not on this issue...'

'Remember your divorce, Pa. I begged you both, for my sake. I'm *begging* you now.'

I stare. My divorce! If only she knew. If only she had begged me one more time. If only Ruma had returned just one call without that prefatory growl. In the end it had come down to my divorce lawyer. He had worked so hard... the earnestness... it had seemed a shame to pull out... and yet...

Yet, this was not the divorce, this was *the birth*. I was too old for this raging fever, this pounding heartbeat. I wanted nothing more than to bury this mildewed history forever; but I knew Ruma. If Aka read Ruma's version first, she would never see me again, 'I just want to tell the truth, now,' I say, miserably.

'If this is true, then my whole life was a lie.'

'My love for you was not a lie.'

There is a long silence, then she laughs quietly. It is a fuchsia warble, like all her laughter, but it goes on too long, like a blunt knife worrying a taut umbilicus. 'Surely, Mr. Dibia,' her voice is emptied of heat, amusement, 'there's a difference between *loving*, and *coveting* someone else's child.' She shrugs indifferently, 'tell me your truth then, and be done with it.' The cord severs again and I am peppered all over with a damning, fine crimson mist. I shiver.

***

'I'm telling this how it really was, Aka. You were born in a small maternity home within an hour of our stillborn son. I was there. Ruma's spirit was broken by our loss. It was our last try: the doctor had been very clear. The midwife was drunk, and two women going into labour at the same time didn't help matters much. Your real mother probably bled to death. When you started crying, I took you across to Ruma – to suckle you; at first it was just to keep you quiet until the midwife recovered her wits, or your mother's family came for you... but you fell asleep and Ruma refused to... and anyway, it... looked so.... It seemed so... right... I think I felt God say... I just knew...

*'I swear this, Aka, that was how it happened. If Ruma says different it's her way of getting even for the divorce. Now she's dead, she'll say anything to wreck my relationship with you, but you must believe me... she was in on it from the first. She **knew** our child was stillborn, she saw me take you from your mother cot. She knew you were not her natural child...*

'I did not plan for us to... keep you... It was just... you know... one terrible thing leading to the other: your real father coming in so suddenly, for instance... seeing my stillborn son in the cot by his wife, seeing Ruma suckling you... he immediately assumed that both his wife and child were dead... then he was rolling on the ground, sobbing... it was hard to cut in then, you see... not that I didn't try – of course I did... but you've got to believe me, Aka... things happen that are so difficult to undo...

we registered you Aka Dibia. We took you home. We never spoke of it again, until… the divorce…

'No one reckons the suffering of men. I suffered birth pains too, I suffered with Ruma, through two miscarriages, throughout labour… I'm not making excuses, you understand? But… when I held my dead son, I… it is worse that men bear no scars: so there's no allowance there you see… so I held my stillborn child and… you cried, and… something broke, and… I am not making excuses, you understand?

'But… look Aka, what's done is done. I'm ashamed and sorry, but it was a different man that stood in that labour room fifty years ago. Let's have a good weep and put it behind us, Aka…'

***

'Put *what* behind *who*?'

Her voice is a slow, inky citrine. A year passes between the utterance of each nuanced word. Afterwards, the silence continues forever on the darkening beach. Ruma's subterranean island rams my shore with a malevolent judder – Aka's icy voice is the temperature of Ruma's, in that terrible terminal week of our marriage. White seagulls gyrate gracefully upwards, riding the elevators of my seismic chaos.

'I… was only twenty-three,' I offer, lamely.

Deliberately, she pulls out the sealed envelope from Ruma's lawyers. She prises away the seal and extracted a cardboard case. It was fat with the expensive rings that had distinguished Ruma's every hand gesture. Aka glances at the letter and tosses it to me. The rings she tips indifferently onto the beach sand. I scan the letter hungrily. It is quintessentially Ruma: baby blue stationery, taut and teary lines… a goodbye letter from mother to daughter. There is nothing about the events of a half-century ago. Ruma had lived and died our lie; despite her angry threats, she had carried our deception to the grave.

'Turns out I didn't even have to know,' Aka says coldly. She rises then and looks up the cliff. I look up as well. I can see the pearly-white glint from her car, parked on the roadside near my home. This is strange. Her car is orange and yet what I see is a pearly-white. My colour sense is now suspect after all. The accuracy of my primary colours is off; everything is muddied… tints of grey, shades of ochre. I glance around the darkening beach, hungrily. The bench is a dull gray. The sea is the colour of dirty sand. The palms are smudges of early darkness. There is no vividness.

Colour-blindness. The first death.

'Do you want a push up, or what?' she asks.

Aka is so detached, it is unnatural. I look up the cliff. The ascent has never looked more perilous. I cannot risk her behind my wheelchair, all the way up… somehow, I cannot trust her until she has lost it, cursed me, raged…, 'Wait. Aka. Please, don't go yet.'

'Goodbye Mr. Dibia.' She says and walks away.

There is a strange silence. I look around. The sea rushes into my consciousness, knowing everything, feeling everything, lifts itself with the shame of the expired moment, and brains itself against the buff shore. A gush of frothing grey matter hisses and splutters down the beach, expires. A silver corpse of broken waves rolls back, lurching into the womb of the amnesiac deep. Ruma's letter flutters from my nerveless fingers onto the sand, gusting several metres before its flightiness is tamed by the wet. A lapping wave drowns it. I try to remember her last words to Aka. I give up. Goodbye Ruma.

The gulls are gone. In their place a flock of raven-black birds circle an iridescent fish stranded by a wave. The fish flips spastically. The birds keep their distance. Was my stillborn child male or female? I rack my brains desperately. I cannot remember. The posts of dementia shift again. My island shrinks further. My magistrate grows smaller as she rises up the footpath to the cliff. Goodbye, Aka.

The fish tires. The birds grow bolder. A brown thunder rumbles as from a distant country, then all the crows in the world cawed once, and all was still.

THE PROVOCATION OF
JAY GALAMBA

All morning, Jay Galamba watched the lizards come and go. They were human enough when they entered the governor's lodge. He watched them on his CCTV monitors as they strutted through the anterooms teeming with his underlings. The transformation happened as they entered his office, and it was uncanny to behold… those hunching shoulders that sucked in the neck and shaved three inches off the height, the tremulous voice, the shuffling gait… but most spectacular of all was the lizard-like nodding of the head as they agreed with everything he said and did, even before he had said or done anything.

Jay saw at least a dozen of them daily. He had to reserve his mornings for this salving of the pathetic egos sprinkled through the top echelons of the state. In the beginning he used to get a kick from the prostrate performances of company directors and distinguished clerics, but in this eighth year of his governorship, enduring their sycophancy was just another chore of governance. Yet, he could imagine what the visits meant to them, they could now pepper their conversations with the priceless… *As I said to Governor Galamba only yesterday…*

He tired of the interminable wait for his last guest of the day. The corpulent visitor stood just outside the governor's office, taking ages to compose himself, arranging and rearranging the beads on his chest. Jay turned from his CCTV monitor to the back page of *The Guardian*. He'd had to ask for *The Guardian* twice that day, which told him there was probably a deeply unfavourable article about him. He was often irritated by the over-protectiveness of his staff, but not yet cross enough to sack anyone. He pushed aside the rest of the newspapers on which his staff had red-lined saccharin stories for his attention. He went straight to Kayo's column in *The Guardian* — the hungry man seemed to have a Galamba-obsession — and he was not disappointed. The offensive phrase was four paragraphs down,

> *Governor Jay Galamba, also known among his staff as 'The Bore'...*

He looked up at the traditional ruler that now stood before him, sweating despite the air-conditioning, weighed down with a wheelbarrow-load of coral bead necklaces. Jay accepted a palsied handshake, resenting the smell of a cheap eau de cologne that thereafter remained on his hand.

'Your Royal Highness,' the governor said curtly,

'Your Excellency,' the traditional ruler said reverently,

The exchange of superlative greetings went to and fro, although neither was in any doubt as to who, in that room, was truly both 'the royal highness' and 'his excellency'. The traditional ruler wore his full, punishing regalia of office, and the tassels of his crown kept rhythm with his bobbing head. Three minutes into his visit, as the overlong greetings and mutual enquiries into the well-being of extended families tapered off, the aging monarch hinted heavily about a leaking palace roof and a commissioner-ship for a favourite son. Jay noted the requests on the back of an unopened envelope. They discussed the last night's television: the Inter Milan match and the judges' scandalous choice of beauty queen. Finally, on the dot of five minutes, the governor rocked to and fro in his trademark laughter and rose, signalling the end of the visit.

> *Also known among his staff as The Bore?*

Jay was completely mystified. *The Bore?* He could not begin to understand the origin of such an alias. His speeches were witty and punchy. His delivery was constantly interrupted by wild applause, and crowned by standing ovations. He binned the unopened envelope, which clearly contained a get-well-soon card, and reached for his intercom. He paused with his finger an inch from the button. Then he sank back into his chair and raised his furrowed eyebrows to the ceiling, as he recognised one of the few boundaries to the near-omnipotence of the office of governor: this was not the sort of question he could ask his staff. It was demeaning in the extreme. Indeed, as he thought about it, he realised there was nobody he could talk to about this. His real, irreverent, friendships had atrophied in his years in State House. Today what passed for 'friends' were more re-strained species of lizards who could still not be trusted to be frank with the truth. He was pretty close to his military attachè, but asking Denle about this alias was not the sort of thing Jay could do without losing face. And whatever else one did as State Governor, one could never afford to lose face.

Idly he wondered if this would provoke a reaction from his vari-ous self-appointed committees of friends. Six months earlier, the Sun had published a report about his hernia, triggering a flood of thousands of get-well-soon cards, which were still arriving to the day. Back in 1998, when the Vanguard claimed that his 'first lady' was actually a third wife and the governor was technically a bigamist, *forty-two* full page adverts had appeared in national newspapers to refute the allegation, which was true anyway.

Considering the trials of his past, it was strange how such a small and insignificant thing like an alias could prey on the mind of such a personage as governor. His state was no ordi-nary state. It was probably the richest in the federation and had received no less than seventeen billion dollars in revenue over the course of his first term, three and a half billion of which were securely stashed in various holdings all over the world. He was now engaged in a private contest with himself to top that total, as the last year of his second term ran out. He tapped his lap-top awake and added the so-called alias to his name, which was permanently in the Google search bar of a laptop that he used solely for ego-surfing. The combination came up blank. Then the trays for his second breakfast began to roll in and he sighed and pushed the alias from his mind. It was probably another in the long line of Kayo lies.

***

That evening, he lay on his bed digesting his dinner and watch-ing what he could of the television over the rotund plateau of his belly. He dallied as usual on the dilemma of whom to invite into his bed chamber for the night. Yet, it was not as delicious a dilemma as it normally was, and he realised that he was still distracted by the question of the alias. He smiled at the irony that the peace of mind of a Jay Galamba could be compromised by staff so ephemeral that they barely had job titles. That afternoon, for the first time in eight years, he had taken a personal interest in his staff. He had been amazed at their sheer number. No less that thirty-seven personal staff had attended to him that day. He only knew four or five by name, but that morning he had actually talked *to* them, rather than *at* them. He had asked their names, which – hard as he tried – he forgot before the end of the conversation. He had also asked their addresses, amazed at the number of ghettoes whose existence he had never even suspected... all the while wondering if the particular staff before him was one of those who had the guts to call His Excellency 'The Bore' behind his back.

At 2 a.m. that night, he elbowed his sleeping companion awake and sent her to an adjoining room, amazed that such a slip of a girl could snore so loudly. He rose and padded over to the book shelf by the TV. He rarely read in bed, but he had copies of all his books in all the bedrooms in the house. He took down his first one, *The Collected Speeches of His Excellency Governor Jay Galamba JP, Bsc. Dipl. Cert, Volume 1*. He could not help the involuntary smile that flowered as he let the leather-bound book fall open. There were university academics who struggled to write a book a decade. Here he was with a book a year, every year without fail, for the last seven. He picked a random paragraph and read aloud,

> ...and in this connection, let me say to the chiefs, the obas, the baales, the obis, the sheiks, the sultans and all the traditional rulers throughout our great land, Nigeria, that I your governor, will never sleep, rest, relax, or take a break until we have rooted out this evil practice...

He read the speech through to the end, then he flicked through the other volumes on his shelf. *The Bore?* Every time he picked up any of his books he lost an hour or two. It was impossible to read a paragraph without finishing the speech. *The Bore?* He stomped to his study, slapping on the lights as he went. He was beginning to get angry, at Kayo who shamed him before the nation, at his underlings who insulted him behind his back, at everyone. He realised that the lizards were probably in on it. When they met his secretaries, they probably asked to see 'The Bore' only to arrive before him and drown him under their sycophantic 'Your Excellencies'? He wished he could add a voice feed to the CCTV footage, but his staff would know, that was the thing; as soon as he awarded the contract the rumour would spread and all the members of staff would thereafter watch their tongues around the cameras. Once again, all he would get would be a sanitised version of the truth. He was darkly sorry for the lizards scheduled to see him later that morning. He searched noisily in his shelves and cabinets and by the time he found a pocket dictionary, he had roused a steward who stumbled up, blinking blearily, 'Anything Sir?'

'Get lost.'

'Thank Sir,' said the steward, nodding enthusiastically as he disappeared.

Jay browsed quickly to 'bore'. He stiffened as he read the first meaning,

Somebody considered to be annoyingly tiresome and boring.

… yet, there was another meaning,

The internal diameter of a gun barrel

He snapped his fingers and sank into his chair in relief. That was it of course! He owned not one, not five, but *eleven* rifles of various *bores*. Of course it was years and years since he went hunting, but his staff knew everything about him. Over the last five years he had added quality merchandise so that if he ever went hunting again, he would required a specially adapted van to carry his rifles of various *bores*. He was not a man of leisure, not with all the responsibilities of state that haunted his every waking moment, but if he had to pick a favourite hobby, it had to be the shooting, of course. Any staff who entered the Residence and saw the sophisticated gun cabinet would have known that. He kissed the dictionary and returned to bed. Ordinarily he did not like nicknames. When he started secondary school his name had been Jamis Galamba... until he realised that the 'Jamis' in his birth certificate was a corruption of James by his illiterate parents. – But this nickname had gone national and he decided to roll with it. A snore racketed from a neighbouring room but he fell into a sleep too deep for the discomfiture of noisy nymphs.

In the morning his guests found him unusually affable, and at the end of their more leisurely visits he walked each lizard the full fifty metres to his door, detouring to the new, glass-fronted gun cabinet where he displayed a handsome .22 bore carbine. He had been tempted to put his more imposing 600 calibre dangerous game rifle on show, but all Kayo probably needed was a picture of it to inspire more fictions with seditious pieces like *Governor Galamba Plans Secession*.

It took a while for his staff to pick up the vibrations, but Denle, a veteran of the Liberian Peacekeeping, was the one bold enough to take the plunge. Two weeks after the appearance of the gun cabinet, he called across to Eunice, the P.A. 'The Bore wants you now!' It was well within earshot of the governor, and the jaws of six underlings dropped open as they waited for the explosion, but the governor carried on as if nothing had happened. Indeed, that weekend when Denle went to visit his wife who was on bed-rest at the maternity, more jaws dropped at the sight of the 'little something' the Governor sent the pregnant wife. Suddenly the offensive sobriquet went mainstream.

It was not to last, though. Within three weeks Denle was sacked, and his terminal benefits were never to be paid. No one knew just what happened, but in all probability it had to do with the visit of a guest who was not quite a lizard. Dr. Marcia Gudembi was both young and beautiful, and she had spent a disproportionate part of her life abroad, where there were scant opportunities to learn the traits essential for a successful political career in Nigeria. She did not pause at the door to check her make up in a mirror; neither did she break the gait of her confident walk as she passed the threshold into The Presence. Still, he found her exuberance refreshing and thought her beautiful, if a little arrogant. After a twenty-minute chat, Jay promised to support her charity with the ten million naira in seed funding she needed to open. He then took her on the gun-cabinet detour to his door.

She never did get the money, nor did she get any further audiences with a previously accommodating governor. When she replayed that first and terminal visit in her mind, it was clear to her that she had blown it in front of the gun cabinet. In her favour it must be said that she had never liked guns – and had worked late the night before – so when he launched into the penetrating power of various bores, from the Winchesters, through the Remingtons, to the Sakos, an involuntary yawn had prised open her firmly clenched jaws. She had put three manicured fingers in front of the calamitous yawn but it was too late: he had seen her. The governor's reaction had been immediate: from his ashen, thunderstruck silence, to his swift stalking away... even her quick-fire questions about the weight and the balance of the gun had bounced off his gunmetal back.

Later that same day, six-point-eight-billion-dollars of gubernatorial fury fell on a stunned military attachè in an earthquake that cost him his job and shook the administration to its roots. Six other personal staff of the governor lost their jobs before the canny secretaries figured out the score, and the word went round, quietly retiring the offensive alias from the public to the private domain where it belonged. Dr. Marcia Gudembi wrote many more prostrate – and blatantly suggestive – letters, asking to see the rest of the governor's impressive collection of 'masculine' guns at the official residence, but they all ended up at the Governors elbow, where they served as notepads for the requests of visiting lizards.

COUSIN KAŞHIM

We are going to the burial of my darling sister Kaboss this very morning. Later we are going to the jail sentencing of her killer and husband, Aliu. After that we may be going to the burials of many of my other darling sisters, even including me.

My mother born us plenty, that's the thing. And if her husband didn't pack her bag and baggage out when Kaboss was only one years old, she would have born us more, that's also the truth. But because that her husband pack her bag and baggage out when she was just twenty-five years she only born Salia, me myself, Rekia, Fafa, Shatu, and our baby sister Kaboss, making six of us. – My baby sister who has now brought this graveyard problem on our head.

My eyes are full as I'm writing this secret that I swore to Mama (God bless her soul) that I can never, never say, even to the fada at confession. But I will say it now. Now that Kaboss has leaked our family secret, what more is there to hide?

And am telling this story for a good reason, not just that I like to gossip, because of all these young girls like Kaboss who think that just because a man has said *I love you* is why he should know every family secret.

All this started when my oldest sister Salia packed her load back to our house, crying that her husband has thrown her bag and baggage out. And this was not even one week after her wedding feast, of which even the photographer has not even finished washing the wedding pictures. My mother shouted, 'Hah! What happened?'

And my sister, Salia, said, 'Was it not just because we quarrelled and I called my husband *Alhaji Mongoose* because of his long neck?'

So Mama (God, bless that woman's soul) abused my sister left, right and centre, saying that a woman must never use animal to abuse her own husband, because a wife knows her husband so well that the animal she will use will be the real monkey that will wound her husband most. Salia was still saying, 'No,' that it was not like that, but my mother said, 'Shut up,' that the very mouth she was talking with was the same mouth that called our daddy 'Billy Goat' because of his strong B.O. which made the poor man break their wedding photograph and pack our bag and baggage out.

So Salia began to cry and cry, 'Is this how my own has spoiled? When me myself I haven't even borned at all at all?'

But my mother said, 'Don't worry, I will call your cousin, Kashim.'

'My cousin Kashim?' asked my sister, Salia, her eyes stopping to cry and looking wonders at her own mother, 'which cousin Kashim? I didn't even know that we have a cousin call Kashim.'

'I didn't tell you about your cousin Kashim?' My mother said, although she couldn't look at us as she blew this fabu, 'I'm a foolish, true. Come inside the room with me, these small childrens are still too young to know the inside and outside of your cousin Kashim.'

That was how they went inside the room, Mama and Salia, and they talked and talked and talked, and not even two days after that talk, Salia's husband, stood on the doormouth of our house on his own two feet, and behind him was a Kombi bus, true, true. But to look at his face, it was difficult to know whether he came to make peace, or whether Salia had carried one of his own portmanteaus by mistake; if you see how angry was full in his face.

Mama opened the door. 'My in-law!' she cried, 'come in, come in! Kaboss! Bring whiskey for my senior in-law!'

But our in-law was still raking: 'Is it now that you will know that you have in-law?' he asked, 'Me and my wife quarrel, and she pack from my house and you can't even try to settle the quarrel!'

Inside the room we were jumping and pinching our sister, Salia who was smiling for the first time since she came back with her bag and baggage. For two hours, Mama (that woman can talk *sha!*) and her in-law were talking and talking, then the whiskey finished and our in-law carried Salia and all her load and luggage home, and that was that.

Thirteen years! That's how long they have lived together since that day that Cousin Kashim visited Salia's husband! Thirteen good years, plus two boys and three girls! And Kaboss has to catch lovingitis and open all her mouth!

As for me myself, was it not three months after my own wedding that my marriage ended. I think it's a family problem, this our sandpaper mouth. So on my own divorce-day me and my husband we were not talking, but the little we were saying to each other was like small, small daggers that we were chukking ourselves, true. Then I pulled one very long dagger and chukked it inside the very soul of my own marriage.

What I said? He asked me for sugar, but my Tai can stammer a little when he's angry. So I asked him if it was sugar he wanted or *susugar*.

Yes, I know it is not as wicked a thing as buying maxi with the chop money or friending another man behind your husband back, but Mama said the truth, *to God!* A wife can find the sharpest dagger that can make her husband mental, true. My Tai can forgive the wearing of three months' chop money as perfume… he can even forgive the having of a small boyfriend – at least, if nobody else have heard the story *sha*… but to make mockery of his stammering? *Hai!* That susugar of a thing just chukked our marriage dead, I'm telling you. When I saw my Tai's eyes I didn't need reverend fada to tell me that church has finished! Before one hour has passed, before the cocoyam I was cooking has even done, me and my luggage were looking at ourselves in Mama's house. To cry was even hard for me. Come and see the shame! That they have drive me from my husband house because of *susugar!* Which mouth will I use to say that one!

So Mama took me inside her room (God, bless that woman, please) leaving Rekia, Fafa, Shatu and Kaboss to be thinking *what can that woman be planning now?* 'You see yourself now?' My mother said, doing her "I'm warning you" finger like the head of fowl that is eating corn.

'I sorry, Ma,' I said, as she brought out her mobile phone that was fat like plank from building site. 'She put her glasses on her nose, making her eyes times four so that she was looking like Mrs. Babalola from my primary school. Then she began to dial Cousin Kashim.

'He's not your cousin at all,' said Mama as we waited for him to come. 'What he was to me is too heavy for a mother's tongue to tell a daughter's ears. But is business between us now. You will see. Is only business between us now.' And my mother made me watch – as she made all my sisters watch when it was their turn – as she counted most of that month's salary into the hand of Cousin Kashim. To see him was to shake, that's how tall and dark and moustached a man he was, with his eyes like two black bullets looking for their antelope.

And I thought of my darling Tai, with his voice that can break into pieces when fear catches him. And, true to God, I was afraid for him, I swear to God. 'Please let me come,' I said, remembering how the man-mountain that was Salia's husband had run and chartered Kombi bus to pack his wife's bag and baggage back, thinking that my darling Tai could get heart attack by the time Cousin Kashim had finished with him... but it was not like that.

It was not like that, at all.

That very evening, as the *omolanke* boys were finishing their business for the day, the longest Mercedes I have ever, ever seen carried me and Cousin Kashim to my husband house. Even to shake the hand of Cousin Kashim was hard for my Tai, because his hand was oily from the bus-corner akara that he was eating like bachelor from the inside of the newspaper on the centre table. It was not the best way to meet Cousin Kashim, whose Mercedes was long like the street of our house, the glass and the stones of whose lace was shining like the gold teeth of a Mecca Hajia.

'I didn't even know she had a cousin called Kashim,' said my Tai.

'*Okpenke*,' said Cousin Kashim, which was a word that he could use to mean anything he wanted; of which, then and there, he meant: "What you know or don't know is your own problem, not mine". I had enter the house like thread that follows needle inside tough leather, but as I poured brandy for them I could still see the vex sitting like cobra in my Tai's eyes and I knew that, so far so bad, I was still going to follow that needle out as well.

Cousin Kashim opened two long artillery shells like that and brought cigar out from inside them. Slowly-slowly, he began to remove their foil. And if you see as he did it, it was as if he was undressing a woman! He cut the mouth of the two cigar with one wicked blade razor like that. Then he gave one cigar to my Tai.

The Tai that I know has never smoked common cigarette before, but is not after all Cousin Kashim's cigar-ceremony that somebody can just say 'No thank you'. So my Tai took his own cigar. Cousin Kashim set fire to it, and to his own as well. Even his lighter was like the shape of somebody's skull. Two by two they slowly-slowly filled that room with smoke, and although my own condition was to cry for, come and see me struggling not to laugh as I watched my Tai just struggling not to cough.

Then when their two cigar have burned like one or two inches, Cousin Kashim cleared his throat and said I should give them chance to talk their man-to-man. Me I left the room for them and closed the door. – God can punish me for this, but the next talk-talk was not the type that Comfor can miss. To miss that talk has passed the power of this poor sinner-girl. So softly, softly, I jam one tumbler on the door and gummed one ear to the tumbler.

'I got the invitation to your wedding,' Cousin Kashim was lying,

'I cannot lie.'

'So why didn't you come?'

'That torture is more than a human being can take.'

'Torture? To come to the wedding of your own cousin?'

'I can lie and say I was busy at my cement factory in Islamabad, but this is man-to-man talk, not so? The time for joke has come and passed. If is not that my Comfor is my aunty Maria's second child and that we forbid such a thing, I would have married her since she was sixteen years of age. Why do you think I packed to Islamabad? The torture of seeing that beautiful girl every time was too much a torture for a human being to take. To see her and know that I can never marry her! To see her and know that every night, that another man... *no!*'

'I... I didn't know that you felt like that about CoCoComfor...'

'To attend Comfor's wedding was to risk your life, by God who love me!'

'To risk my own life?'

'I cannot lie to you, I'm a violent man,' confessed Cousin Kashim so quietly that I almost wounded my ear, the way I was pressing it into the tumbler, even. I heard a brandy glass conk on the glass centre table. I heard the springs on my Tai's chair creak and creak again as Cousin Kashim said again, 'I'm a very violent man.'

'Is... is that so?'

'*Okpenke.* All my childhood fights must end in the hospital – and the wounds are always on the other person, not me, by God who love me! One of my friends is still in wheelchair, even. Just because of me. That's why I joined army. I would have gone to prison otherwise. That five years of killing people on government licence is what save my life, it has reduced my tension a bit, but I'm still a violent man, as for.'

'I see,'

'No, you don't see anything,' explained Cousin Kashim very gently, 'you see, when I heard my darling cousin crying on the

160

phone to me, when I heard that she was now divorcee–'

'*My wife? Divorcee?*' shouted my darling Tai – and come and see his angry voice! 'When it was only one small quarrel that we quarrelled? *Divorcee?*'

'But that was what I heard...'

'If she is divorcee, then where's the cocourt papers? Is it ordinary mouth that husband uses to divorce his wife?'

'But what about her bag and baggage?'

'Bag and baggage! You know these foolish... I mean, you know these wowomen, you say one woword to them and they pack their bababag and baggage to their mother's house. Me that I even thought you brought her baggage back to settle the quarrel.'

'*Me,* Kashim? To settle a marriage quarrel? God forbid! That's one thing I will never do. A man must rule his house, that's what I always say. What I have come to do is to tell you that you have cause me two sleepless nights...'

'Me? Tai Azeez?'

'...the first night was your wedding night with my Comfor. I cannot lie, I did not sleep that night and for that, I cannot blame you. The second night was yesterday, when I thought you have made my Comfor divorcee...'

'See me see trouble! These women can add pepper to story! I can never divorce my Comfor!'

'Is twenty-one years since I left army, twenty-one years since I killed another man, and me, I really don't like how I'm feeling now,'

'I really must say that...'

'Is it not funny how a man can love a woman to pieces and can never marry her, whereas the man that marries her does not even love her one tiny bit?'

'Me?' shouted my darling Tai, 'Me that I love my wife to pieces?'

'Are we talking about the wife that you throw her bag and baggage out, or the other one you marry yesterday?'

'Me?' shouted my dearest, dearest, darling Tai, '*Me?*'

At this very juncture, to tell the truth, my hand was shaking so much that the tumbler scratched on the door and I ran away on my hands and knees before Cousin Kashim opened the door and caught me listening to their man-to-man. By the time the door opened in another ten or fifteen minutes, I was already cooking cocoyam in the kitchen, of which Cousin Kashim totally refused to eat, despite all the raking and begging of me and my Tai. He just shook his head and said, *Okpenke*. Of which I think at this time that it means "No" and "Double No."

He shook hands man-to-man with Tai, and as he was doing that, his hand was on my waist, of which it made my knees to weak like pap. That I did not cry at that moment was miracle, true, true. Then I saw Cousin Kashim off to his Mercedes Benz, of which his door was opposite number 5, even though his front bumper was opposite number 11. As he entered the car, he aimed his black and wounding eyes on me and I couldn't breath again, and he said, 'Your mummy hasn't got the money to pay me to come out two times for one daughter. You hear me so?'

'I know.'

'If I hear that you make fun of your husband's stammer again, I will tell him the truth, that you are not my cousin at all at all.'

'But he will kill me,' I whispered.

'*Okpenke*,' he said. Of which, I think he means "exactly".

Except that it was Aliu that killed Kaboss first. Because, me myself, I never quarrelled with my darling Tai after that, or my Salia with her husband, or any of my other sisters with their own husbands. When it was Kaboss' turn for my mother to save her marriage, Mama did what she did for all of us, but did Kaboss keep our family secret as dead people keep secrets? You're asking me! She went and caught lovingitis. Then thinking that she had reached that mountaintop of love that nobody else had ever reached before with their own husband, where it becomes sin for her to have a secret that her darling Aliu did not also know, she opened her mouth and said what she had sworn to Mama that she would never, ever say. 'Is that so?' asked Aliu, remembering how he had knelt down to beg the very woman that called him 'orang-utan' to pack back into their marriage house.

'Yes o,' said my darling, but really, really stupid sister, Kaboss, and she went on and on, saying how she was really very sorry and how she was really very happy she had told him everything because to keep a secret from Aliu was to carry a luggage heavier than stone...

And she was still going on and on like this when her darling Aliu put his hands, which, to tell the gospel truth, were long and large and powerful like orang-utan's, and strangled her and put her body in his pick up. Then he drove to Mama's house (God rest her precious soul), 'I have a message from Cousin Kashim,' he said to her.

'I can explain,' said my mother (God rest her strangled soul), and she tried, she really tried, as all we witnesses can swear, but he just raised his orang-utan hands again, and when he finished he carried the two both of them to the police station.

So we have buried Mama this last Monday. Today we will bury my darling sister, Kaboss. Is difficult to know who we will bury next, because despite that Salia's husband is a huge man-mountain of a man, the nickname of Shatu's husband is "Matches", because of how fast and quickly his anger catches fire: and all our in-laws, plus including Tai, are wondering how and why that gentleman Aliu has done such a wonderfully terrible thing as this to an innocent family as ours, and they are waiting, really, really waiting for tomorrow's date to go and hear Aliu's story in the court of sentencing.

As for me myself, I'm thinking hard, that is either I just run away, me and the five children I born for my darling Tai, or... *Okpenke!* – as Cousin Kashim would have said... which in this case means: I just don't know what to do or think or say at all at all.

URBAN ARCHITECTURE

Finally you buy the plot of land of your dreams. It is 100 x 75 square feet, somewhere in Lagos or Ibadan – anywhere you happen to be posted at the time. It is a lovely spread, this land of yours. It is a big enough architectural playground for that old friend of yours from your university days, who made his fortune converting Victoria Island residences into banking halls. Yet, you despair. The ink is still wet on the contract, you are standing in the middle of the plot, up to your chest in angry elephant grass, and you despair: where will you find the money to build a dream "villa" which will fit in with the expensive piles of concrete your neighbours are building, up and down the street?

So you start where you can: with the fence. Six months pass and you manage to raise a four-foot-high wall around the plot. You are tempted to raise it higher, but the excitement takes over and you want to get started on the house itself. Your architect schoolmate is a friend indeed and he adapts for you a plan which he originally created for a retiring super permsec. It is complete with car porches and Roman-style entrance columns. Of course you will have a terrazzo finish rather than marble – and you will manage without the swimming pool – but it will do.

So you hire some labourers and sink the well in the front. In two short days they clear away the unruly elephant grass and the ferocious thickets. They chop down five or six trees and cart them away for firewood. This is when you find a small surprise waiting for you at the back of the plot: a small mud house with fat adobe walls and tiny windows! It has probably been there one or two hundred years, and the thatch roof has rotted away. You haven't seen one of these antiquities in decades! On a whim you tell your labourers *not* to knock it down, for now. It is there in a corner of the plot anyway. You will probably put a zinc roof on it and store cement bags there till your mansion is finished. It will be an interesting curiosity to show friends: your very own back-yard architectural museum. There is also a shade tree in front of the hut with some low-hanging mangoes. You will save the tree as well – till it ripens its fruit later in the season.

You are now ready to build, but this – of course – is the point at which reality hits you. You are just a senior protocol officer after all. It has taken you most of your career to save up for this plot of land. You have no former classmates in the building materials trade, and what you have left in your bank account is only good for a modest bungalow. You are torn by the dilemma: do you accept reality and dig the foundation for the small bungalow you can afford, or do you walk in 'faith' and start the imposing three-level-mansion that your children may have to finish, long after you are dead? You have only six years before your retire-ment, so a mortgage loan is out of the question.

While you vacillate over the decision, you hire a live-in guard and begin to mould sandcrete blocks on your plot. Your guard was a thatcher, back in his village, and he harvests palm fronds and fits a thatch roof on the mud house. This costs him nothing. He sleeps there at night. He digs fresh clay to patch and render the circular walls. This also costs him nothing. You watch him prime the clay by stomping on it for hours. He seals it in with lime. He raises a clay platform for a bed. Heck, he even goes on to acquire an earthenware pot to hold his drinking water! This loving restoration begins to rile you. This is your modern prop-erty, not some village house. But you ignore your house-proud guard and install an imposing gate. This costs you an entire month's salary, by the way. It is five feet higher than the current fence around the property, but it is an eye-turner, and hints at your ambitions for the house to come... yet, you still cannot de-cide what type of foundation you want to build. For six months, you lose interest in your plot of land.

At this point, fate takes a hand in your affairs. Something happens to justify your sixty years of patience with the shambolic state of affairs in your country. You have always defended the corruption and nepotism in the system, despite its terrible impact on you, because you lived in the hope that someday it might be your turn. That day arrives in a flush: a second cousin of your mother-in-law's school daughter becomes minister for health and you get to supply toilet rolls to the local teaching hospital. From the staggering orders you receive, there is clearly a worrying amount of shitting per capita going on at the hospital, but you are the contractor not the health inspector, and you address your own business diligently. In no time at all you are able to put the marble back into the specifications of your house.

When you return to your plot of land, it is with much more confidence. Your guard had been rearing goats there and the place is full of their black droppings. (You don't like the irony of a toilet paper contractor being overrun by the faecal matter of goats, so you compulsorily purchase his animals. For some days, the aroma of barbecued goat meat overpowers the smell of goat shit.) The mud house now wears a cap of palm thatch. Your guard has polished the mud walls to a smooth finish. You walk into the adobe hut. There is not a scrap of paint on the walls, yet it does not look 'unpainted'. You, kind of, like the earthy smell of it, the lime with which the external walls are varnished. You cannot get over how cool the interior is, despite the tiny windows, as you walk in from the blistering heat of your Kano or Enugu day. The fat walls of clay, the thick roof impregnated with dead air pockets, they all drink in the heat, leaving the inside of the adobe as cool as an egg. The last time you felt this snugly comfortable was in the womb. It will be a pity to demolish it when the time comes. Yet, it is clearly too small to shelter the cement and other stores for your mansion, so you crane in a container. You hire a building contractor. Construction begins.

Between your regular job as a senior protocol officer in your ministry and your evening job as toilet paper contractor, you have no time for your house during the week. But you never fail to visit on Sundays, with your friends who have become hooked on your weekly barbecues. You will walk around the empty site, inspecting the work done during the week, then you will retire to the shade of the mango tree at the bottom of the plot. You have set up some chairs there.

Eighteen months pass and thanks to your hard work – and the apparent epidemic of diarrhoea at the teaching hospital – your dream house is complete. *Look at me! Look at me!* cries your house, and everybody does. It occupies most of the plot now, an imposing, muscular building – concrete window arches, aggressive jutting balconies, and a very red, long-span aluminium roof. You can see the top twelve inches of the twenty-foot-high Greco-Roman columns of the grand portico from halfway down the street. Of course it looks like a jail-house, what with three-metre-high walls and the no-nonsense burglary proofing that ruins the views from every window. But it is an impressive jail-house, and you prefer "safe" to "pretty". It stands shoulder-to-shoulder with all the other expensive piles on the street – nobody can mistake this for a house built from a salary. Although your children have all left home, you have fifteen en-suite bedrooms. The windows are large, aluminium and tinted; but because they are sliding windows, they will only open halfway. The house is as hot as an electric oven in the day and airless and humid at night, but you have installed air conditioners and air monitors even in your toilets and there is a generator in the backyard to cope with the regular power failures. (You have supplied enough toilet paper to keep yourself in diesel, well into retirement.)

The air conditioners work hard: the height of your fence, and the three feet between your house and the wall, means that there is precious little by way of breezes.

Your friends still come, although you now spend your Sunday evenings in the cossetted lounges of your new mansion, where you drink your beers and eat your takeaway suya while you soak in hour after hour of satellite television. There is little conversation, but when you talk it is often to reminisce about the "good old days" under the mango tree. You know that this is ordinary nostalgia, another manifestation of the deceptive "Old-is-Best" syndrome. Yet, as you return this evening to the rumbling hubbub of dozens of generators and air conditioners up and down the street, as you drive in and your guard locks you into your fortified dream house, as you try to decide where – as between the ground floor, first floor or penthouse lounges – to unwind with a beer, you have a sneaky feeling that in truth, those evenings with friends in front of the mud house at the bottom of your house were probably the best days of your life. You recognise that this is both silly and illogical, but it is difficult to argue with a feeling.

You reach for the beer and remember your doctor's frightening warning. So it is the mango juice you take from your bedroom fridge as you walk out onto the rear balcony. A small breeze stirs the leaves of the mango tree. You hear it, but it is too wispy to ease the clamminess of the collar that sticks to your neck. Despite the airlessness, you will like to stay on this balcony, but over your generator, you are assaulted by the chorus of six or seven other monstrous generators that will run through the night. Generator sizes are indexed to the prestige of their owners and though you are a Big Boy now, you recognise that you are a newcomer to the league. The loudest generator belongs to your neighbour four houses away, who works for the Power Holding Company of Nigeria. You will have to seal yourself into your grand mansion to escape from this mad racket. As you turn to go in, you can just make out the thatch roof of the mud house. It is all brown now, the thatch. You cannot see your guard, but even over the generators, you can hear his uncouth laughter from under the mango tree. You feel a sudden – and very strange – stab of envy. You wonder why this is so. You still don't know how to swim, but you decide to dig that swimming pool in the backyard all the same. The blasted mud house will have to go.

A TASTE FOR LEFTOVERS

If he hadn't cooked the mush himself, Bedi could not have eaten it. As it was, he knew that the ingredients were perfectly healthy – even though the combination of mincemeat, kuse and shredded spinach had somehow overpowered the red beans he had warmed over from dinner. He had risen an hour too early so he was able to breakfast on the balcony overlooking Sekondi beach. It was too early for the Alleluia chorus, but a small throng of gulls quarrelled over a grouper. It was not terrible, he decided, after the third spoonful. Of course he would never have taken this from a steward – or his Ga or Ethiopian ex-wives – but in spite of his six bedrooms and three living-rooms he lived alone. And it was not that bad, really.

Down in the yard, and out of his line of sight, his driver ran a bucket of water with which to wash a Mercedes that was not dirty. Over the gentle roar of sea and caw of seagull, over the rush of water into bucket, he heard the fart and he sighed and pushed away his meal. Now he could hear and not smell. During the long drive to his Accra office he would regularly smell and not hear. The sense of impotence inspired by his father returned. He did not know where he found the strength of character to run a major corporation, but not enough to tell his chauffeur to stop fouling up his car.

The ingredients of his life were perfect. Yet, Bedi could not deny the obvious: his many houses, the fleet of cars, a dream job... none of them masked his overwhelming depression. He was envied from Takoradi to Nandom, and he could drive across his country without seeing a single car, house, or asset of any description that he couldn't afford. Yet, the one thing he desired in all the world teased him from an admin cubicle in the Takoradi office. She was sixteen no longer, but he could still fillet the inflection of her voice from the hubbub of the staff, and it still twined him with regret. Her laughter still stabbed him in the soft organs. She was a slip of a girl no more. And his father was right, of course: her family was wrong. In the end, she had made nothing of herself. Now and again, he passed her in traffic, two noisy boys in the back of a smoking station wagon... He was right to walk away back then.

Yet, he could not forget their mornings after. The tang of her tongue. The way she melded mincemeat, kuse and spinach with any leftovers in the fridge, evoking flavours that calcified even the most tumultuous memories of sex, flavours that sent him questing from Ga to Ethiopia – and almost into faraway France – before he realised that what he was seeking in his future only existed in his past... his father was wrong. Downstairs, his chauffeur switched on a tinny radio and whistled along to a song. It was time for work.

Bedi rose with resolution.

***

His reception seemed more like a fashion show than an office. Sama sat there and stewed.

Perhaps it was a mistake to take the job after all. It had seemed perfectly safe at the time: the opening was at the Takoradi office while Bedi was based at the Accra Headquarters. It was a nine-month maternity cover and she was to be strictly small fry. How hard could it be to pull a steady salary for a few months until her restaurant turned the corner? The Akumaka Group had close to six thousand staff and she had a new surname. Surely she would be long gone before he even realised she had worked in his company. In any case, Bedi sat on the boards of a dozen companies on the Ghana Stock Exchange. If she really wanted to get away from the shadow of her first boyfriend she would have to leave the country of her birth.

Yet, within four days of starting at Marine Admin, Takoradi, he was in their conference room for a briefing. She twirled the ring on her critical finger as the memory burned again. Had she really added so much weight? Or was her dread braids and new surname the perfect disguise? During the thirty-minute meeting she had not said a word, and afterwards he had gone round the conference table, shaking her hand without a flicker of recognition in his eyes. It had been the closest of many calls. Until the email arrived that morning.

She looked up from her ring and caught the lady opposite staring at her with a grin that was more smirk than smile. Sama nodded a greeting but the woman raised her Ghanaian Chronicle and disappeared superciliously behind her newspaper. Sama's eyes dropped directly to the other woman's shoes: sure enough it was the ruinously expensive brand. Her legs were crossed with easy confidence, the red toenails were ten oblong smarties. Power briefcase, rich navy blue skirt...*Stop it Sama!* She forced herself to shut her eyes, and to keep her hands from smoothing her own crumpled skirt. She had a lot of work on her desk, but it was his business, not hers. If he chose to have her wait in a reception for an hour while he saw one husband-hunter after the other, each masquerading as businesswoman, it was his own funeral.

'Chief will see you now.'

She rose stiffly. *Chief.* With the death of his father, *Chief* only meant one person to the staff of The Akumaka Group. That was why she had waited three hours, wasn't it? Because *Chief* was all grown up now, had to show his ex- who was 'big boss' now. Miss Chronicle had gone in first, even though she was the last to arrive. Indeed Sama was the very last visitor to be shown in. As she approached his office she tried to bite down the anger, but when she stepped in, it was the sheer grandeur of his accommodation that subdued her. The office was easily half the entire penthouse floor. She had never been in a private office that large. He was not sitting behind a desk as she had expected. Instead he sat in a small, intimate, suite of chairs, and he rose as she approached. She wished he was fat, balding and pot-belied, but all she could hang on to was the wistfulness in his eyes, which could very easily have been merely a reflection of her own eyes.

'Hello Sama,'

'My name is Samantha Wolio,' she wanted to say, but her jaw seemed locked down with a monkey wrench. She smiled tightly and shook hands with him. He sat down opposite her and she set the ship register surgically in the centre of the coffee table.

He ignored it. 'Would you like a coffee? Tea?'

'No thank you, Sir. I've already had four coffees and a tea in your reception.'

'Ouch.' His teeth flashed apologetically. 'I'm sorry about that long wait – my secretary mixed things up. I told her I wanted you as my last appointment... but I didn't realise she kept you in my reception for so long!' The apology seemed overlong too – teenage anxiety underneath the veneer of a lifetime of success.

'I wasn't complaining, Sir.'

'Please. Drop the "Sirs", Sama.'

'My name is Samantha Wolio, Sir.' She was surprised to hear the words resound in the room, but pleased with the confidence in her voice. At that moment, she realised she was ready to walk away from the job. – And to turn her back on corporate Ghana, for she also knew how long a shadow a vengeful Chief could throw. There was a long silence, then he smiled and breathed deeply.

'How are you, Samantha?'

'Fine, Sir.'

'I want the long answer.'

She hesitated. His voice was an amenable coo, not at all the voice of a one who had hauled up an ex-girlfriend to gloat over the present gulf between their lives. *What did he want?* Then she crossed out the thought angrily... it didn't matter what he wanted! She leaned forward, pushing the register towards him, 'I brought the ship register, personally, as your P.A. requested...'

'Forget the bloody register!' he snapped impatiently, slapping the table with four fingers. She flinched, and hoped he did not notice. She would rather be angry than nervous. He had not had a temper to speak of, back in the day. This was the capitalist backlash that masked the gentleness of the human. There was no Bedi here any more, then. He was all Chief now. She rose.

'Sit down.'

'No, Chief Akumaka,' she said quietly. 'You can't give me any more orders, because I am going to my office to write a final letter to Human Resources.' She watched his face as she spoke. She knew she was being irrational. She could so play this differently, fake some simpleness, humility, and leave that room with her job, maybe more... but, *God!*... that would be not be human! That month end would be very difficult, but she was drinking in the mixture of shock and speechlessness on his face, bottling it up. This memory would carry her through the drought. It would fire up her stalled engines. She would run for many years on the fuel of it. She turned.

'You don't even know why I called you here!'

'And I don't even care.'

'Why can't you be professional about this? Whatever happened between us happened twenty years ago! We were teenagers!'

She whirled about, grasping at her self-control, scared at the elemental thing that surged inside her, 'I was the teenager. You were three days away from your twenty-third birthday. Our child would have been your age today...' she broke off as he rose. She had said too much already. She could not afford to let her guard down, to uncork twenty years of rage. She turned. At the end of his tennis court of an office she took the knob of the door.

'Listen,' he said urgently, from paces behind her, 'I called you here for one thing only. To say I was sorry. Okay...' he broke off. Just then he looked more angry than sorry.

She felt the blood rush to her face. *He was sorry.* 'Why? Did your pastors tell you that my forgiveness would open the wombs of your barren wives?'

'I hoped you wouldn't still be bitter, after all those years.'

'*Bitter? Me?* Listen, Bedi. I waited for you for only six years so why should I be bitter? *Only six years.* I had thought that sooner or later you'd realise that what we had was... different. Sooner or later you'd grow the balls to tell your father what the king of England told his country. He gave up his crown for the love of a woman. I thought you would call your father's bluff. But you didn't, did you? So I moved on. I filled my life, and my body, with all manner of animals. Because I needed someone... some- *thing*... beastly enough to replace you.' She show him her cheap wedding band. 'But eventually I found Steven. I don't love him. – Thanks to you I can't love anybody any more. But he is a great husband, and we have two great boys. So I am not just bitter, Bedi. I simply hate you with every fibre in my body. And if my forgiveness has anything to do with it, your great Akumaka em- pire will never have an heir – because you and your father or- dered me to abort your true heir.'

She walked out, shutting the door softly.

There. She had said everything after all, delivered the speech she had dreamt at least a thousand times. Yet, as she dropped slowly to the ground floor, she did not feel better for it. Instead the con- tentment that had filled her life in the past decade seemed to take flight. She had stood in that vast room. Spoken again to that great man. Spied again that alternate destiny that had been so rudely snatched from her...

The elevator paused at the fifth floor and three middle-aged women debarked, decongesting the cage and revealing the mir- ror side of the elevator. Sama sized up her profile. She had defi- nitely gained weight. And it was all going to the hips by a factor of three to one. Of all days to have worn the corduroy coat! That was clearly what the Chronicle woman was staring so contemp- tuously at! And her face... she tried to smile but the result was more ghastly than friendly. Why did she have to carry the woes of world on her face! She had nothing to set beside the Chronicle woman. Not in looks, not in poise, not in prospects. Her father was a carpenter. She had brought his forgotten spirit level to the Akumaka's speedboat which he was repairing. The young lovers had met. Months later, she had made love for the first time on that boat. She remembered private meals she had rustled up in the galley of that boat, anchored in a secret cove of his own discovery. They had gone out until the day of her graduation... she caught herself. She was reverting to Bedithink... the day-dreams, the reveries, the recriminations that had possessed her for six years until it gutted her life of its promise.

Resolutely, she evicted him from her mind once again. She drew her twins onto a centre-stage where her psychiatrist was inton-ing a stark voice-over: she had a duty to Marko and Matt to stay in the real world, to figure out how to pay their next school fees... Bedi was her past, not her future.

The lift doors parted on the ground floor and there, barely five paces before her, was Bedi Akumaka talking to a minion. He was not even breathing hard... his express elevator would have done all the work. He broke off, 'Oh... Mrs. Wolio?'

'Yes... Sir.'

She had to admire his play-acting skills, as the throng of staff and visitors washed past them. What a prostrate people we are, she thought, as passing heads bobbed deferentially, like Agama lizards. Was it the first billion cedis, she wondered, or the sec-ond, or the third, that made us so subservient to the wealthy and the powerful. Her own neck was riveted by rage, as though her head and spine were fused into a single bone.

'By the way,' he was saying, casually, 'I have finished with the register, you can pick it up upstairs and take it back to Takoradi,' he waved a hand in the direction of the two Grecian columns that hid his elevator, 'this way...' he paused and held her eyes, 'please.'

He turned for the elevator, without waiting to see if she would follow. Because that was what chiefs did: take their minions for granted. The significance of the please had not been lost on her. It had been invested with special, shorthand powers. It was the sort of please a big man could dispense to a small girl in a public lobby without losing face. It was different from the teary, de-meaning pleases she had poured out two decades earlier, over the weeks it had taken for her to realise that she was indeed to be left in the lurch. A backwash of rage began to swell, enough to tell him publicly, and colourfully, what to do with his bloody register, enough to burst onto the front pages, if not of the next day's Chronicle, then at least The Mirror... For a split-second she saw herself as she once was... not the bitter shrew in the elevator mirror, but the confident, sassy girl with the world before her – more confident indeed that the Chronicle woman – ready to take on all of Ghana, quick-witted, good-humoured, but with eyes only for the most handsome man in Africa...

Yet, she was no longer that lady. She was now the matronly type in the elevator mirror. *What did he want from her!* She had reached a precious accommodation with her true reality and she wanted nothing of the scary bitterness she saw in the mirror. She would live out her lot with dignity... but... w*hy had she lied to him?* Before her, the revolving doors beckoned her out into Accra's sunlight. Behind her, the CEO express pinged as the elevator doors opened. In a trice her mind was made up.

Sama moved with resolution.

***

In the bathroom, the escort dressed slowly, humming *Night Nurse* under her breath.

Sometimes he wished he had a cancer of some sort – not the sure killers like late diagnosis prostrate, which had killed his father – maybe an early tumour which would be quickly taken out and fried by a course of chemo. Six to twelve months of uncertainty hell and he would get his life back. This depression just went on and on. Plus he got neither public credit nor private understanding from friends for his suffering.

Some diseases had prestige value. Others were guaranteed to elicit sympathy when people spoke about it at the golf club. Almost any cancer would do. But anything that took a man into the psychiatric hospital was not good for business. Hosni was the son of a Lebanese family of truckers who had checked into the high-brow Mt. Sinai Clinic fifteen years earlier. He had won his struggle against addiction and drugs and taken the family business into the airline sector... but he was still "Junkie Hosni" to this day, still suffering a whispering campaign that started up once he left a room and questioned his business judgements.

Yet, Bedi could not argue with the oppressive reality of his depression. He saw his doctor every last Sunday of the month. Mostly they just played chess. It was out of the question for him to confide the truth. Bedi's doctor was very confidential: a sensitive secret confided to him could take all of a year to reach the motor park, but reach the motor park it would. Bedi had considered confiding in his foreign doctors. He had an annual Harley Street check up, but he knew how those ones operated. Nothing was done off the record. In no time at all the information would be in his insurance paperwork and once their computers got it, that was it. There had to be a dozen Ghanaian clerks in London alone who had access to the data in his insurance files.

So he lined up the self-medicated drugs he had got on the internet and downed them one after the other. *Whatever it takes to pull yourself together!* He stared at his reflection in the black glass of the hotel room. He did not feel like one of the richest men in Ghana.

The escort finished dressing and stepped back in shyly. He wondered how a woman who was so brazen, naked, could be so shy fully-clad. 'Thanksir,' she said, almost kneeling. She was holding her fees in her hand, and she was helplessly smiling, as well she should. He had been generous.

He tried, desperately, to remember her name and failed. 'Go well, my dear,' he said finally, and she did, closing the door carefully. He knew that this rendezvous could be buzzing within a select grapevine within hours, but this was Ghana. Liaisons like this could be good for business, especially for a man whose marital status was providing grounds for more unpalatable rumours.

He sat in front of the television and stared at the screen for thirty minutes.

He was tempted to switch it on, but the silence was strangely balming. Eventually he decided on a bath instead. As he stepped into the water, her name dropped into his mind. *Anelie.* He decided it was a business name. Her accent was Ewé and he did not know many Ewé men who called their daughters Anelie. It had been a fiasco after all. He had been responding to Sama's humiliation when he booked her. He had closed his eyes throughout, but this time it hadn't worked. Now that he had met Sama again in the flesh, he could no longer sleep with a woman as though he was sleeping with her. The new Sama was woman to the girl he had known. The new Sama was as mysterious as the old had been known. Her curves were newly virginal. The Sama that humiliated him in public completely defeated his imagination in the privacy of his hotel room, and despite Anelie's best efforts, he had been completely slain. That was why he had been so generous to Anelie: to make her public memories of this night more flattering than the reality.

As he towelled himself, his PDA chimed an alarm for his 8.30pm meeting with the Natural Resources Minister, but he knew that if he took a critical meeting in his frame of mind he would be slaughtered. He called Kwesi and told him to cancel.

'Do you think that is wise Sir?'

'What?'

'Sorry Sir!'

He paused. Then he snapped, 'Tell him I had food poisoning, okay? I'm with my doctor right now.'

'Yes Sir.'

He switched off the phone and glared at it angrily. Anger. This was good, very good. Anger was a good antidote to the apathy that was suffocating him. It was the first time his deferential P.A. had dared question his judgement quite so boldly. It was a meeting to renegotiate the Akumaka Group's mining licence. His father would never have cancelled, that much was clear: there were three viable competitors standing in the wings. There were thousands of employees relying on his judgement. The anger began to swing around, to confront him... *Pull yourself together, Bedi! Do whatever it takes!*

Whatever it takes! It was like trying to inspire a spine of steel into a stalk of boiled spaghetti. The office hours were fine and he seemed to run well enough on autopilot, but after hours, he was a mess. A man like him needed a woman. His favourite home along Sekondi beach, needed a soul. He texted his driver and dressed swiftly. His friends had warned him after his last marriage broke down: he had to start dating immediately, to get over it. Well he would start now. The Asantehene's cousin had been leaving messages every other day. He would schedule her immediately. He restacked the files he had been prepping for the meeting with the minister. There was also the Gambian businesswoman who had come in earlier that morning. Her handshake had lasted a full five minutes and she had engineered that full-lips accident in the middle of the cheek-kissing routine. She should be up for a weekend up in his ranch. A slow courtship... see if there was anything there before he embarrassed himself again... he picked up the last of the folders. It was Sama's personnel file.

He paused. Perhaps he should start here. He was slightly embarrassed now. That afternoon, after Sama had walked out of the Headquarters he had called up his HR director immediately to deny her the satisfaction of resigning. He opened the file. The top letter was the termination that would have been waiting for her when she got to her desk in Takoradi. Gross insurbordination. Somehow that did not quite describe what had happened between them that morning. He was suddenly overcome with shame. His driver came in and left with his briefcases and files. Bedi followed, holding on to Sama's file. With that termination letter between them, he now had to face facts. From what he knew of the new Samantha Wolio, there was no longer the possibility of a relationship. He would get on with his future... but he would sort out this last page from his past, first. He would not wait twenty years to right this most recent wrong.

Besides, she had to understand that he knew all about her Lie.

***

After her termination, Sama left her Takoradi office two hours early and was buzzing with too much angry energy to go straight home. All in all, it was the worst possible day for her restaurant manager's boyfriend to park his seventeen-year-old Toyota in

Sama's slot. The large-boned clearing agent who generally had too much time on his hands spent a lot of that free time at the restaurant – although he rarely ordered more than a beer, which was usually flat by the time his long visits were done. When Sama finally entered her restaurant, she found his table decorated with empty beer bottles. He was also in the middle of a meal more elaborate than anything on her menu. From the state of her till, it was mostly complimentary too. Akan, the manager, was defiant to boot – apparently other restaurants laid out free food for staff and "family". As Sama drove home that night, she was aware of the irony of firing her manager on the same day that she had been fired herself.

They rarely had late visitors and when the doorbell rang at 10 p.m. she was ready to succumb to the prostrations of a more remorseful Akan. It was true after all that Akan was more than a "manager" – she was also chef and waiter, purchasing officer, kitchen hand and sole staff. Truth be told, she was actually more of a friend and in the last few months of her employment at the Akumaka group, Sama had not so much delegated, as abandoned, the restaurant to her. Despite her indiscretions with her boyfriend, Akan discharged her other roles well enough. Rebuking and reinstating her was suddenly a far more sensible prospect than replacing her. When Sama opened the door and found Bedi on her porch, she could not have been more shocked had it been her late father standing there. She recovered quickly enough though, and shut the door in his face.

He knocked again and again, but she just stood there, breathing shallowly, trying to come to terms with the fact that only a door panel stood between Bedi and Steven. Her husband looked up curiously from television. 'Who is it?'

'None of your business,' she said in a low voice, in the first words she had spoken to him all day.

'Is that so,' he said mildly, flicking through the channels.

Bedi continued to knock. Finally, she walked across to her boys' room, Steven began to rise from the couch in which he had spent the last four hours. He was wearing his "I'm the man of the house" scowl, but Sama only said, with a smile that did not reach the eyes, 'There's a mad man behind that door; open it at your own risk.'

Her husband rearranged the cushions and sank back down. She locked the bedroom door behind her. The two boys were already asleep in Marko's bed. She killed the light, sank into Matt's bed – which had been hers for the past twelve months – and tried to sleep. Yet, the incident at the restaurant, and the strange presence of the man at her door, was dissipating the rage that was supposed to power her through her challenging circumstances. Her porch was a small forest of potted cacti. It was harshly lighted and buzzing with moths. She pictured him there now, knocking. Why was he there and why had she acted so precipitately? She had a sudden moment of panic: what if Steven had let him in after all? What if, even now, the two men were talking in her living room? She started to her feet and crossed to the window, teasing aside the curtain in time to watch Bedi stalk across the darkened shade of the jacaranda in the yard. Momentarily, he disappeared from view before reappearing beside the outline of the small, anonymous Peugeot beyond the dwarf wall. She felt her lips curl into a sneer. It was the sort of car that was normally beneath people like Chief Bedi Akumaka – until it was time for the anonymous, night-time crawl through the slums. It fired into life and pulled angrily away. It did not look like she would be getting any more unexpected visits. She returned to bed, feeling around her mind for the totems of her own rage.

Her secret was safe. For now. Yet, her anger project was struggling. The infelicities of her life crowded in on her until she could hardly breath. How much of her dysfunctional relationships and marriage could she legitimately blame on Bedi's twenty-year-old betrayal? Yes, Akan's boyfriend was lazy: he cleared one container at the wharf at 11 a.m. and came back to gloat over a bottle of beer for the rest of the day... but who was she to judge how ambitious a man should be, and how much time he should spend with his sweetheart? And what was so wrong with a manager knocking together leftover pottage and *banku* for a friend...

She longed for sleep, but when the muezzin cried at 5 a.m., she did not have to open her eyes. It was a while since she had to leave the bed so early, but if she was to open the restaurant alone at 7 a.m. she had to open her kitchen two hours earlier. And since she had to sort out her children she had to start the work in her own kitchen. As she groggily soaked the beans and steeped the kuse leaves in goatmilk she realised that she had been punishing herself when she sacked Akan so precipitately. She turned the marinaded meat into pots which she parboiled, then she packed them into cellophane bags and left them to cool. She spent thirty minutes chopping chips and the vegetables for her sauces. Then she tossed a portion or two of mushrooms and shrimps into the cooler she was taking to the restaurant – she didn't yet know what she would eat for lunch, but she was damned if it would be anything on her own set menu.

Finally she slipped back into bed to pray. She was finally sleepy, but she did not dare shut her eyes. Already the children were stirring as their inner clocks wound down. She looked at her boys and a sudden wave of guilt engulfed her. How long could she sleep in her boys' room without causing them irreparable harm? She felt pity for the next generation of women, for her boys had been nurtured on her poisoned breastmilk. She could not recall the last time she had prepared a family meal with the same passion she had just invested in a meal for her business. *Family.* The word curdled in her mind. There had not been anything like a "family" outing, meal or occasion with her husband and the boys in a year. The mother tongue her boys had acquired from growing up under her roof was not the language for successful marriages... it was a lexicon for dysfunction.

She sat up, trembling. *Was it too late?*

The fuel of her anger was compromised by the remorse in Bedi's eyes. He had not said a word, but his presence, his eyes had been enough. She could not say just what triggered the slammed door... was it her principled hatred, her frayed night dress, or perhaps the embarrassing distance between Bedi and Steven, between the tennis-court-sized office and her sagging sofas... but if the hatred was not enough to drive her to succeed at the restaurant, perhaps the love of her children could do it – a love unadulterated by her revulsion for their father.

Across the room, Marko sat up sleepily. Before his eyes were properly open, he was feeling around his pyjamas. He grinned gummily. 'Mummy, I'm dry!'

She tried to smile, properly, 'That's my boy.'

***

By 6.45 a.m., Marko and Matt were safely at breakfast club and Sama had dug in at The Kitchen, hosing down her worktop and clearing out a small sackful of expired spices. She clucked at the colour of the frying oil as she poured it down the drain, despairing at the fish dishes Akan would have sold that would have been marred by the aftertaste of blackened oil. It was a flurry until 7 a.m. when she opened her doors, but there were no customers for another hour. That slow start was an anticlimax after the hectic hours of preparation, and as she polished and repolished her clean hobs, as she compounded her soups and sauces, she thought of all the marketing she should be doing for the outdoor catering end of her restaurant business. She sat in the empty saloon and began to phone around for a replacement for Akan. By 8.30am a regular customer finally came in and she retired into the kitchen to prepare his quick fry-up.

She was serving his order ten minutes later when she noticed that Bedi had installed himself on the same table the clearing agent had occupied the day before. His silent P.A. glowered from the doorway, his face gravid with dark thoughts. Bedi's face for his own part was more inscrutable than the night before, but Sama was too experienced with the male gender of her species not to recognise the markers of the masculine sulk. Yet, she was in her own shop and did not miss a beat. She served her first customer and then paused by Bedi's table. Not for the first time, she wished she had hired a dedicated waiter.

'What do you want?' she said, keeping her voice neutral.

'How about better customer service?' he said lightly, but she stared balefully and the joke fell flat. His voice fell lower, 'Yesterday I came to apologise about the letter – and to offer a reinstatement.' He shrugged, 'today I'm hungry. Am I in the right place?'

She continued to stare. It was easy then: she could never forgive, never go back to work for his company, and never serve him water willingly... yet if she told the truth, it was easy to see how he would keep on pestering her. The thing was to lie – and to serve him such a meal that would send him directly to his posh toilet at the HQ Towers downtown. 'I accept your apology,' she lied evenly, 'but I don't want your job anymore. – I was going to resign anyway.' Then she took a dog-eared menu from the rack and placed it before him.

He waved it away without a glance, 'Just knock something together for me, please. Something with a hint of... lagoons... I'm happy to pay for the trouble...' he broke off.

A hint of lagoons. Without warning, something deep and undefinable flumped inside her, as though her intestines had become a python flexing in orgasmic agony. She could barely breathe. Her vocal cords seemed to belong to another. Neither pure memory nor naked longing, the feeling was too amorphous for words, yet far too physical to ignore. None of this fit into the plan she had mapped out in the long hours of her insomniac night, and she wanted nothing of it. But she was in her professional space, under the gossipy eyes of a curious customer, the unreadable gaze of a stolid P.A., and far from slammable doors and allied boorishness. It was far easier to nod professionally, retreat into her kitchen, and sink into Akan's 'sleeping chair'.

Ten minutes passed. She was seventeen again. She was as light as her clothes, which they were flying like flags to dry, ten feet above deck. She was in a bikini in his galley kitchen. They were in a cove on the Songor – back when it was still beautiful! Did he remember? She groaned, *You're too old for this, Sama...* She staggered to her fridge. She opened it and stood there, twirling her wedding band round and around her middle finger. A hint of lagoons or a stint on the loo...

Two more customers walked in and hollered. Breakfast or no breakfast, they wanted their fix of *banku*. She laddled some sauce from the fridge and dumped it in the microwave. The kettle whistled and she whipped up two white steaming mounds to accompany the meat stew. As she bore their plates into the saloon, she saw that between a standing I-pad-weilding P.A. and Bedi they had converted a wing of her saloon into a branch of the Akumaka group where calls were processed from three mobile phones between Man-Friday and boss man. As she turned for the kitchen, the P.A. – who had never seen his boss treated so shabbily, and in such a squalid eatery too – complained: 'Chief was here first!'

'He said he could afford a special.'

The P.A. pulled out a wallet. 'How much is it?'

Bedi scratched his forehead in embarrassment as Sama scoffed, 'It not the money, it's the time,' she looked directly at Bedi, 'So. Can you afford it or not?'

'I can afford to wait,' said Bedi quietly.

'And sit down, you,' she said to the P.A. as she turned away, 'you're driving my customers away.'

Bedi sighed, 'Kwesi, go get my signature file,' then, as she entered the kitchen, he tossed her an unfortunate aside, 'I hope it's worth the wait.'

She did not deign to reply, but as she passed through her beaded curtains she was muttering vindictively, 'I'll give you *worth the wait!*'

Her mind was made up. She went through the yard and, leaning over the far wall, sent the amiable security man in the adjacent churchyard on an impromptu trip to a nearby streetmarket. She compounded fresh and sun-dried tomatoes and sautéed mushrooms and prawns in groundnut oil until the aroma of it filled the kitchen and wafted into the saloon. That was when Akan arrived, nose twitching, eyes sharp and parrying.

'Akan!' she cried, scarfing her delight with prefabricated indignation, 'Why are you so late?'

The other woman stared incredulously. 'Late? You sacked me yesterday!'

'Stupid girl. So you took me seriously?'

Akan rocked stubbornly from side to side. Sama chopped the

last lemon in the fridge finely, all the while watching her ex-staffer from the corner of her eyes. Her heart pounded. She was unused to encounters of the emotional kind. Why didn't the silly girl just apologise and get on with things.

'You're just wasting the lemon,' Akan muttered, 'you can't even cook anymore. Why do you need so much lemon anyway?'

'I know what I'm doing,' Sama replied testily. Why couldn't she just apologise and get into her apron!

'I came to collect my two weeks salary, that's all. This is seventeenth...'

'I told you...' she broke off as the security man hailed her over the wall. '...get that for me, will you?'

Sama turned to the oven without waiting to see if Akan would obey... then she remembered Bedi walking to his lift, assuming she would follow and she felt a chill, despite the heat of the kitchen. Fortunately, Akan fetched the plastic bag, but she simply dumped it on the worktop and folded her arms once more, waiting stubbornly for her terminal salary. Swiftly, Sama cleaned and filleted the fresh oilfish. Turning on the grill, she ground fresh ginger for pepper, then she seasoned and set the fish on the grill and turned up the heat. She turned to Akan and sighed, 'Put on your apron, please. And chop the goat meat, I haven't started the pepper soup and the lunch crowd will soon start...' she broke off, realising that the other woman was crying.

'You sacked me. Aunty Sama. *You!* Because of a stupid plate of rice.'

She wanted to mention that there were also three or four bottles of beer involved, but she didn't. She willed herself to hold the younger woman, but her feet refused to move, instead, she said earnestly, '...how can I sack you, Akan? You are like a small sister to me, I was angry that's all, because... because...'

There was an impatient call from the saloon and Akan wiped her eyes and snatched her apron as she went to attend to the new customer. Sama felt the pang of a lost opportunity, but the fish wanted attention. She hastily glazed it with the herb marinade and layered it with lemon and kuse. Then she replaced it in the grill for five minutes before shielding it from burning with a foil mask. Minutes later, she laid the fish to rest on a sauced bed of coconuty rice. Things didn't get more lagoony than that. A subdued Akan was back, watching beadily.

'Serve table seven,' said Sama wiping her hands self-conciously.

'It's not on the menu. What is it?'

'It's a special. Just serve it, okay?'

Akan moved to comply. Sama slipped into the disused cubicle, hating herself for doing so, and watched discreetly though the service hatch as Akan served Bedi. He took the first morsel to his mouth, paused, and addressed a quiet comment to Akan. They continued to talk as Sama returned to the kitchen. Slowly she began to clean the work top. Akan returned and joined her wordlessly.

'Did he like it?' Sama asked thoughtlessly. The words were out before she realised her indiscretion: in all the years of running a restaurant, she had never asked whether a customer liked a meal. The Kitchen was not that type of place.

'What?'

'Don't bother,'

'No, let's bother,' she said angrily, 'You're doing exactly the same thing you sacked me for!'

'Akan!'

She whipped her apron off angrily, 'You're just a hypocrite! I don't even want your job anymore!'

'You don't understand...'

'Well, he said it was just like he remembered it, just like old times... *and you're married!*'

In spite of herself, she managed to say the wrong thing, 'He did?'

Akan whirled around and stalked away, snatching her handbag as she went. Sama managed to catch her inches from the door,

grabbed and embraced her from the back. Akan fought silently to break free, but Sama was the bigger woman. Slowly she
hauled her affronted mentee back into the womb of the kitchen.
Akan struggled to break free – until she realised that her boss,
fifteen years her elder, was actually weeping great racking sobs
that had to be about more than a lousy plate of fish and rice.
The fight drained out of her then – and she became afraid, of
the enormity of the thing that was happening... for in all the
years she had known Sama, tears were something she simply
did not do. She turned around for her first sight of them, and she
hugged the other woman wordlessly.

From the saloon an impatient newcomer called for service. 'Just
sit down and wait! I'm coming!' shouted Akan impatiently, for
the regulars of The Kitchen came for the old-fashioned good
food, and were not hung up on new-fangled notions of customer service.

Sama broke away then, and wiped her eyes fiercely, 'You'll
stay?'

Akan nodded dumbly.

'Thanks. I'll phone you.' She grabbed her own bag and headed
out through the yard entrance.

'Where are you going? What if he...'

'I'm going to sleep. Tell him I was long gone, that you cooked
the food. Tell him I rarely come here anyway, that I only came
today because you had to take your HIV shots... drive him away,
Akan. I'm a married woman. Charge him five times...'

'Okay, okay, bye bye!' snapped Akan, who had stopped listening after the HIV comment.

The new customer was slapping the table for attention when
Akan entered the saloon. He was one of her regulars and they
traded good-natured insults. 'The usual?' she asked eventually.

'No, I want that one,' he said, pointing at table seven where Bedi
was eating his meal with religious reverence. That gave Akan
pause. It would not do to start a run on Sama's Special; in desperation she raised the price to ten times the cost of his usual

fare. 'What did you use to cook it? ' he laughed incredulously, 'Elephant testicles? Bring my *kenkey* and tilapia!'

Afterwards, she returned to the kitchen with professional pique. Nobody had ordered the special she had served her boyfriend on the strength of a sighting. She brought down the grill tray and spooned the second fillet of oilfish onto a plate, noting the spray of fresh herb, the translucent glaze, the aromatic charge… she served up the rice, sniffing at the sheer waste of the coconut paste clogging up the serving spoon. She sat down for a late breakfast – and an educational tasting.

She ate swiftly, the way she always did. Halfway through she decided that if she were rich enough to start a restaurant she would probably hire her boss as a cook, but she would certainly hire their new customer to eat all his meals for free, right at the entrance of the restaurant. He made a dish more desirable than it actually was, just the way he ate it.

***

'What's so funny?' Bedi asked.

'This is so teenage, it's hilarious. It's 11pm, and I'm too old to be eaten alive by Sekondi mosquitoes… goodnight Bedi, have a good life.' She turned to go, and hesitated, 'Was it worth it after all? Was I value for money?'

He laughed, 'Are we talking about the catering, or this thirty-minute pleasure of your presence.'

She did not laugh. They were standing on his Sekondi balcony with the view of the Atlantic ocean. Behind them was the tasteful wreck of a dinner party for fourteen guests from a Mining Conference at the International Mining Convention. The guests were all gone now, and even as they spoke, servants moved quietly and efficiently, clearing up plates and glasses. In the distance, a glass fell and broke. In the further distance, the music from a more boisterous, longer-lasting party boomed. Bedi was slightly miffed at that. His wealth and the size of his estate should have insulated him from such neighbourly nuisances, but his neighbours were also rich – and irresponsible enough – to buy powerful enough speakers to constitute expensive nuisances.

She stared at him intently. 'I am serious, Bedi. When your people approached me officially, I gave them an outrageous quote. When they accepted it I... well, I had no choice.'

'You think it is outrageous. You should see what our usual caterers charge,' he paused, and added mischievously, 'but you didn't have to come personally. That was not a part of the contract, was it? There was enough in it for a subcontract.'

She smiled. 'If I was taking all that money, I had to make sure it went well, didn't I?'

'And yes, the food was worth it, there will be other functions. From other departments of the Group.'

She hesitated, then she shook her head. 'I am going to be frank with you, Bedi. I think you deserve it. I am old-fashioned this way: I am married. I will never divorce my husband, and there will never be 'something on the side' for me. Maybe I am being presumptuous... I don't know what's going on in your mind, but I think I have to make it clear that no catering contract is going to change that for me.'

'Well,' he laughed uncertainly and raised his wine glass, '...that's intense. Here's to fidelity.' They chinked glasses. As he drank he realised the painful irony of those words. It was Sama who taught him the meaning of the word infidelity. It was a curious paradox, no woman had ever betrayed him as painfully as Sama had. And yet it was only her ambiguous presence on that balcony, his favourite place in the world, that made him feel so light, electric even. He remembered his first Harley Street full medical with his father. It had been a bit of a game at first: a fifty-three-year-old fitness-freak tycoon comparing lab results with a son in his early twenties. Then the doctor dropped the bombshell: *Mumps Orchitis*. Bedi was completely sterile. Yet, how could that be: Bedi's fiancee was back in Accra, pregnant for him. His devastation in that London lab redefined his life, put him under a cloud from which he never totally emerged. His father had been great: Bedi had been determined to return to Accra and have a showdown with Sama, but his father pointed out how damaging that would be for his reputation. If he had an open confrontation with Sama on the ownership of the pregnancy, it would involve her parents and family. It would become public knowledge that Bedi was less than a man. For the most eligible bachelor in Accra that was social suicide. The pregnancy was still early. It was far better to pay for an abortion, end the relationship discreetly, surgically, and get on with his life. So he had done just that.

Except that life had refused to get on with him. Nenghi left for Addis within six months of his confession, and his first marriage was over. She was an only child and she simply couldn't contemplate a life without her own children; the Akumaka fortune couldn't change that. She was now remarried... four children from her last Christmas card. On his second try he tried honesty, and his second wife knew exactly what she was going into: his sperm count – which had been non-existent – was rising ever so slowly, but there was still the prospect of a lifetime of childlessness... yet, every single time they quarrelled that was the first abuse on her tongue.

Fidelity... As he drank the empty toast, he realised that both his wives had been faithful – as far as he knew – but none of them could give him the raw pleasure that the unfaithful woman opposite had given him simply by sharing a bottle of wine after the formal function was done, 'You'll get our business, Sama, even if I never see you again, if you continue to cater like you did tonight.' He continued, lightly, fishing for a twenty-year-stale confession, 'Some say fidelity is over-rated... are you saying that you have never ever, been unfaithful?'

She did not even blink, 'Never.' She drained her glass slowly.

'Even with your boyfriends?'

'Never,' she smiled, 'I probably gave you a wrong impression that day in your office but that was just the jilted woman sounding off. I'm sorry, I had to say it like this, Bedi, but you had the first shot at me, and you turned me down.' He was silent, biting down the refutation, even now resisting the possibility of hurting her, of spoiling the moment. She took a deep breath and put down her glass. 'Goodbye Bedi,' she hesitated, 'and thanks for being a good sport.'

She walked slowly away, wondering. *He did not say goodbye.*

From the balcony she entered into the vast mezzanine lounge that had swallowed the party of fourteen and their baby-sitting complement of servants and bartenders as though they were a family of six. This could have been your life, she thought, but it is not. Your life is an empty sham, emptier now because you can no longer hate the man who emptied it, who – barring that terrible, *terrible,* Jilting – has been a gentleman. More of a sham now because you can never love the man who makes it a sham.

She walked through a white-carpeted stairwell that was plush enough, wide enough, even for her tall husband to roll down, locked in an embrace with Andy, the 'distant cousin' who had lived with them from their wedding day until that day, barely one year ago when she returned early from her restaurant to find them rolling about in her marital bed. He had wanted a divorce at first but she had refused. He would not take away both the joys of her marital bed as well as the respectability of the marriage shell. He would have been less discreet, outside the walls of a marriage, and she had their sons to think about. She walked downstairs into the front hall where a single, vast canvas depicted a regal princess with an overlong neck with a crown nestling in her coiffured hair. This could have been you, she thought, smiling brightly at the teenage servant running a vacuum cleaner down the strip of carpeting, but you are no teenage waif hard done by the world. You are a mother who will do her duty to her sons: if you can forgive Bedi, then you will forgive Steven. You will return to The Bedroom, taking one step at a time. You will stop beating him around the head with the baton of The Offence and give a future, any future, a chance. She walked onto the granite porch thinking that she would have grown a single, giant cactus here, and hating herself for the thought. As she stepped beyond the overhang of the balcony, his voice came, low and condemning. 'I know your secret, Sama.' She stopped and looked up, Bedi stepped over the railings and dropped four feet onto a promontory from which he dropped to the Tarmac. 'I'll walk you to your car,' he said stepping up to her.

She did not move. Her throat was suddenly parched. 'What secret?'

'I mean,' he said bitterly, 'I'm not taking anything away from your grand speech. This is not about blackmailing you into bed or anything, but... *dammit Sama*, we've known ourselves so long there's no point in all the bullshit, I know your big secret!'

He spoke with such exasperation that there was no point in pretending any more, but the admission was a gulf of such enormity that she turned and walked towards her car, blustering, 'I don't know what you talking about.'

'You were lying about all that fidelity bullshit, and you know it,' he said, keeping pace with her.

She wished now that she had left this catering to Akan. Up close, she was defeated by the knowing in his eyes. She let out her breath slowly. She felt naked, dirty. Bedi was the last person in the world she wanted to know about her husband. It did not change anything about her convictions, but it had been so important for her that he credit her with some marital felicity, something that had eluded him with all his wealth and privilege. She sighed 'I suppose with your intelligence department you would have found out sooner or later.'

'I don't go out to dig into anybody's life, Sama. I located your house and your restaurant simply by reading your personnel file. But why? Why did you have to deceive me about something like that?'

Suddenly she resented his wounded tone. What right did he have to her confidences? She turned to confront him, 'It's my privilege,' she said tautly, 'who I choose to share my truths with.'

'*Your* truths? And that's it, yes? Not even an apology for the deception?'

Her anger flared, but she remembered her outburst on the day of her termination and took a deep breath. She would not lose control again, but she would end this quickly, while they could still be courteous to each other. 'No sir,' she smiled tightly, 'I have nothing to apologise about – and I'll appreciate it if you can keep my secrets confidential!' She really tried, but it came out nonetheless, 'And no, whatever you choose to do, you can never blackmail me into sleeping with you!'

'Keep dreaming!' he said angrily, 'You're nothing but a hypocrite!'

She jumped into her car and slammed the door. The engine fired into life. The wrought-iron gates parted as she approached, but her car braked to a halt there on the lip of the highway with two milky headlights glaring into the night. He stood there waiting for her to drive away. His heart was pounding, the clouds of depression were descending with a vengeance. *When will this end?* he thought. Indeed, would it ever end? A minute passed and then the reverse lights blinked on. Smoking generously, the station wagon rolled back until she was looking up at him. 'If my husband is an active homosexual,' she demanded, 'how does that make me a hypocrite for wanting to stay faithful to my marital vows?'

He swallowed, discomfited. 'Your husband is a homosexual?'

Her jaw dropped, she killed the headlights, the engine, and stepped out of the car. Her legs were suddenly rubbery and she did not resist when he took her arm and led her to a bench under a coconut palm. The catering van she hired had gone, with all the sessional staff she has recruited for the event. As they watched, the company van bearing the stewards pulled up to the gates as well and drove off towards Takoradi. The gates rolled shut. 'What secret were you talking about?' she asked.

'Our affair could not have been that perfect, Sama, if you had another lover.'

'What are you talking about?' she whispered, 'You were my first lover, and the only man in my life. Till you left me. There's never been any question about that? Why are you doing this, now?'

'I know the truth, Sama,' he was suddenly exasperated. 'At least some of it. And don't worry, I forgave you years and years ago, otherwise we won't be sitting here now. But don't deny it... don't make this so... tacky!'

Sama blinked rapidly, 'If anyone told you...'

'The child you aborted was not mine. You were clearly sleeping around!'

She slapped him hard across the face, and jumped to her feet. Her face was clouded with fury. She tried to storm away but he caught her by the arms and held her tight.

He was even angrier than she was. He glanced at the gatehouse and his guards were studiously looking the other way. He was a veteran of two tumultuous marriages, and it took an ex-girlfriend to slap him for the first time, close to midnight, on the lawn of his Sekondi home. 'Mumps Orchitis, Sama!' he whispered fiercely, 'I am now a living expert on the disease. I was practically sterile when we were going out. Confess! Who was the father of the pregnancy you tried to foist on me? Are you going to cure me of my infatuation by making me lose the last shreds of respect I have for you?'

The physical change was so dramatic. She seemed to wilt physically, to sag from the inside. Without warning a copious stream appeared on her cheeks. 'Please, Bedi,' she whispered, 'let it go.'

'How truly hypocritical,' he said bitterly, letting her go, 'for years you give me this guilt trip about breaking up and forcing you to abort our child. Now that it is time for some honesty all you have to offer is manipulative tears and let-bygones-be-bygones!'

She sat down suddenly. She fought for self control but the tears came nonetheless. She looked at him, reading the growing rage in his body language. So many things were buried under the weight of years. That terrible occasion had been buried so deep it didn't exist any longer. All that existed was her single story of The Jilting, which she had rehearsed and rehearsed until it became the only reality... until now. She wept bitterly. Bedi shook his fists in frustration. 'Am I missing something here?' he said irritably, 'I thought I was the injured party!'

'Please, let it go.'

He glared at her. 'I will.' Then he spat on the ground. 'Goodbye.'

He turned and walked away. *He had finally said goodbye.* Suddenly, she was alone on the lawn. It was close to midnight and he had let it go just like she wanted, walking quickly down the drive toward the main house. It was perfect. She could go now, and be absolutely certain that there would never be another ambiguous contact with Chief Bedi Akumaka. There would never be another heady *Special*, cooked with teenage passion, another three hours spent choosing an outfit for an ordinary catering... and yet... Bedi's attentions had done immeasurable good to her self esteem. She could not deny that. Suddenly it was important that he did not think so ill of her.

She rose and chased after him. Her heels rang out on the Tarmac and although he must have heard them, he did not turn around. She was almost there when he entered the house and slammed the heavy timber doors shut. A bolt shot home and she knew from the finality of the sound that she stood less of a chance of entering that house than he had on her porch those many nights earlier.

She stepped backwards, wondering how many minutes she had before the guards in the gatehouse came for her. *Go home*, said the rational voice in her head, *now*. But she was already peeling the shoes off her feet, tossing them up onto the balcony, and mounting up onto the rocky promontory. From there she clambered onto the ledge of the balcony, ruining her pin-striped trousers as she drew herself up the rails. As she pushed herself over onto the balcony, it was to stare at the open mouth of the teenage servant who was standing with the vacuum cleaner in the middle of the lounge. Bedi emerged from the stairwell. 'Breaking and Entry...' he said derisively, 'where will you draw the line?'

'Leave us now,' she said quietly to the servant.

'How dare you order my staff around!'

'Now!' she shouted stepping forward, and the boy fled, shutting the door behind him.

He advanced on her then, towering, his rage stoked by the impotence of being slapped, wronged and then upstaged before his personal staff, *in his own house* by a woman of no integrity, with whom he was so totally besotted.

She met him halfway, and looked fearlessly into his eyes. Without her heels, she was a full head shorter than he was, and for all the weight she had added, still woman to his bullish male. 'You want to know it all don't you? I'll tell you. I never willing slept with any man while I was with you, but I was raped once. And if you were sterile then, I could only have been pregnant for the rapist. The timing checks out...'

'How convenient. Who was this rapist? A nameless stranger, no doubt. Someone who caught you in the dark on your way...'

'We both know the rapist,' she said quietly. She pointed at a portrait of Bedi's father on the wall. 'There he is-'

He slapped her hard so hard she fell backwards on her buttocks. She looked up, more shocked than hurt, despite the red trickle from her nose, and she thought how odd it was that the first two acts of violence in their relationship should occur twenty years after it was dead and buried. She stared at him fearlessly from the ground. 'Like father like son, this was how he started. I screamed for help and he slapped me hard. So hard my ears rang. Not once, not twice, not thrice. It was the weekend you went to Lagos for the Polo tournament... you won't remember. I came from Legon to spend the weekend as usual. He came to your chalet that night...'

'Liar! *Liar!* You dare to lie on Dad because he's dead! *How dare you!*'

'I see your eyes Bedi, you know it's true. You father never made a pretence of faithfulness to Mama. We both know this. You would have hoped he drew a line at his son's girlfriend, but I *know* he did not. And you know I could never tell a lie like this.'

'How would I know that? What do I know about you – except that you deceived me for twenty years about something so fundamental. If he... if you were raped, why didn't you tell me about it as soon as he... as soon as it happened?'

Her lips trembled, but she reined herself in and rose. 'What would you have done? It would merely have broken up your family. Afterwards he begged me, it was the Devil, he said, and all those bikinis I wore on the boat. And then he threatened me:

if I wanted to marry you I'd keep my mouth shut. And if I talked it was my word against his... who was going to believe a carpenter's daughter over Chief Akumaka?'

'Pathetic liar, what are you trying to do? I told you, I forgave you years ago!'

'So should I invent a fake lover so I can continue to bask in your false love? You wanted the truth, Bedi, and I'm done protecting your false image of your father's integrity! Until I left university, the only sex I ever had with any man apart from you was once with your father, *and he raped me!* I swear to this on my own parents' graves!'

'Shut up, you! You have no respect for the dead!'

'I can prove it, too.'

'How?' he sneered, 'By swearing on the Bible? That's proof indeed!'

She pulled a chain bearing a tiny silver locket over her head and held it out to him.

'What's this?'

'A keepsake from the son I killed for you,' her voice was trembling. 'I kept a lock of his hair, thinking he was yours as well. If you were truly sterile during our years together, there should be enough DNA here to prove that my child was your halfbrother. After that you will only have to decide whether I seduced your father, or whether he raped me.'

They stared wordlessly for a moment, then he took the locket. She turned quickly then, without hesitation, and picked up her shoes from the balcony. Then she walked barefoot down the stairs. Presently her car started and rolled towards the gatehouse. Bedi stared at the intercom for what seemed to be minutes, then he crossed resolutely over to it. Her car approached the gate, but this time it stayed shut, instead a guard approached her door and crouched at her window. Presently she reversed back towards the main house once again. She mounted slowly up to the upstairs lounge, using the stairs this time, 'Bedi,' she said tiredly, 'let me go home, plea...' she broke off. There was something different about the room... she looked up at the blank wall from which the senior Chief Akumaka had glared at her a moment before, at the portrait whose broken pieces littered the floor... 'You believe me... without testing...'

He nodded solemnly. 'I thought about it. The only reason why I didn't confront you about the pregnancy was because my father forbade it. Now I know why. And I remember the Polo tourney I returned from, to find you with a bandaged face...' he wiped the slick of blood from her nostril, tenderly, 'you said you were... mugged? ...I apologise for my father, and for slapping you tonight.'

'And I too...' The clocks chimed, 'God, this is teen-crazy! It's midnight, Bedi! I really have to go now!'

'Yes, I know,' he walked her downstairs slowly. 'This changes everything you know? Are you going to divorce your husband, or am I going to have to kill him?'

She looked at him sharply. 'I know you're joking, but you shouldn't even say things like that in jest.'

'I'm only partly joking. I know you Catholics don't joke about divorce.'

She laughed then, 'Does it really change anything?' she asked gently. 'You know why I told you the truth? Every time I feel driven by lust, or love, to do something that would hurt my children, I think of another man, many years ago, who was driven by lust to rape me, who did not care whether he destroyed his own son's happiness... Look at us now, Bedi. What if your father had not come between us? What if he had been more disciplined?'

The thought was so affecting that he took a deep breath and fought manfully for self control. Eventually, he exhaled through his mouth. 'I'll never do anything to hurt your sons, Sama,' he said thickly, 'You know that.'

'I believe you,' she replied. She squeezed his arm and tapped it twice, in a gesture that took him back decades. Then she got into her car and started the engine. The weary gates rolled open.

'I love you, Sama.'

She considered deeply, then she shrugged. It was true anyway. 'I'll always love you, Bedi,' she said softly.

She drove away. For once the darkness of the night did not seem to blend into his soul. The way to a woman's heart was to put her children at the centre of yours. He looked up at the balcony, at the house where he had both slapped and been slapped, in the sight and to the hearing of the most gossipy class of people in Ghana and he couldn't stop grinning. It seemed to have a soul for once, his house, and it had never seemed more a home than it did at that moment.

MARITAL ACCOUNTS

If you want me to be totally honest, I love hijabs. I think they are sexy outfits. Once or twice a month, I won't mind wearing one myself. – And don't get me wrong, I'm not that bothered about men seeing some skin... not that I'm a loose woman, you understand: just that I like to be practical about things like that, that's all. What I find totally seductive is the idea that I can pull a wall of secrecy down when and where I want. And what I cannot have... what kills me dead, just to think about it... is the idea of anybody leafing through anything as private as my bank statements. Yet, that was exactly what Denle was doing. He was sitting on the floor by the bed, where the shock of the statement must have dropped him, and he was still on page twelve or something when I returned from walking the dogs.

He showed no shame. This was a grey area of our marriage, truth be told. I read his own letters – of course. And because I have always been on hand to pick up the mail, I had not, in the four years of our marriage, tested his awareness of the golden rule that a husband should never, ever, read his wife's mail. Now for the first time in months and months, the mail man was early, my statement was on time, and Denle, home sick with the flu, was on hand to prove that he had no shame whatsoever. Instead, he turned a thunderstruck face up to stare at me. 'Is this a mistake? Is this your own Fassi Jekujo? What am I reading here?'

'I think the right question should be why are you reading my mail?' I was boiling myself, and I knew that if by the next morning I was still happily married to my third husband it was going to be a major miracle. – don't get me wrong: I am not the kind of woman that goes around marrying rich men... but unlike quite a few women I can name, I refuse to sleep (regularly at least) with a man who is not my husband. After a while, that type of policy tends to run up the marriage mileage. I tried to snatch the sheaf of my bank statements, but his fingers were like an industrial stapler. 'Denle Dearie, can I have my statements?'

'Fassi, are you into... 419?'

My jaw dropped, 'Is that what you think of me? '

'What am I supposed to think!' He shouted. This was pathetic. His mother died six months ago and he did not cry. The stitches of his appendectomy tore during a silly celebrity football match last month and he didn't cry. Now he was about to break down over his wife's bank statements! He voice was cracking, 'I am your husband for god's sake!'

'You're my husband, not my accountant! We've only been married four years, Denle, you can't know everything about another person in forty-eight months!'

He tried to stand up, but his legs were still weak and he staggered back onto the bed, on top of the half-eaten plate of akara that the arrival of my bank statement had interrupted. He did not seem to notice. 'What about the two years we courted?' he demanded, I hated the shrillness in his voice. I did not know that I had married a man whose voice became shrill under stress.

'That doesn't count, I was still married to the Ivorien ambassador then,'

'Fassi, Fassi...' He cleared his throat – I was getting worried myself. His voice had not been as unstable as this even when he was negotiating with the drunk robber who woke us up at 3 a.m. last June with a gun at the foot of our bed. This was the problem with men. Because of this bank statement he will soon forget that I fried akara for him. And I can count on the fingers of a bird's four-fingered hand the number of wives I know who will take time to fry akara and make a fuss just because their husband's nostrils were blocked. I give him all the babying he wants, and yet here he was, bleating, 'Thirteen million naira was paid into your account two weeks ago, Fassi, *two weeks ago!* You couldn't fix your tyres two weeks ago!!'

I relaxed slowly and, against every screaming instinct in my body, let the statements go. God be praised! He was griping about the thirteen million naira deposit from the rent of my small London apartment...! Was it really possible that he hadn't seen the forty-six million capital gains tax refund, or the total balance of the bank account? I took a deep breath. It might still be possible to save this marriage after all. His net-worth was only eighty or ninety million – if he included inherited masonry that he could never sell. With adequate massaging, his ego would be able to live with what he knew – so far. I sighed dolefully, 'I always get it wrong!'

'What!'

'My first husband complained that I insulted him by picking up my own bill in the restaurant... I didn't know you wanted me to service my own cars-'

'That is not what I am saying at all!' He shouted, 'You know that!'

At least he was becoming defensive now, not holier-than-thou. I reached out my hand once again, and though his fingers tensed on my statements, I only palpated the knotted muscles of his biceps. There were better ways of prising secret documents from the grip of a hulking six-footer husband than wrestling him for them. 'Do you want me to tell you the truth?'

'I am listening,' he said. His voice was still angry, but his biceps were softening.

'I'll tell you, but first get up from your akara. Get up, you're ruining my bed sheets.'

Tentatively, he put the statement down on the couch and he must have liked how I didn't dive for it immediately. He must have also liked how I instead helped him out of his soiled pajamas and into a fresh one. Men always like that kind of attention. I changed the bedsheet like your average village wife and joined him on the couch... when I squeezed in between him and my precious statements, there was a tense moment when the fight in him reared up, but my hands and attention were all over him, not my statements, so that moment passed. I breathed a sigh of relief. It would be downhill from here onwards, or my name was not Fassi Blanchard – sorry, Fassi Jekujo.

But, first thing tomorrow I will have to get a post office box and notify my banks. I'm too young to be a widow; and Denle's going to get a heart attack if he opens any of my fixed deposit slips.

HIGH FIDELITY

I want a divorce,' I will tell her.

She will not understand. She will sit there in the sofa where the shock has dropped her. She will breathe quickly, waiting for the rumble of my laughter that would have signalled that I was only joking after all. It will not come. Then the pin-pricks of sweat will appear on the tip of her nose, as she cross-examines me closely,

'Is it the loan to Shafia that I didn't tell you about?'

'It is not.'

'Derin! So it's that old quarrel!'

'It is not-'

'-that quarrel about me laughing at your-'

'-It is not about any quarrel Magiya and it is not about the children that we don't have that I've told you for years and years that I'm not bothered about; and it is not about that nineteen-year-old secretary either-'

'So what is it then? Why do you want to do this to us?'

And at that, I will look at her and fall silent. Because it is difficult to explain that you are divorcing your wife over of a pot of soup, and how she looked at armed robbers in the way she used to look at soldiers in uniform... in a way she had never looked at you.

***

They had been at it for hours. I had wired my music system into the walls and they were determined not to leave without the cables, so they followed me from room to room, as I painstakingly prised the wires from their crevices with long-nosed pliers.

'This wire won't cost more than three hundred naira, *kpata-kpata,*' I suggested politely. I was dripping sweat. My fingers were slippery with fear. The nervous tension of a home-made pistol in my back, and the sheer intricacy of the work.

'Is okay,' sniffed the leader, his voice distorted by his mask, 'I like this particular colour.' They certainly had something about colour. They wore up-market Nike footwear with the most garish of stripes. Their sneakers were more expensive that anything I had ever owned and I did not know whether to be grateful or embarrassed that they showed no interest in my own footwear. When the wires snaked under the bed, he crawled in ahead of me, stabbing a torch into the darkness, checking for weapons that might change the dynamics of our little situation.

Midway through the operation, the leader sneezed explosively, sending his mask scuttling across the room. I could not look away fast enough and there was a moment of alarm. Ordinarily, that could have been fatal for Magiya and I. Robbers who had to protect their identities either wore masks or left no witnesses. But this thief was probably persuaded of our impotence – or such was the heat in our little apartment that rather than retrieve his mask, he pulled off his shirt with a chuckle. It was a signal and suddenly we had two young men in the flat with us, stripped to their jeans. Their resemblance was unmistakable. It was clearly a family business. The younger of them had barely sprouted a moustache.

Somehow we no longer feared for our lives.

That humanising of the robbers did something to Magiya. I suppose it must have been all the adrenaline. Or the breathless proximity to death, and the sudden reprieve. Or the gratefulness that they were more interested in my expensive hi-fi system than the dread of all womenfolk. Despite my preoccupations, I noticed her lingering glances, the lilt in her voice and the new flightiness that accented her gestures.

'What's that smell?' called the younger of them from my wardrobe where he was expertly rifling the pockets of my clothes like a valet preparing his master's suits for the laundry..

'Ugha,' replied my wife.

'Ugha soup?' There was something in his voice. He was tall and rippling. Even if he owed his clothes to burglaries it was clear that he worked hard for his body.

The leader snorted from outside the toilet. 'Not everybody can cook ugha. '

'This one really smells good,' returned the younger, stubbornly. I shut the toilet door against their argument as I contorted around the toilet bowl, straining after the wiring.

'Why do you put loudspeaker inside your bafroom?' asked the elder as I tottered unsteadily on the bath while unscrewing the unit in the ceiling.

'I like it like that,' I grated, trying to remind myself that I was talking to an armed robber and so sarcasm was not an option. I was grateful that I was unlikely to die that night, but I had worked for years and years to acquire this lifestyle and my flat was never going to be the same again.

Eventually, they had the best of our clothes and everything else they wanted in the centre of our living room. There was the croc-skin briefcase containing my cash and documents. There was the raffia box that would normally contain Magiya's gold trinkets, but which now also held our wedding rings. There was our electronic universe: the mobile phones, television, DVD player, laptops, and the crème de la crème, my wall-to-wall integrated-apartment hi-fi system. They even had our passports which I had secured five years earlier. We had saved and saved for the cruise but the visas and passports had expired before we quite put the money together. I told the robbers that they were mere mementoes, but they said they liked the colour of the passport holders. So there they were; all they had to do was go.

Instead, the leader scratched an itch in his crotch and yawned liberally. 'Maybe you should bring the car to the frontage,' he said reluctantly. He looked at his watch.

Yes, I thought, *you should.*

'I am still hungry,' complained the younger thief.

The leader grinned and winked at him. 'Is that soup eh?'

The boy grinned back.

The leader looked at Magiya.

If he had ordered her to make them a meal, my marriage would have survived, who knows. But it was she who offered, and I could hear the pride in her voice, that the aroma of her Ugha had stopped flint-faced robbers in their tracks. I could hear it every time she retold this tale. It got so that the enormity of our losses shrunk with every relating until it was all about her Ugha soup. In recent months, my hi-fi does not even merit a mention. The incident of The Day the Robbers Came could be related without a nod to the grievousness of our loss. Nothing about the rape and plunder of our home, the seventeen thousand naira in my wallets, the irreplaceable wedding rings, nothing about the hi-fi they had taken. Nothing except the, what? three hundred naira pot of soup she had weaved into a snare for armed robbers. And the praises ("They said it was better than their mother's soup!") and the five hundred naira (from my wallet) they had flamboyantly pasted on her face when they were done.

It was a small kitchen. They had all crowded in there and left me alone in the living room. I heard Magiya bossing the young men around her domain in much the same way that she would me. The normalcy of the banter jarred. These were not lads from the office over for a meal, yet that was how they sounded. They left me alone in front of our almost-stolen property, beside an unlocked main entrance, in a final sneer of impotence. Yet, the most heroic scenario that flashed across my mind was the possibility that I could sneak my sim card from my mobile phone without the larcenous brothers noticing.

And yet, I had not dared.

Hours after they left, we sat on the sofa and talked as we waited for dawn. My stomach growled from the experience of watching other men eat my dinner but I did not move for the leftovers – she had served them in her dowry china, the beautiful decorative plates that had been too precious, before that day, for regular use.

Then she clumsily took my hand, and we made love for the first time in many months. It was our first time without the ethereal accompaniment of my hi-fi, but she did not seem to miss it. She seemed different: animated and aggressive. Not brief and businesslike as she had been in the years before our medical assessment, or bored and indifferent as she had been in the years since. And it was the first time in our marriage that her eyes were tightly shut, throughout.

***

I will sigh and shake my head again. How do you explain that you want a divorce because of the best love-making of your marriage?

THE FALL OF PHIRI BOMBAI

Phiri took Abe's promotion to Grade Level fourteen very badly indeed. He got the news on his return from his annual vacation and locked himself into the senior staff toilet to recover from the shock. He stared at the mirror. He tried to turn on his automatic smile. It didn't work. He tried to flash an *Imsohappyforyou* smile. He couldn't either. He looked gaunt and devastated, quite the loser. His charisma was gone. It had been atrophying for years, but it was all gone now. – And he knew what to blame for it: he had not been promoted himself for close to a decade. It was enough to break anyone's spirit.

At first the lack of promotions had not bothered him. He was after all, Phiri Bombai, six feet two inches tall, and at forty-three only the vaguest hint of a pot belly. He had passed his school certificate exams with distinction and every year he still checked the results from his alma mater to see if his old department at the University of Lagos had awarded another first class degree since he left. The smug grin with which he scanned the top of the results list had not slipped once in the twenty-one years since his graduation. In his two decades at the senior levels of Nigerian civil service, he had survived all the isms, from tribalism to nepotism. He had shrugged off the Federal Character caps on his progress, and although he had no godfathers, he had weathered two civil service purges. He had seen off every challenge to his progress by the sheer brilliance of his track record, the comprehensiveness of his credentials, and the charisma of his personality. He had proved that, even in Nigeria, there was no keeping a good man down.

Until his nemesis joined the department. Abe Araguna had only two assets to speak of: a Ph.D and an uncle who happened to be the Minister for Solid Minerals. Abe was a slow-thinking, slow-talking historian who could not in all honesty be called a fool, because he did, after all, have a Ph.D. While he was never wrong about anything, his answers were also so long-winding that he was usually in the middle of it when someone else solved the problem. Phiri had sat on the panel that employed him. He still remembered, with shame, the post-interview discussions of the three-member panel hurriedly recalled for a last minute candidate after the regular interviews had been concluded. The Director-General had been the keenest to hire:

'Ph.D Medieval History!' he had repeated, over and over, 'Very impressive!'

'Although, he did spend thirteen years on it,' Mrs Lenton had observed timidly.

'That shows doggedness,' the Director-General had replied, 'we need some doggedness around here.'

Phiri had cleared his throat with some irritation. 'I don't want to sound petulant,' he had said, sounding petulant, still smarting from his cancelled vacation, 'but his so-called university was still a college of education when he first enrolled for his teacher-training certificate, sixteen years ago…'

'You don't need to be jealous!' The Director-General had snapped, in the rudest put-down Phiri was to receive in his entire career, 'This department is big enough for two Ph.Ds.'

'That's not the point, Sir,' Phiri had continued when he found his voice again, unsure what he had said to so upset his Director General, 'but the candidate is a historian and this is the Ministry of Solid Minerals — compared to the man we had already selected-'

'Rubbish,' the Director-General had snapped, 'what this ministry needs right now is a new sense of history.'

When Abe Araguna joined the service, it did not occurr to Phiri that the slow Ph.D (who quickly earned the sarcastic sobriquet *Please help Doc o*) could – in a hundred years – be competition for

224

him. The gulf between them was that wide. They were the same age but while Abe had spent a decade contending for his Ph.D from a former college of education, Phiri had acquired his own doctorate in Geosciences from his respectable alma mater, in a part-time programme that did not cost him a day in the office.

Phiri had joined the service on Grade Level eight. By public service rules staff were supposed to spend three years on each level before promotion to the next. On average most of his colleagues spent much longer but Phiri aced his promotion exams and returned from every annual vacation with a fresh diploma. He had skipped through to G.L. 14 on an average of two years on each level. When Abe joined the service on G.L. 10, Phiri was already on G.L. 14, within shouting distance of Directorship. In civil service terms, that four level gulf between the two men was like the ocean span between Brazil and the Bight of Benin. In knowledge terms, more cosmic metaphors were relevant, for Abe was a square peg in a round ministry. A historian in the Solid Minerals Ministry was like a fly-catcher in a nuclear lab. Abe took a week to get a grasp on problems that Phiri could solve with a phonecall. They were not 'mates' in Civil Service terms.

Yet, Abe was not merely introduced by the minister. He was the *nephew* of the minister.

Grade Levels fifteen, sixteen and seventeen were the director-grades, the Eldorado of the Civil Service. Public servants on G.L. 15 could fly First Class, were supplied with the full complement of personal servants from drivers, through gardeners to house-boys – with some of them monetized. There were only three directors ahead of Phiri in the Department of Solid Minerals, and they were all older than the D.G. In six years when the D.G. was due to retire, the most senior person in contention would likely be Phiri – if he continued on current form. It was clear that he was on track to becoming the youngest Director General in the history of the department.

Then strange things began to happen, a stratosphere beneath him. Abe Araguna was appointed a 'chief' by a village nobody had ever heard of before. Phiri got the invitation to the coronation, like everyone else in the department, and snickered before tossing it into an overflowing drawer. (His relationship with Abe had been delicate from the beginning: the D.G., trying to curry favour with the minister, had related Phiri's opposition to Abe's appointment, and the steps he had taken to overcome it) On the Monday afterwards, the event was all over the papers. The D.G. and the Minister had attended! Yet, that was not the most surprising thing, for the President's Senior Personal Assistant had also attended! And those were just the faces that Phiri could make out from the photograph in the Vanguard newspaper! Phiri's hands were shaking slightly as he filed the newspaper away carefully, for future rumination.

Things gradually got worse. Abe retired his English suits in favour of heavy white robes that slowed his already slow locomotion and work output further. But where he previously looked like a corpulent toad, his resplendent robes now lent him a regal bearing. He adopted irritating – and suspiciously fetish – mannerisms, like the sinister necklace which he touched before and after every handshake. He was now addressed, even by the D.G., with the deferential moniker, *Chief*. This caused Phiri no little aggravation, especially when official circulars put out by the pool typists began to put the name Chief Dr. Abe Araguna above Dr. Phiri Bombai, contrary to protocol. On several occasions he was on the very brink of storming down to the secretarial pool, but he always held himself in check, recognising, quite rightly, that it was beneath him to notice such little-minded machinations by the *hoi polloi*.

Unfortunately, little-minded machinations began to occur higher up in the service as well. Every time Phiri went off on a business trip or annual vacation he returned to find a more senior Abe Araguna. Although he was Abe's direct supervisor, promotion assessments "just happened" to be bought forward to hold during his absence. The result was that – despite his atrocious work output, all Abe's assessments were glowing and he was rocketing through the cadre at an even more precipitate speed than Phiri himself, a travesty that kept at least one civil servant in the ministry of Solid Minerals awake at night. For, while Abe was moving up, Phiri was going to pieces. His personnel file had never before accommodated a bland recommendation, how much more a query. Now, his directors seemed to find fault with every thing he did. He now lurched from query to query, and there were currently three pending anonymous petitions taking issue with his retirement of festival funds.

Phiri spent eight years on G.L. 14. He was still there when Abe received the promotion that brought him level with his former mentor. Nobody called him *Please help Doc o* anymore, whether behind his back or otherwise. – Although there was no shortage of people ready to help him. Even new entrants to the service quickly discovered that the best way to get ahead was to write brilliant memos for lucrative new committees, get Abe to sign them, and get appointed a deputy to Abe when his uncle approved it – as he inevitably did.

That morning, as Phiri stared at his face in the mirror of the senior service toilet, he realised, with a grieving spirit, that Chief Dr. Abe Araguna was going to become the next D.G. of the department. He raised his hands to his cheeks to wipe away the tears and noticed, again, the trembling that had started those rumours – made known to him only the other week by his secretary – of an early compulsory retirement on medical grounds for the former rising star of Solid Minerals. With a flash of insight (which had become rare these days) he realised that his hands had never trembled before Abe's chieftaincy. He shut his eyes, heart pounding, as he tracked back, realising with shock, that it had all started with the handshake with which he congratulated Abe on his chieftaincy.

He was the subject of an occult attack!

He left the office immediately, at a loss as to his next step. Now that he had traced his problems back to that handshake, it was easier for him to admit that his performance had taken a downward spiral. It was years and years since he last came back from a vacation with a diploma in anything. The anonymous petitions were not entirely without substance – and he had fallen asleep while in charge of departmental minutes at a Federal Executive Council meeting!

Yet, this was not simply Phiri going loco. It was an occult attack.

He was suffused with a perverse relief. The ability to identify a fault outside himself galvanised him. He went straight to church, surprised to find it in full session at 12 noon on a Monday. Although he was a Christian, he himself only went to church once a month or so. He was not a particularly religious person, but he knew instinctively that this was a peculiarly spiritual problem.

The church was a beautiful, new denomination, barely six years old. The pastor-in-charge was also the general overseer of the ministry, and although he was barely greying, he had a look of great sagacity and an aura of imperturbable calm. Phiri waited impatiently at the back of the church until the prayer meeting ended. The congregants broke up abruptly, as their lunch hours expired, and drove off without the usual hanging around at the end of the Sunday services. It was not difficult to secure an audience with the pastor. Indeed it was as though he was expected, for the pastor called him by name, remembering to add the title, Dr., a feat of memory that both humbled and gladdened Phiri.

'I have a big problem,' said Phiri.

'Tell us all about it,' said the pastor. Phiri looked around self-consciously, then realised, stupidly, that the pastor was referring to himself and God. So he did. And it was such a relief, speaking about it for the first time, that he gushed on and on. By 4pm, the pastor, who had to start preparing for his evening service, spontaneously broke into prayer and prophecy. Regarding the prayer component, he prayed fire and brimstone; concerning prophesy, he foresaw death and damnation. He prayed with such ferocity and rage that Phiri swiftly went from relief to apprehension about the Angel of Death on His way to "uproot and destroy" all his "enemies" at the office. After twenty minutes of the prayers he was able to break away from the maelstrom of curses. He arrived in the office just before closing, half-fearing a pandemonium of felled corpses, but the first person that he saw in the senior management corridor was Abe Araguna, who was looking particularly chipper as he touched his hand to the amulet of dense obsidian on his necklace and offered a handshake.

Phiri turned and bolted again.

He went straight back to church. The pastor, who was just about to start his evening service, was not quite as receptive as he was in the afternoon.

'With a serious case like this, you have to make a serious sacrifice,' he explained.

Phiri was incoherent with sincerity. 'I will give up anything: beer, cigarette…' then he noticed the pastor's humourless eyes and checked himself. He pulled out his chequebook and made a serious sacrifice.

It was no good. The next day, he noticed that he was the subject of long significant glances. The women in the typing pool who used to look at him with forlorn lust were now looking at him with pity. As he arrived for the departmental executive briefing, Abe (who by virtue of his promotion, was attending for the first time) offered a handshake right in front of the D.G., so Phiri had no choice but to accept it. As the meeting broke up, he even tried on a "goodbye" handshake which Phiri pretended not to see, causing Abe to lay the scorned hand on Phiri's shoulder. That very evening, Phiri burned the jacket that Abe had touched, and spent the better part of thirty minutes washing his hand; but his right arm, from the shoulder, seemed to grow heavier and number by the hour.

Yet he couldn't avoid handshakes in his office, and he couldn't very well keep burning his suits either. That Sunday, on the recommendation of a lettuce-seller at the evening market, he tried another church. The Prophetic Latter End Miracle Centre did not hang about. Before Phiri had been in the congregation fifteen minutes, the ecstatic minister of God had purged a womb of fibroids and cast out an infestation of demonic spirits. Phiri felt a warm tingling all over. When the chants of praise began, he rose to his feet. Afterwards, he was one of a long line of people waiting to see the minister. Phiri was taken aback by the harried and morose faces on the queue, and hoped that he looked nothing like them. He tried on his *itsawonderfulday* smile, and was somewhat relieved that there was no mirror to assess it in.

On Monday, he arrived in the office with a lot more confidence than he had had in a few years. When it was time for the dreaded handshake, he not only took it with gusto, he clapped his left hand on the shoulder of the startled Abe, for both his hands had been liberally pomaded with anointing oil blessed by the minister of God. He walked around his office with an over-full glass of water, to disguise the liberal sprinklings he had made earlier that morning with the bottle of the minister's holy water. It had been dark when he carried out the protection instructions, and he had not counted on the noticeable splotches on the carpet.

***

He was okay for the whole of that year; indeed, his greasy palms dissuaded many a handshake. Then, the following year, he and Chief Dr. Abe Araguna were promoted to Director grade G.L. 15, on the same day.

His joy at this long-awaited promotion was swamped by his dismay at the premature elevation of his bitter rival. It was the first time in the history of the department that a civil servant would spend just a year on a grade that required a three-year maturation period. He knew very well that his own promotion was window-dressing; he was most likely going to retire at that level, while Abe moved on to bigger things. He felt a little light-headed as he folded away the official gazette, and then he blanked out, and found himself (quite suddenly) in the observation bed of a mustachioed civil service doctor.

The doctor was grinning genially, 'I also fainted myself in medical school when I saw my first corpse,' he said helpfully. 'Take these tablets-'

'I want to rest for one week.'

'No problem,' said the doctor, pulling up his sick leave booklet.

He took the medical advice. There were no more churches for him. The anointing oil and the holy water, he saw now, were passable defensive shields; but they were not proof against the pernicious patronage of the Minister for Solid Minerals, who was at that moment lobbying the national convention of the ruling political party to become the next presidential candidate. Phiri knew he was going to die the day he had to answer sir to a roach like Abe Araguna. He moped in his bedroom, already feeling like guest of honour at a wake. Then his secretary phoned with the warning that Abe and other senior colleagues at the ministry were planning to come the next evening on a get-well visit.

More like a kill-and-go visit, he thought, fleeing to his village.

Because it was more than fifteen years since his last visit, he had to spend the first night in the hotel while his country home was scrubbed and cleared of the dust and cobwebs from a decade and a half of neglect. Yet, the change did him good. On the second day, he was actually well enough to walk, on tottery feet, along River Ukagba, for which the village was named. It was so peaceful, so far away from ministry politics, that he sat there under a gnarled mahogany, and fell asleep. It was already dusk when he was roused by a gravelly voice, 'Phiri Bombai? Is that you?'

Phiri started awake. The elderly man in front of him was bald, but in revenge he had grown his beard with an obsessiveness that had no place for niceties like combs. The result was a tangled grey-black horsetail that hung down to his navel. Phiri recognized the other man immediately, despite the extra six inches of beard. 'Uncle Menire!'

'So you remember us today.'

'Don't mind me! Civil service life is terrible!'

Phiri found it convenient to go along with his uncle's assumption that he had rattled his gate a short distance away, and finding him out, had fallen asleep while waiting for his return. In truth, Phiri had forgotten all about this distant cousin, until that very moment; had forgotten that his family had worshipped the deity named for the river. Three decades earlier, when Phiri's father was still alive, Menire was one of the last adherents of the river deity, and his loyalty had driven a wedge between him and Phiri's more Christianized section of the family.

Now, as Phiri paid his impromptu but quite agreeable visit, a radical and alarming idea began to grow in his mind, but it was an idea of such brazenness that he was unable to speak of it until close to midnight when he was several bottles away from public service sobriety. Menire had found a carton of beer of reasonable antiquity under his bed. A family of rats had nestled in it, but the liquid contents were fine, really. It was warm, but the evening was cool, anyway. They sat in the front yard of Menire's lonely, riverside bungalow hedged around by a rustling wall of browning maize. A chittering monkey chained by the waist ate groundnuts and threw the husks at its captor. It was suddenly aeons away from cosmopolitan Abuja. It was suddenly the place for brazen propositions. His uncle heard him out and grunted dispassionately, 'The deity is dead, Phiri.'

'What about all those stories you told me when I was a child, of how Ukagbani put children in wombs, how Ukagbani put yams in barns...'

'They were true – then. But Ukagbani is dead. Many years dead. You don't leave a baby in the bush without food for forty years and come looking for it- '

'A deity is not a baby –'

'But it feeds on offerings. On worship. Every god needs worship, Phiri.'

'A real god cannot die just because we don't worship him. That means he's not almighty-'

'Who needs an almighty god? So long as he's mightier than your neighbours, that's mighty enough... and all I know is that after one hundred years of worshipping America, Almighty God is not going to part any more Red Seas for Israel. That's my finger! Let's bet!'

Phiri did not accept the bet.

Menire rose and shuffled into his bungalow. He bumped into barrels that weren't even in the way, and Phiri knew that his uncle was even more drunk than he sounded. He came out a few minutes later bearing a dusty sculpture the size of a fair tuber of yam. He dropped it dramatically on the ground before Phiri, the way one could never drop a tuber of yam. 'This is Ukagbani,' he said. 'Remember that iroko in the village square? Our great grandfather carved Ukagbani from one of her branches.'

He resumed his chair. His lips were pursed and swivelled swiftly in circles, making a comic feature of his face, but Phiri was not close to laughter; indeed, he had never seen his uncle so close to tears. They both swigged huge gulps of beer. Then, losing his fight for self-control, Menire sniffed and broke open a can of snuff which he applied liberally to his nostrils, promising, 'The last time, the absolutely last, *last* time!'

When he had sneezed – and wiped his tears like one that cleaned away the products of a good snuffing – he shook his head and rolled the wooden idol with his toes until its terrible face looked up at the two men. Its bottom half was still black from decades of poured offerings. Its black eyes stared vacantly at them. Menire shook his head ruefully, 'Look at him!'

Phiri did, thinking that their great grandfather was not exactly a gifted sculptor.

'It is only good for firewood now,' said Menire bitterly, '*Hai!* I remember when Ukagbani was Ukagbani! In those days, if I touched him without first killing a cock, eh? That whole week, headache won't let me sleep!'

Phiri looked longingly at the prostrate idol. The very land on which they sat had been disputed with a powerful family. Their great grandfather had ended the dispute by setting Ukagbani's shrine in the middle of the land. Phiri's spine tingled at the memory of that acquisition by divine fiat, that gem of family history. This was the sort of godfather Phiri needed! He remembered Abe Araguna's obsidian necklace and obstinate uncle. The parochial unfairness of life suddenly bore down on him with grinding vindictiveness. Abe Araguna's village was not dead. It was there, investing him with an empty chieftaincy that gave him prestige and respect in a bereft Abuja. His ethnic gods were not dead. For all his stately Christianity, he wore one of them around his neck, wearing down the potentials of his more intelligent rivals in the most parochial way. His uncle was dressed in ministerial pomp, not an unkempt beard. Phiri was suddenly overawed by his sad lot in life, 'I need a godfather!' he groaned, 'that civil service is a terrible place! A very terrible place!' And at that moment he was grateful for the beer, and for the scandalous depth of confidence it empowered him to share.

'But you are a Christian, not so?'

'I am,' said Phiri equivocally.

'That's good,' said Menire approvingly, 'I am now a deacon my-self.' He kicked Ukagbani again. His lips began to twitch again, 'We were idiots before, worshipping sticks and things that we can hold in our hand. Now we worship an international God. I still put children into barren wombs, sure, but now I give God the credit. We are-'

'I want something that I can hold in my hand,' blurted Phiri. He swallowed. His fists trembled from the ferocity, and sinfulness, of his need.

Menire looked at the younger man with some alarm. Then he looked around the empty courtyard with drunken discretion, 'Okay now,' he said, teary eyes gleaming with alcoholic resolve, 'bring your bible and your cross tomorrow. There's no need to look for our gods inside the grave, eh?' he kicked Ukagbani again, 'After all, we were more Christian than the missionaries that brought Christianity here. Eh?'

'Yes,' said Phiri without conviction.

The following day, the influence of beer dissipated, Phiri remem-bered his idolatrous conversation with Menire with deep embar-rassment. He instructed his driver to tell all visitors that he was sleeping, and took to his bedroom, deep in depression. An hour passed and a trembling driver came to report the presence of the Director-General and a party of commiserating senior staff from the department in the living room downstairs. Chief Dr. Abe Araguna did not just shake his hand. He hugged Phiri for the first time, and the full bodily contact with the obsidian neck-lace dried out Phiri's mouth and set off palpitations in his heart. He realized that nowhere, not even his village, was beyond the swathe of Araguna's oppression. Much later, as the delegation left for their cars after leaving behind a get-well card signed by the entire staff, the D.G. took Phiri aside and reminded him of the generous civil service provisions for early retirement – and the party convention to select a presidential candidate, which was in progress as he spoke, 'You have a nice village house,' he said gently, 'it's better to enjoy your pension, you know.'

Phiri thought that was very rich, coming from a D.G. who had, at the age of forty, sworn to an affidavit that he was actually thirty-five, and who was dyeing the last of his hair to wring out the last years of his working life without provoking anonymous petitions. As the delegation's convoy left his house, Phiri hurried over to Menire's bungalow with his bible and cross. His uncle was waiting patiently, tossing grains of corn at an overweight cockerel whose crowing sounded like the strumming of a bass guitar.

'You have come,' he observed, unnecessarily.

'Yes.'

They retired into the parlour which, Phiri was relieved to see, did not have a cock or goat tethered for sacrifice. When he spoke his thoughts aloud, his uncle smiled indulgently. Without opening the bible, he quoted, 'Sacrifice and offering You did not desire, but a body You have prepared for Me.'

Phiri was duly impressed. He had dismissed the claim to deaconship as empty puffing.

Menire started the ceremony. He inspected the bible. *NIV version*, he muttered approvingly. He dressed his centre table with a white cloth and set the bible and cross on it. An age passed in the course of which the deacon struck a desultory gong and sighed heavily from time to time. Suddenly he snapped his head upwards and to the left of a bicycle hanging on the wall, 'Tandi,' he said curtly, and made a clicking sound. An hour passed, and he smiled and bowed deeply, 'Mehu-Mehu!' Phiri recognized his father's nickname, but he could not turn his head. He swallowed, waiting patiently as his uncle greeted many more ancestors, seeing off the more undesirable elements.

Then he set down the gong and began to chant. Disjointed passages from the bible flowed around the praise names of dead ancestors. Phiri felt a peculiar crowding in of memory. He knew very well that his father was *not* standing to attention to the left of him. He knew that his mother was *not* floating in the air, where Menire addressed his praise of *Mother with the Heart of Water*. But it was nice to feel that wholeness again, for the first

235

time since he was a child in the hearth of his parents, it was nice to be – confirmed bachelor that he was – secure in a womb of family that death could not dissolve.

It was almost a rude shock when Menire broke off his chant and rose. An expression of incensed rage grew on his face and he began to harangue the air around him, speaking in a language that was neither English nor any other language known to Phiri. After ten minutes of this, he seemed to reach an accommodation with his spiritual collocutors. Taking up the bible, he kissed it and opened it wide to the ceiling. Then he lowered it, blew into it, and shut it gently. He gave it to Phiri, who, instinctually kissed it thrice before handing it back. Menire looked around the room which was now peopled with pews and pews of genial ancestors. He made his choice, and kissed and opened up the holy book again. Five times he invited ancestors, five times they entered in, and five time Phiri kissed them welcome, dropping tears of gratitude onto the holy book. He welcomed in Mehuni, his father and Raisa his mother. He welcomed in Kaabaka his step mother, and his great grand father Atima, who had led Ukagba in the last communal war that humbled their upstart neighbours to the north. He welcomed in his grandfather Akarjo, who had retired a chief clerk, the highest ranking Nigerian civil servant in his province, at a time when the forbears of the Solid Minerals Minister were most likely peasant farmers. When all that was done, Menire gave him the book. 'Open it and read,' he said.

'What verse?'

'Any verse. Just open anywhere and read.'

Phiri hesitated, then he cracked opened the bible centrally. His eyes fell on a verse from Psalm 144:

> *Reach down your hand from on high;*
> *deliver me and rescue me*
> *from the mighty waters,*
> *from the hands of foreigners*

Menire grinned happily. 'You see? God is here. That is your war cry. That verse is your amulet. It is your special word from God, from the Great Beyond. Don't forget it.'

Later that evening, they sat in the yard, enduring the jabbering taunts of the captive monkey, and reflecting on the portentous events of the day. 'What about the cross?' Phiri asked.

'It will sleep inside your bible. In the morning, you will put in on a chain and wear it everywhere. Your ancestors live in that bible now, so you must honour it. It requires serious sacrifice.'

'I know,' said Phiri, reaching for his wallet.

Menire waved it away disdainfully. 'Not that type. The bible must never leave your bedroom. You understand? It must never be touched by anyone else. You understand? And your beard...'

'Yes?'

'You must grow a full beard. That was Atima's condition. He didn't want to enter your cross, so I asked him, what about your beard? At first he wanted it like mine, but I told him that you're a public servant, and that Abuja is not like Ukagba. So that is the deal. He will fight for you, but you must grow a beard.'

Phiri paused. This was heavy. 'So I will be a nazirite like Samson, eh?'

Menire's beer was almost at his lips, where it paused. He grinned, 'But no Delilah, o!'

They laughed. 'The iroko is too big,' he explained, 'so we cut a branch from her. God... the Bible... they're all too big, eh? Who can obey every law? Eh? So we take a verse, a thing and hold it tight eh? That what every church does. Select. And who knows God eh? So we bundle Him with our ancestors that we knew very well, eh? They may be ordinary people when they were alive, but they are near God now, eh? So maybe it is idolatry, okay, but who can obey everything in the Bible? Eh?'

'Nobody.'

'Exactly.'

The goat farted an amen.

The next week, Phiri returned to work, to a disciplinary hearing on the first of the anonymous petitions. He got a two-month suspension and a serious warning. Yet, he did not throw away his ancestor-infested bible and cross, for on that same day, the Party convention announced the new presidential candidate and it was not Abe Araguna's uncle. That same day, the sitting president announced a cabinet reshuffle in which the Solid Minerals Minister and a few other Presidential aspirants lost their jobs. – Although the president was at the tail end of his maximum of two terms, he had expected his ministers to spend their energies campaigning for a constitutional amendment to allow him to run for a third term. So Phiri grew his beard assiduously. It was clear that they were not almighty. He did not expect his ancestors to win every battle. All he needed was a few solid punches landed on his behalf.

As for the rest, his name was Phiri Bombai. He would take care of it.

GOING STRAIGHT

I remember as clear as sin the day I went straight. I can still see myself sprawled across that double bed in Hotel De Beeg's room 403. Through the open windows I could see the car park, the green village and – if I squinted hard enough – the rusty zinc roof on Caraposa Street where my cousin lived. I was still dressed, if you discount the scarf by the door, the jacket on the carpet and the crepline blouse draped across the sofa. (My heels don't count: I never take them off, anyway.) Yet, that was nothing that couldn't be quickly fixed. Mutoni had just popped down to the reception get a "surprise package" from the porter's desk. Besides, I was waiting for the meal of skewered brill we had ordered on room service. It was going to be a long night.

I did not set out for married men; it's just that marital status was not a question on my dating form. I did not, for instance, *know* whether Mutoni was married or not. The pale band of skin on his ring finger could have been a fungal problem; and the ferocious-looking woman I saw glaring from his wallet as he paid for the room could just as easily have been his mother. I usually never asked, and they usually never told. Life was complicated enough, without adding the various permutations of fidelities. It was enough for me that two adults pursued their mutual pleasures happily. So there I was, sprawled out, waiting for the meal and the man, or the man and the meal, whatever the order in which they arrived, when the room telephone rang.

It continued to ring as I took off my pearl hoop earrings. After a painful accident in my first year it was now a settled, pre-liaison ritual. I usually would not pick up a phone in a man's hotel room, so I didn't; but it rang eight times, which was an unusually lengthy stretch of time for any phone to ring, so I thought to pick it up if it rang a tenth time, which it did; so I did.

'Is that housekeeping?' demanded an angry voice. I recognised Mutoni right away.

'It's me, Muti – but you have my mobile-'

'Housekeeping!' he snapped angrily, 'This is the third time I am calling your office-'

'Muti-'

'-can you please fix the door lock in my room 403, *immediately*,'

'It's me Shanta! What's the matter with you?'

'Good, because my wife is here now. Please fix the lock so I can get into the room, okay?'

'*What?*'

'You'd better get it done in *ten* minutes,' he said curtly, hanging up.

I replaced the phone. I was angry to see that my hand was shaking. I was no coward, but I had seen wife/mistress confrontations in the past and I was in no mood for high drama, bloody noses and scenes of public nudity...

So that was his "surprise package". I supposed I ought to be grateful that the canny receptionist had not allowed her to come right upstairs! I was not feeling very grateful just then.

He should have told me he was married.

I stood up and looked at myself in the full length mirror. I deserved more than this. The year before, I had reached the final round of the university's Miss Hot Legs competition; and I did look better, the less I wore. I stared long at myself. I stripped slowly. The better I looked, the better I felt. I don't know how long I stood there dressed in the killer jade-green heels I won in the beauty pageant – but my feeling of well-being ebbed suddenly as I became conscious of passing time. I dressed quickly.

Perhaps that was the problem. It should not matter *how* I looked.

I should not have to dress down to feel good. The ten-minute quit notice had something to do with my uncharacteristic soul-searching. The life of an aspirational undergrad was such a struggle! If I started drawing moral boundaries who was to tell where it would lead? Married men were a large, lucrative demographic... ruling them out would be a game-changer for my lifestyle... In a few months I was due to graduate, hopefully in the third class... which would be a bonus really after four years of partying interrupted by nasty snatches of exams. I was almost out of the classroom, perhaps it was time to graduate from the hotel room as well...

There was a knock. Anxiously, I pulled on my blouse, wondering if I could pass as 'the woman from Housekeeping'... but it was only a waiter from room service with our brill. After he left I realised that although my appetite for both man and meal was gone I could not muster the anger to leave Mutoni to explain the second plate of fish to his wife, so I took my tray and left the room, plunking down on a lounge chair just outside the lift. I had just started eating when they appeared, man and wife. They were a power couple alright. Mutoni was thirty kilogrammes or so heavier than I, but he had his match in his wife. She had no eyes for me and motored past on her husband's arm with a bosom as aggressive as a pair of boxing gloves. I was suddenly grateful she had not burst in on us.

Yet, it was Mutoni's glare that cured me, and killed the married men scene completely for me. When he tore himself away from me fifteen minutes earlier he had been in the middle of a declaration of undying love... now he sneered at me with a look of condensed hatred and disgust, like an arachnophobe trying to decide between fleeing a spider and squashing it underfoot. I got that he was terrified of his wife, that he wished me a million miles away at that moment... but I was only twenty... I could not process the transition between his love and hatred. I had never felt lonlier in my life than I did at that moment.

They disappeared into my room and I put down the tray. My appetite was totally gone.

So the *Married Question* is now up there on the top of my dating form... they have continued to proposition me since, these philanderers, but I have kept my distance – because I know that what lies beneath the love lie is the *Mutoni Glare*.

And if that does not work, I usually recall the *Shanta Sprint*. – After Mutoni and his wife entered the room, I was good for another round of self-pity, but it was not to be. The next moment, my pearl earrings emerged, held high in the red claws of the wife. She was an experienced madam alright, and all she needed to see were my guilty hands rising to check my ears and then she was screaming as she kicked off her shoes and thundered towards me. I had the wisdom to lose my own shoes before beginning the most embarrassing sprint through the labyrinthine corridors of Hotel De Beeg. It was touch-and-go on the narrow corridors, bumping into startled guests and almost getting caught by the screaming madam... but once I hit the gravelled car park the advantage of being barefeet and twenty years younger kicked in and I made my escape, running all the way to Caraposa Street where I was spending my Easter vacation.

So I'm a relatively good girl now... I still miss my pearl earrings though. – And I cannot count the number of times I have opened my wardrobe for my favourite jade-green heels, only to sigh and remember the *Shanta Sprint*.

CONFESSIONS OF THE
GENERAL'S MARABOUT

Good, sit down. I've said it many times, you journalists will kill me one day. What time is it? Very good. 3 p.m. is a good time for an interview. You have been chasing me for this interview for the last ten years, not so? Well I like your spirit. And your cunning too. I noticed when you started buying gifts for my little Aisha years and years ago... you saw she was my favourite granddaughter, didn't you, and you used her to get to me... ha... you're a snake, you! Now she is a grown woman and doesn't stop talking about you, and reading your articles to me. She told me I can get more money from talking to you than I got from working for General Sani Abacha all those years ago. Well as they say, talking about money and counting out money are two different things entirely. Let me see your cash.

Good... very good... it isn't money I have not seen before, but it will do for a tale or two of the good old days. You like fried snails don't you? Well, eat. Aisha fries them very well. She will make a lucky man a good wife someday. Let me see those hands of yours. I know you don't believe in palmistry and stuff but... what harm can it do? Go on, bring those handsome hands! Indulge this old man who doesn't get many quality palms to read these days... *O my God*... Okay. Let's leave your palms for now, let us talk about Sani Abacha. Don't bother about the horror of what I read in your palms, that is not what you came here for, is it? Let's talk about my time with Sani Abacha; the secret of this business is victim-knowledge, take it from me. Of course, you also need luck, but all your good luck will soon spoil if you can't acquire victim-knowledge, that's the truth. You have to really get to know your victim. Yes, I call them victims, not clients. I am retired now, so I can be as honest as I want... Look, do you want to hear about Sani Abacha or what I read in your palms?

I admit it was something serious, but you didn't come all this way to read your palms did you? I am sorry that my face was so open – I wasn't on my guard... it isn't every time I see graphic images like what I saw just now. You educated types don't believe things like this anyway, do you? And it doesn't concern you personally in any case; it only concerns your wife. So let's just forget about it!

About my time with Sani Abacha, I was researching him for years and years. From the time when he was Minister for Defence, I was researching him. I started by standing at his Ikoyi gate, then I began to following his cooks, to befriend his mistresses... I had dozens of smart helpers all over the streets watching their every move... in this business you never eat alone, you see... until I knew everything there was to know about him – and the people around him. It was only then that I made my move. That's the other secret about this job: if you haven't got your information, don't keep the appointment. I have seen young fools who treat their craft like it was a spare parts business or something. They sit in their 'shop' and see everybody that comes along. Throwing prophecies left right and centre, like 419 letters, in the hope that one or two will come out right. *Fools.* Me, I don't do that, I only see those I am ready to see... that's why my results are always fantastic! I was one of Abacha's all time favourites, I'm telling you!

Enough about these palms of yours, mister journalist! You really try my patience! Look, I don't ply my craft for free, that's the truth. If I read your palms for you, then that's your money on the table gone. Are you prepared for that? Naturally, I only charge if I can prove that what I see is true. So choose now between your palms and an Abacha tale. Is that your final answer? Good, bring your hands again. Look, are you really sure you want to do this – after all the years that you've spent chasing this story? I have the real secrets about Abacha, you know. What will your editor say? Aha... I see the old cunning in your eyes. I can see the cynicism all over your face. I remember all those articles my Aisha read to me. This is part of your first paragraph, isn't it: you will say how the old marabout tried to pull a fast one on you, how you exposed his tricks and then, on to the main fare, the Sani Abacha secrets! Well we shall see if I am a total fraud! Sit still now! Give me your palms.

You see this thumb and index finger? They will send you to jail. When? That's a bit cloudy... it could be for battery and assault, it could be for wife-beating... it's all in the future, it all depends on you... You see this small finger, it will bring you out of jail. I am not speaking in riddles... don't you know poetry when you hear it? Look, I know that a prophecy of death is no 'prophecy', since all will die... but look carefully at this wedding band... it lies. She was wearing a yellow wedding gown at your wedding, was she not? And she made a long and flowery vow of fidelity, did she not? ... all lies! I see her now... hold your hands steady! ...long of hair, no real brows, just two pencilled lines erased by sweat and shame, she is full of bust and broad of hips isn't she... she's your wife all right! I see she's wearing an identical wedding ring! ... but it is all she's wearing right now – apart from the *jigida* on her waist! ...and she's not alone! I see him too... this big, great, sweating... no!

Enough! Take away your hands! I don't like these X-rated auguries! Ask me anything of Sani Abacha! Even now, let's forget this horrible vision I see in your palms, I'll give you an Abacha tale for free! Okay? I was his favourite marabout for years and years! The things I could tell you of the dictator, Sani Abacha! I saw his own death approach... but of course I held my peace... you don't become someone's favourite marabout by telling them they will die next month... *don't phone her!* That is such a bad idea! You will surely hear the panting in her voice... and she will never admit. Why do you want to torture yourself like that? The secret to a happy marriage is spousal blindness... He answered her phone? What an imbecile! Who would answer a lover's phone in the middle of an... what a fool. What an *Imbecile!* Don't go now, mister journalist, it's not a good idea to drive in this state of mind... well, goodbye then.

And good luck.

Sit down Aisha. He's gone now? Very good. That was my wedding present to you, wrapped and presented five or six months in advance. My panting helper will have her phone back in her bag before she is back from the gym, before she even knows it was stolen. – If there was one lesson I learnt from Abacha, it is 'never eat alone'. Innocence won't help the missis now, poor thing. I hope for their sake that the divorce is swift and painless. All you have to do now is to be nice and nearby. Hopefully the man who stole your heart so calculatingly ten years ago will chose more wisely next time.

DIARY OF AN HONEST GIRL

Post-coitus, Paul watched a cockroach cross the pitted lino of her bedsit. Little things like this that told him that, however good the sex, he and Sara belonged in completely different worlds. He smiled back at the girl-woman hurrying anxiously from the kitchenette. It scared him that she had believed his lies so easily. Why would he fracture the ready-made perfection of his life and leave his wife and daughters for her? Didn't she see how anyone would say anything in the throes of *that* hunger?

She brought in dinner on a gaudy plastic tray. However poor her dinner service, Sara was an even better cook than she was a lover and Paul's bowels, primed by the red aroma of *awaii*, heaved in anticipation. Then he saw her lovesick face and his heart began to race – at the stressful mismatch of casual sex on his part and an all-consuming love on hers. Despite his groaning bowels, his saliva dried up. He became so guilty he was scared, and he became so scared he was angry. – With himself, most of all. His usual dalliances rarely lasted longer than six months... after all, brevity was the whole point of the fling. Now here he was, in a relationship that had lasted twelve months already. He was almost in danger of falling into a routine! It was most marriage-like in the number of impossible promises he had been forced to make. It was time he moved on. He had to end it now! The anger pushed him right to the cliff of decision, yet, he refused to jump.

He had to finish the yam pottage first.

Post-dinner, he sighed as he poured a glass of Gulder. He drank slowly, watching her lips and her green-rimmed eyes while her dextrous fingers remoisturised themselves after the trauma of cooking. There were still two bottles of beer in her fridge and she didn't drink any alcohol at all. He stared idly at the fingers, the lithe fingers, and wondered who would drink the beers eventually, who would tend those moist lips... as his imagination flared, his resolve began to weaken, and he sat up abruptly and cleared his throat. 'Are you okay?' she asked solicitously, 'Was the food nice?'

'It was very nice, Sara, but we have to end this affair tonight. I'm very sorry.'

He watched her nervously, heart racing as he downed the rest of the glass of beer. He remembered drunken debates with mates on the subject of ending affairs. He was an experienced man in his own right and could have written a book on the subject. – Every affair was unique and had an ideal method of termination, but there were only ten main variations on the 'It's all Over' theme. With Sara, he had been tempted to go for the Implied Termination: he would lie about a sudden transfer abroad and disappear – simply blank her out... she would discover the lie within a few days of course, but she would have got the message all the same... hatred would replace the lovesickness... job done...

Yet, he prided himself in his integrity, that was why he used the Magic Bullet termination – he got everything out in the open in one sentence delivered out of the blues. The downside was the emotionally-wrenching tears and hysterics. That evening, as his family ate dinner alone (because of his training programme on some new radiological equipment) he sat across his soon-to-be-ex-lover and waited for the tears. They did not come. Instead, she poured the rest of his beer for him and smiled, 'What did you say?'

He was too sensible to repeat the hurtful words. He just apologised for them, 'I'm really very sorry.'

His Relationship Termination textbook would have said, stop there, don't go waffling on and on, but he couldn't help himself. Her continence made him garrulous, 'You know I love you to bits, but... I have to be honest, Sara, my Christian upbringing is giving me sleepless nights. To make matters worse, only yesterday she told me she was pregnant again... I know I told you there were no intimacies between us anymore but... you know how it is when you are sharing a bed... I'm really very sorry... in fact just last night I had this nightmare: I was standing behind a reverend father and I couldn't-'

'That's okay,' she said softly. She rose and smoothed down her dress, 'I have something for you.'

He rose as well, trying to keep the alarm from his voice. 'What is it?'

'It's a surprise. Just wait.'

She turned into the corridor of the small flat. Still standing, he downed the rest of his beer and watched her narrowly. She passed the entrance into the kitchen and he breathed more easily – she hadn't gone for a knife after all. Then she entered the tiny bedroom and shut the door behind her. His alarm redoubled. He went to the entrance of the corridor and listened raptly. He heard a distinct grating and he racked his brain. Only the box under her bed could make that sound... a box secured by a combination lock... *she was going for a gun!* Of course! She was too slight of build to take him on with a knife! He tensed for flight, but the entrance to the flat was halfway down the same corridor. She only had to push open the bedroom door at the right time to be able to shoot him at point-blank range. He couldn't take the risk. He turned urgently and crossed the parlour to the balcony. It was a second floor flat but it was better to break his legs and live, than to be murdered in cold-blood by a vengeful ex-lover.

Once again, he hesitated on the cliff of decision, as she entered the parlour with a notebook. Her jaw dropped slowly, 'What in the world are you doing?'

He recovered quickly enough, inspecting the hanging basket of flowers just above his head. 'I thought so,' he said, climbing down from the balcony railing and dusting off his hands, 'the soil is bone-dry, you'll need to water it soon.'

'They're artificial flowers,' she said with only the faintest mockery. She sat down and crossed her legs. Her long, lean legs. 'Listen Paul, my bye-bye gift to you is the diary I've kept since we started going out.'

'A *diary?*'

'What did you expect?' she smiled, 'A gun?'

Paul smiled back sheepishly. It was an old-fashioned notebook, with the image of a long-jumper on the cover. 'A diary,' he repeated. His relief was making him stupid. His own traditional affair-termination gift was a Seiko watch, which (he had found from long experience) compensated adequately enough for a wedding ring. It still sat in a case in his hip pocket. He usually pulled it out when the tears began to flow, that way it had the most dramatic impact, but so far it seemed that Sara was still in shock.

'I started it the night you came here for the first time,' she explained. She opened the book to the most recent entry and put the end of a much-chewed pen between her lips. Her moist lips. She pursed the lips hesitantly, 'I was going to fill out today's entry before giving it to you but...' she shook her head, '... no. That would extend our affair by thirty minutes at least. I like your approach: clean and surgical. You can fill in today for me.' She rose and, laughing nervously, offered him the gift.

As he took the book and walked backwards, he imagined the future nights locked in his den reading her lovesick scribblings, and he was overcome by a pre-emptive nostalgia for those moist lips, overwhelmed by his bereft tomorrows when the cockroaches and plastic trays would have paled against the absent technicolour of her laughter. Against his better sense, he confessed, 'I really love you, Sara.'

'That's nice,' she smiled, and he realised that she had walked him to the entrance of her flat, where she was now waiting patiently. Was she trying to hurry him out before she burst into tears? The Seiko dug into his left buttock. Something was not quite right about this final goodbye, yet... he could not hang around by her door forever, waiting for her to cry. He opened it. He had also planned to make the loan of the generator permanent – to convert some tears from despair to gratitude; but in the absence of any tears at all, he was a bit at a loss. 'You can keep the generator,' he said anyway.

'Oh. Okay,' she said. There was some surprise in her voice: as though it did not occur to her that the generator still belonged to him. He felt his rep slide significantly. She ran her hands through her short afro and her breasts strained inadvertently against the muslin of her nightdress. Her boyish breasts. He wondered if he should hug her a final time, for a valedictory feel of that firm bosom, but the generator comment seemed to have released a noxious fume into the dying relationship and he knew it was wise to get out while he was still ahead.

As she closed the door in his face he realised that this was the fastest termination of an affair in his long love life. He waited there for several minutes, still trying to understand what had just happened, still trying to negotiate the disproportionate sense of loss that made him feel as though he had just been jilted, rather than the other way round. He listened for the faintest sniffling from beyond the door, which would have mollified his loss somewhat, which could have given him an excuse to open the unlatched door, hug and comfort her, and make his dramatic gift over one of the last two bottles of Gulder... instead he picked up the strains from her favourite keep-fit video. Perhaps he should not have ended it tonight, he decided eventually, but what was done was done. He trudged downstairs. In the air-conditioned comfort of his Mercedes, he touched on the reading light and opened the diary. Her handwriting was girlish and immature. He read the first entry,

> *'Where's your housegirl?*
>
> *That was the first thing he said to me when he finally entered the flat he had been begging me for weeks to enter. I was already lighting the candle in the parlour and I returned to the entrance and there he was standing with his jacket held out in one hand and the briefcase full of seismograph charts in the other. Housegirl? What's a single woman living in a one-bedroom flat doing with a housegirl?*
>
> *So I took his coat and briefcase (why I did that I still don't know), and he took my candle and went ahead into the parlour.*

I put the briefcase down where I stood and thought about the jacket: I could have hung it up in my wardrobe of course, but the way he was going I wasn't sure I wanted to let him past the Cape of Good Hope after all. So I folded his jacket carefully and set it on his briefcase.

I followed him into the parlour and he was standing there, waiting for me. I thought it was a polite, class thing – standing until your hostess sat down or something, so I sat down. It would be a new experience, being wooed by a soon-to-be-divorced man with some class – but he remained standing after I sat down.

'Where's your generator,' he asked gallantly, 'I can switch it on for you.'

When it dawned on him that I had neither housegirl nor generator he took off his waist coat and tie. He made conversation for a while. About how much the oil company was spending on his department to provide advance notice of the earthquakes that we never had. I noticed that he was sweating unnaturally and realised that his third question was probably going to be, 'Where are your condoms?' so I got up and confessed to a sudden, blinding headache. He tried for a goodbye kiss but I just held my head in my hands and winced.

Didn't let him near the Cape of Good Hope after all. Don't think I will be seeing this one again. Handsome fellow, but every time he opens his mouth he puts his foot in it. Plus I've never seen anyone stare so long at my breasts. Must be one of those poor kids who were weaned too early. Pity about the flash car, the class, and all that jazz...

Paul rolled up the book angrily and wound down his window. He was taking aim to lob the diary into the over-flowing bin across the road when his second thoughts arrived. There were dozens and dozens of close-cropped entries, and he realised that he *did* want to know what she thought of him, however painful it was to read. But not now. Just now, he couldn't handle it. He flung it into his glove compartment instead, killed his reading light, and fired the engine into life. By a fluke he glanced up and saw her watching him from her balcony. There was the same smile on her face that had fired his passions through the months of their relationship, but in the context of her diary it acquired a uniquely malevolent gleam and he realised that the mixture had not been casual sex and all-consuming love after all. How blind he had been. How thin the line between love and contempt.

She waved at him but he drove away without waving back. His own churlishness amazed him. As he swerved away from a lamppost, he realised that he no longer felt any nostalgia for her lips and breasts and things... it was truly over! Then it struck him... the girl was even more of a pro than he was! *The honest diary*... She had just taught him the eleventh and most effective way to end an affair.

MAN RATING

For their first date, Alasa took Sheri to dinner at the new Hotel De Beeg along Waterside's marina and she scored him his first point right away. This man was no cheapskate.

At thirty-six, she was a handsome, engaging conversationalist, and if she was still a spinster it was mostly down to her sentimental heart, which seduced her time and again into relationships with wharf rats creeping around in the guise of men. Fortunately, she had developed a scoring system to separate rodents from the real McCoys. She genuinely liked Alasa, but that would count for nothing. These days she was led by her ratings, not her heart.

The restaurant was laid out on deckings overlooking River Niger and they both ordered the chicken peri-peri while listening to Sweet Mother and watching half-naked men diving for sand just off the riverbank. He said to make his own chicken "five-pepper spice". The waiter checked his menu diffidently, 'Sorry sah, is only one- two- or three-pepper spice, sah.'

He got a little angry then, 'Tell the chef I said "five-pepper spice",' he snapped, and she gave him another point. He was clearly not intimidated by the plush Hotel De Beeg, which was an expensive tourist trap planted in the middle of what was really a big village. She liked men who knew what they wanted, and were not afraid to insist on it.

He ordered a Star and she hesitated. She was realistic enough to accept that in all probability he was also rating her. Two years earlier when Boyfriend No. 5 got drunk enough, she had learnt how much he despised 'beer-guzzling, pot-bellied women carrying around permanent three-month-pregnancies'. Yet, she was wearing her corset that evening, which took her from 'three-months' to 'barely-a-hint'... and... dammit, she wanted a beer, so she compromised and ordered a half-pint Harp.

A suicidal cockroach crawled up from a crack in the decking and sped towards her high heels. She crushed it underfoot without drama. Fifteen years was such an age in the dating game. She remembered her only real love, BF1, on whom she had upturned a fully-laden restaurant table when a praying mantis alighted on her lap all those years ago... She smiled. She now knew how to deal both with bugs and rodents.

'I like your smile,' he said, and she smiled wider. Gratuitious compliments... that was good for a point.

He conversed well too. This was a point she had added to her man-rating formula after Kola, BF7, who could only talk about football and Manchester United. She steered the conversation apprehensively from medicine through solid minerals to Asian politics and he had an intelligent opinion everywhere she went. She tossed in the fourth point. It was too early to get excited, but... could this be the man to rank 10 on her man-rating? It had never been done before. The sheer possibility that here was the first true marriage material since she started her scoring system made her nervous. She began to regret the beer. It would be rich irony indeed if he passed her test with flying colours and never called again. Between the flutter in her tummy and the iron restraint of her corset, she did not know how she would eat dinner.

The Indian chef came out, worried. Alasa assured him that he had Oyo State and Rivers State parentage – he could handle pepper.

'But,' said the chef, wringing his hands, 'even Indians can't...'

'I'm not an Indian,' boasted Alasa curtly, 'when I was born, the first thing my mother put on my tongue was pepper. When I was circumcised...'

Sheri had a fit of coughing in the course of which the chef departed for his kitchen. Then Alasa's phone rang. She had introduced a point for phone etiquette since Uti, BF6, who multi-tasked blackberrying and love-making, to distracting effect. She liked how Alasa asked her permission, kept the call short, and switched off his phone when he was done. Of course he had neutralised the point on offer by his public (and premature) reference to his genitalia... but she was really digging him now.

The food arrived. The waiter was ill-trained and served Alasa first, with pity in his eyes. She liked how he ignored his meal until hers arrived. She knew she was being hasty now, but she couldn't help it: she tossed in the fifth point.

The chicken was good, and no wonder: it was twice the price of Bintu's food, but she noticed how silent he grew as he began to eat, and how quickly he now drank his beer, leaving his mouth open between gulps.

'Is it too peppery?' she asked with some concern.

'Nah!' he said derisively, 'My father is from Ibadan and my mother is from Okrika. I can eat raw chilli even!'

The chef came around to see if they were enjoying their food. She thought she noticed a gleam in his eyes when he asked Alasa if it was peppery enough, but she could not be sure. Her date conceded that it was not too bad and the chef returned happily to his kitchen. Alasa ordered another beer. His conversation was now distracted and he was mopping sweat with his dinner napkin, which was a little embarrassing. Then he rose abruptly and stalked to the loo. He was there for a long time and she dabbed a suspicious spoon in his peri-peri sauce, gasping at the raw, peppery fire of it. She had never tasted anything hotter in her life!

As she sloshed beer around her burning mouth, she realised that, technically, her date was a total write-off. For such a promising prospect, it was a crushing blow, but here was a pig-headed idiot who was prepared to kill himself rather than admit that he was wrong and that 'five-pepper-spice' rated chicken peri-peri was far too hot for human consumption. Yet, she could not get the smug chef out of her mind. He had over-peppered the dish intentionally and had the nerve to come to their table to gloat! Her face grew a crustacean determination. She realised she was a tribalist when it came to male pride: her father was the most pig-headed man in the world and although she knew all about the evils of that peculiarly male streak of stubbornness, it was now a family matter. She'd sort out Alasa in her own good time, but first she was going to deal with the chef.

She looked around and surreptitiously swapped her plate with Alasa's, deftly scraping the dead cockroach from the deck into the over-peppered plate before her. She was smearing it with peri-peri sauce when Alasa returned from the loo. He settled in, took a deep breath, and sliced a tentative piece of chicken from the plate before him.

As he chewed, his eyes darted from plate to plate. He must have known right away that she had swapped the plates, but he said not a word as he lustily ate the rest of the meal. She smiled privately. It was classic, that readiness to die rather than admit that they needed or had received help from anyone. All her brothers had grown into pig-headed men so she knew exactly what to expect. Truly the date was over – this was no boyfriend material, how much more a marriageable man. She hailed their waiter. 'What's this?' she asked him, pushing around the cockroach with her fork, 'it doesn't taste like prawns, and I can't see very well without my glasses.'

The waiter did a double-take and tried to swallow his Adam's apple. Alasa craned his neck, 'wait...' he called, '...what was it?' but the plate was already half-way to the kitchen and accelerating.

The chef appeared three-and-a-half minutes later, bearing a fresh, over-generous, plate of chicken peri-peri. He was sweating and apologetic.

'What's the meaning of this...?' demanded Alasa, adding his angry baritone to the drama, but she tapped her shoe lightly on his and he fell silent.

(That sudden silence impressed her no end. Never did a barrelling automobile respond more intuitively to the tap of a brake pedal – and this from a man who so clearly 'knew what he wanted'. She flipped back through the lives of her parents, for a similar instance where the public thunder of husband had been stilled so conclusively by the subtle wink of wife (ha ha)... and yet: a pig-headed man was a pig-headed man. She leaned forward to engage her food.)

Her replacement plate of chicken peri-peri was also very good. Now that there was no future in the relationship, she forgot about her man-rating, his impression of her, and enjoyed the evening. On her own trip to the loo she lost her corset to her commodious handbag. She ordered a full pint of Harp. When he made a deserving joke, she gave the full-throated laugh that BF4 had considered too masculine. There were three or four more points that he could have picked up himself, but she let them pass, for there was no longer any point. When the waiter brought the dessert menu she ordered the chocolate dumplings but they were out of dumplings. He ordered the cheesy meringue, but the meringue was also out of stock. They laughed at that and threw the menu back at the flustered waiter, 'Just bring us what you have in that bloody kitchen!' he cried, wiping tears from his eyes, and she wondered if they were having that much fun, or were simply prematurely tipsy on two beers apiece.

When they had simmered down somewhat he left again for the loo. He was away for another age and when he returned it was from the direction of the hotel entrance. He put a rolled-up package by his plate without a word. She said nothing on her part, but made a private bet with herself. Their dessert arrived, a disgrace for a hotel of De Beeg's footprint: two oranges per plate, peeled and cut in halves. She took a half, and he followed her cue, 'You don't really like me, do you?' he said, and she glanced up guiltily, wondering if her thought-life was that transparent.

'What are you talking about?' she blustered.

'You've been looking at the naked divers all evening.'

She laughed with some relief, 'They are half-naked, not naked! You make it sound so dirty!'

Although none-too-juicy, the oranges were tangerine-sweet and as she sucked daintily at them she really looked at Alasa. His tone had been light enough, but as between jest and jealousy, she could tell that his comment was serious all right. Despite his own manly physique she could feel the weight of the insecurity in his words. It was another warning flag and she would definitely have docked him a point for neurotic possessiveness – had he still been in contention for her bed.

She took another orange. Yet, it was such a long time since she evoked any jealousy in her men. Her mirror was honest with her and cosmetologists did not get much of her money. She knew she pulled her men with her personality rather than her body, but it was rather... stirring, this jealousy of a man she was not yet going out with. Purely as an academic effort, she scrambled through her memory of the evening, updating his scores [docking him a massive three points for pig-headedness] until he arrived up to the minute with a measly three points. If she docked only half-a-point for jealousy it would still put him at par with Uti, BF6, who had broken up with her publicly at Waterside Market when she touched the massive biceps of an itinerant trader in a flirtatious but innocent attempt to shave a hundred naira off the price of a jeans skirt...

'What are you thinking?' he asked,

'Nothing,' she lied, staring at him, trying to match his intensity. He had followed her cue and was eating his oranges the way oranges should presumably be eaten at places like De Beeg: sucked politely, three or four times and left daintily on plate. He was on the last of his oranges and as he stared into her eyes he seemed to forget that he was at De Beeg. His fingers slipped into autopilot. With a little dismay, she watched him unfurl an already ravished orange, exposing its naked pulp publicly to his strong white teeth. Section by quartered section, he ripped out and chewed up the sweet pulp, masticating with transparent enjoyment, muscular tongue sucking at his teeth, and sweeping the orangey grooves between teeth and cheeks. Her imagination kicked into autopilot as well, and in that hot Waterside riverside, she saw herself in the grip of those strong fingers, of that muscular tongue, the subject of that lusty appetite, and shivered.

'Are you okay?'

'Yes...' she lied, 'but you have some orange bits on your beard.'

He brushed at said beard unavailingly, so she picked it out for him. It was bristlier than she thought, that beard, and he took her by surprise when he took her wrist gently, guiding the fragment of pulp gently onto his tongue. She was a strong woman, and she liked how powerless, how orangelike, she felt in that grasp. As she yielded the fragment of pulp to his tongue, she felt like a reverend administering communion.

Sheri! she admonished herself severely, recognising the onslaught of her sentimental demons, *Shine your eyes o!* This man was no longer a candidate for her affections. All that remained of the date was a terminal handshake at the gate of De Beeg.

Then he raised his hand and the waiter approached with the bill. She tensed instinctively. Normally, this was the Big Test and it carried a massive one-and-a-half points. Curiously, she wondered how he would fare. Six years earlier, at Bintu's place, she remembered how BF3 had flinched at the sight of the bill for her cowleg peppersoup. He had paid the bill quietly enough, but she had never forgotten that cowardly flinch that had made her feel like a glutton, and she had never forgiven it. BF2 was the worst, though, auditing every bill line by line, trying to negotiate service charges, disputing the price of bottled waters... until that terrible day when he quarrelled with her for ordering the isi-ewu peppersoup special, which cost an extra six naira more than the regular isi-ewu peppersoup. Alasa did not even look at the bill. His eyes remained locked on hers as he passed his payment card to the waiter. 'Will I see you again?'

'Of course,' she lied, as he punched his payment through a virtual terminal. They rose. It was always the same answer for failed dates... of course... but she would never take their calls again. The life of a discriminating single lady had to be a ruthless one. He was confused by the two free dinner vouchers that came with his receipt, but he folded them into his wallet with a shrug. As they walked out, he held out what she thought at first was a premature, misaligned handshake. In the nick of time she realised he was only inviting her to step through the door ahead of him. She burned with shame, realising that too long an association with ruffians had made her forget how to be a lady. He gave her the rolled-up bundle as he walked her the hundred and fifty metres to the ferry. As she suspected, it was the same floral shirt that had caught her eye in the gift shop in lobby of the hotel, earlier that evening. Her mother had many gifts like this, and despised them all, preferring the humble 'sorry' to the proud gifts that replaced vocal apologies.

He was such a write-off... and yet she remembered how he had ended his tirade at the trod of her toe. Her own mother had no defences to the swell of her father's rage. Plus, the shirt was... she hated to admit... now the best in her wardrobe. Just out of interest, she tried to reckon Alasa's final position on her man-rating scale. She was not sure if the 'communion' thing was a plus or a minus. Did it rate as a romantic gesture or presumptuous overreaching on his part? ...And the bush way in which he ate his last orange, that was such a massive minus, a total contradiction of his gentlemanly airs... suddenly they were at the ferry. It was time for the final handshake but instead he tilted slowly forward, clearly going for a cheek kiss. High-stakes stuff! On a first date! And within hailing distance of Main Market!

With years and years of dating experience, she knew how to checkmate bear-hugs, waist-grabs, upper-arm-feels, and similar 'current-tapping' manoeuvres from frisky men, but her brain was disoriented by the herculean effort at tallying up his man-rating scores. So between his going for a right cheek and her offering a left cheek (which to her mind was a tad less familiar) they kissed on the lips in a scandalous accident, right there before the Waterside ferry. What was even worse was the eye-closing and the mouth-opening reflex triggered by his orangey lips, and the fleeting thought that perhaps she should eat one more dinner with him – before writing him off – after all, it was she who earned the free dinner vouchers...

Then she was hurrying down to the ferry, muttering fiercely to herself, *Sheri! You see yoursef now? You don start again!*

THE BUTCHER'S REVENGE

When Pito got home that evening, his wife was waiting at the doorway. After his day at the factory he was more tired than God had been on the seventh day of creation and his mind was set on his daily consolation of akpu in okra soup. Yet, there was his wife standing ominously on their porch with a boiled ear of maize and news of an urgent meeting at his clan's longroom. He was vexed about the meeting – but there was no help for it. He supposed it was another inconvenient death of a distant relation which was presently going to cost him money that he did not have. Gloomily, he exchanged his bushel of implements for the takeaway snack, which he ate hungrily on his way to Zetabu's.

He joined the stony silence in the longroom: seventeen adult male members of the Ishu clan of Waterside village. They were usually more talkative, but it was almost 7 p.m. and none of them had properly eaten dinner. When the hour struck, Elder Zetabu grunted and poured a miserly libation. He pulled up the saucer of kola and greatfruit. He hissed and – looking through a low window – raised his voice to catch the attention of the lad playing in the compound beyond, 'Nubi! Did you want me to use my teeth to break kola? Bring a knife here this minute!'

'Use your fingernails and let us go home and eat,' grumbled Iha, 'it's dark enough and we won't tell the ancestors!'

'Yes,' agreed Mongono, taking the gallon of palm wine, 'there's no poison in your nails, share the kola.' He sniffed the wine and poured a dram for Elder Zetabu and himself before passing it to

Padulo on his right. 'Who has died this time – or why have you summoned us for the second time this month?'

But Elder Zetabu was not born yesterday. The same voices that were counselling haste today would accuse him of sacrilege at the end-of-year elections, and he knew it. So he waited patiently until the knife arrived and he performed his office unctuously. As the saucer began its journey around the longroom, he cleared his throat. Even the blind could feel the menace of his voice, 'Today I was insulted by Solo the butcher, from the Zina clan,' he began – so quietly that his clansmen stopped chewing the noisy greatfruit in order to hear his portentous words. 'It is not that I do not have the balls to respond as a man, but the longer I thought about it, the more I realised that it was not just me he insulted, it was my entire clan. – And as our people say, if you fight another man's battle without his request, he has no obligation to bear your burial expenses.'

'What's all this talk about war and burial expenses?' asked Pito, 'Are we not talking about Solo the butcher?'

'Does Zina have two butchers?'

'Solo can never insult anybody. I went to primary school with him. I am married to his mother's young cousin. Solo that prays for his animals before butchering them!'

'Since you have already found your in-law not guilty, perhaps we can all go home and eat.

'No o, speak,' said Pito, backing down, 'speak o.'

'Thank you,' said Zetabu sarcastically; 'my wife gave me a daughter last week so I was duty-bound to kill her a ram today for her feast. That is our tradition in Waterside and I did not fail in my duty. I did not scrimp either – I bought her the tallest ram at the weekly market and her womenfolk arrived to celebrate with her. It was the *biggest* ram in the entire market. Then I sent to Zina for their butcher, whose reputation, before today, was without blemish.'

'Did I not say so?' grumbled Pito.

Elder Zetabu was about to deploy another sarcastic reply when an anguished moan issued from deep within his compound. It was the sort of sound that might slip out of a woman whose husband was giving the beating of her life, while holding a gun to her head with a warning not to make a sound. Half the men in the room rose to their feet, for it was also the sort of sound that made men act like men. Yet, this was the Elder's compound, and it was such a huge breach of protocol to burst into his wife's accommodation, so they looked towards him for permission. He shrugged reluctantly and three men hurried off. More would have gone, but most of the men in the room had not yet mustered the fifty to hundred naira that tradition required near-relatives to use to wipe the natal sweat from the foreheads of new-born babies. Elder Zetabu uncorked the gallon which had returned to him depleted and poured the last drops of wine into his empty glass. He raised it fastidiously to his lips. He was still draining it when the men returned. 'Yes?' he enquired, setting down his glass with the air of a man waiting for an apology.

'It was your wife... but she was alone with her children...'

'Yes?'

'She... said she was just remembering the insult of Solo the butcher.'

'My God,' cried Mongono, jumping to his feet, 'did he... *assault* a nursing mother? This is war!'

'Sit down and listen!' retorted Zetabu impatiently, 'if he touched my wife I would have settled it man-to-man. It was much worse. *Much more terrible.* You know how it is with pregnant women, they have these strange cravings. Well, as for my wife, her cravings did not end with childbirth. This afternoon she was craving the bollocks of a ram. I told her-'

'-that is, the *bollocks* of a ram?'

'I don't have water in my mouth Pito. So I told her that the bollocks and the head of the ram belong by tradition to the butcher who killed and carved up the animal, but she said she felt like stewed bollocks and that was that. And you know how it is with a young wife who has just given you the child you have been waiting for – you have to give her what she wants if you want any peace at all. So I took the bollocks from the pails of meat that the butcher brought in. I weighed it in one hand – did I say it was a very big ram?'

'…you've said it twice, now…'

'That's because it really was a big ram, and so I thought: two or three thousand naira, tops. That was what I'd pay if I had to buy it at the market. So I said to him, "what if I gave you two thousand naira for your bollocks? What say you? My wife wants them you see?" I only said two thousand, mark you, for him to say four thousand like any other Watersider and for me to offer three and for us to shake hands on it, but he was a gentleman – at least that was what I thought at the time – and he shrugged and he said, "if your wife wants my bollocks, she's welcome to them," and we shook hands on it there and then and that was that.'

'What was that?' asked Finiti, who should have been a lawyer, 'did you pay him the two thousand, or was it free?'

'Of course I paid the two thousand!' shouted Zetabu, 'Am I chewing my words?'

'I just wanted to be sure, that's all,' said Finiti.

'If I were you,' grunted Mamba, whose two legs were shaking on account of the two cigarettes that he had not smoked because of the meeting, 'I would not have shaken hands on *that* particular deal,' .

'Which particularly deal? Look, I thought it was a fair enough deal and I shook hands on it. So I gave him the head of the ram and his money – and don't forget the beers: he was drinking throughout his butchering: three or four bottles of my beer he was drinking.'

'Since when does Waterside count beer as part of payment?'

'I am not counting it, I am just saying that he drank them, that's all.'

Pito took the last piece of kola from the saucer and chewed noisily, 'What about kola nut. Did you give him kola as well? I'm just asking to know if I'm incurring a debt myself.'

There was an embarrassed silence, then Elder Zetabu scratched the grey stubble on his chin, recognising that in the private, sarcastic match between him and Pito he had just suffered a humiliating straight sets defeat, 'You're right,' he conceded, 'I should never have mentioned the beers; when you are angry, you are angry.'

'So what is this insult that has vexed you and your wife so much?'

'When he was going he said he wanted to greet the new baby, so I took him into my wife's quarters. So he stood there, and he greeted her. And he asked about her mother and her father and her father's people and her mother's people. Then he looked at the baby and said she looks just like my wife. Then he put his hand in his pocket and he brought out one thousand naira and said, 'This is to wipe off the baby's sweat.'

A staccato of snapped fingers rippled around the room.

'A lie!'

'That is... *one thousand naira?*'

'Impossible!'

'Then he turned to my son, Nubi,' continued Zetabu, pressing angrily through the incredulous interruptions, 'and called down his full name, Nubianya – as if he was the one that gave him the name. "Did you pass your exams?" he asked, "Yes," said my son. "Good, Good," he said, and then he put his hand in his pocket and brought out one thousand naira!'

At this new revelation, the restive room grew silent. At the end of the long room, the unlit cigarette slipped from Mamba's nerveless fingers. He did not notice. Around the room, it was suddenly difficult to swallow. Each man shared keenly the disgrace meted out to their elder kinsman, yet, at the mathematical moment at which the butcher's incredible generosity equalled the elder's unseemly parsimony, none could deny the poetic dignity with which the butcher of Zina clan had crippled the prestige of the buyer of the fattest ram at the weekly market. When this story got out – as it would, now that all their wives would hear of it that night – Zetabu would not be able to hold his head up in

Waterside, for the titters that would follow him around.

Eventually, Ushie plucked up the courage and pulled his chair closer to Elder Zetabu. He spoke in a whisper which everyone could hear, tooled as it was with the resentment of a man who lost the election for the longroom eldership by the narrowest of margins, not that long ago. 'Why have you brought this matter to the longroom, elder? This is a terrible, *terrible* insult, but it was offered to you and your wife in the privacy of your house. You should have hidden this disgrace, taken courage, and moved on. The disgrace of a man is not the end of his life. Remember what the scrotum said to his doctor? – "If sunlight is the only treatment for his paleness, then 'pale' was his natural complexion." Why have you brought this disgrace to the notice of the clan? Butcher Solo is normally a discreet man. He may never have spoken of it, and if he did, who would believe him. Why didn't you hide this thing?'

'Because of what happened at the gate,' said Zetabu, folding his arms.

Ushie paused. He did not like it when the old gossip made him beg for a story. 'Okay, what happened at the gate?'

'That is for Magama to say. I don't like putting my mouth in what is mainly the disgrace of other people.'

Magama carefully pulled down the sock on his left foot. He had stopped working three months earlier when he fell off the roof of the Tourist Board and damaged his back and the clan had kindly undertaken to pay the school fees of his only son until he found his feet. From the sock he took a wad of currency that was bound fiercely in red rubber bands. The Watersiders caught their breath as they recognised the traditional way of carrying cursed money that could not be allowed to mix with the money in one's pockets. He slapped it on the stool in front of him. 'Count it!' he said, to no one in particular.

'Am I a bank clerk?' blazed Ushie, 'To be counting other people's money? Tell your story and let's go home!'

'It is one thousand naira, and Solo gave it to my son at this very gate!' said Magama, pointing, 'My son was coming to play with

Nubi and Solo asked, "Are you not the son of Magama?" and my son nodded, thinking that he was talking to a human being. "How is school?" asked the butcher, and my son said that he had been at home for the last three months while his father's clansmen put together his school fees-'

'We know, we know,' snapped Pito, who was yet to pay his own thirty naira contribution to the fees fund, 'just tell the story!'

'It's the story I'm telling: so Solo asked, "how much is left to complete your school fees?" and my son said-'

'What kind of up-bringing are you giving this your son?' cried Mongono in a strangled voice, 'to be talking to strangers like this!'

'-and my son said, "five hundred," and the butcher said "Only five hundred? Okay, take one thou-"'

'You're spoiling the story!' shouted Zetabu, above a rising hubbub, 'he didn't say *okay, take*... I was there! He said *eiyaaaa*, take!' Zetabu invested the *eiyaaaa* with a depth of pity that would have been more appropriate on a condolence visit to a young widow, 'He said *eiyaaaa*, and then he gave Magama's son one thousand naira! Right there in my doormouth!'

The men of the Ishu clan found their feet, shouting at the same time, and for several minutes it seemed likely that the riot would erupt in the direction of the butcher's house in Zina quarters, for their disgrace was total and unbearable. In the eternal rivalry between the clans, the lowliest butcher of Zina had found an eloquent way to deal a death blow to the prestige of, not just the miserly elder of Ishu, but its entire menfolk. With a generous gesture he had returned a ward of the Ishu clan to school where the entire resources of the Ishu clan had failed. They went berserk. It was ten minutes before some order could be restored – and that only because Mamba and Mongono had lost their voices.

Ushie was the last clansman standing. He wanted dearly to sit down, on account of his right leg, which was trembling uncontrollably from an excess of emotion, but he knew very well that one of his raging clansmen would take the floor, and God knew where their angry counsel would take the clan. Watersiders were hot-blooded, and at times like these they recognised neither protocol nor seniority. 'This is not a matter of beating up people and burning their houses,' he said, hoarsely, 'think how it will sound in the morning!' he broke off and lowered his voice. 'That a clan whose elder served a butcher's bollocks to his wife, a clan *who could not even find five hundred naira to send a child to school*, that that clan came together in the night to beat up their benefactor butcher! And to burn his house!'

There was an uneasy silence in the long room. 'The old man has a point,' conceded Pito.

'I'm not that much older than you,' grated Ushie.

'So what are we to do?' demanded Iha.

Ushie hesitated, but he had not quite aced that portion of his speech. He sat down miserably.

There was a gloomy silence. 'All my wife craved when she was pregnant,' said Mamba, with pious irrelevance, 'was akara and kpuff-kpuff.' Nobody responded to that boast, for his wife was still craving akara and kpuff-kpuff years after the birth of their ten-year-old, with the weight to prove it.

'None of this would have happened,' muttered Finiti darkly, 'if the butcher was not cheated of his bollocks.'

Elder Zetabu was too dispirited to rise to the bait. He glared malevolently, but held his peace.

'I still think we should beat him up,' said Padulo.

More silence greeted that declaration. Earlier, when they were boiling and blustering in the middle of the longroom the door had been open but no one had actually headed out towards Solo's house. Now their rage was spent, even for empty boasting. The proceedings had taken on the gloomy fatalism of a wake. They could bicker and vent all night but by morning the dead man would still be dead.

Zetabu sighed and reached for his fan, telegraphing the end of the meeting. 'Since this is the sum of the counsel of my clansmen,' he began heavily, 'they can go back to their food and their wives, I will sleep on-'

'If we beat him, we lose...' began Amuzu quietly, in his first contribution of the night. There was silence in the room. Amuzu often went five or six meetings without speaking a word, although when he did speak, it was often cogently. He scratched his head and bit his lips until the worst of his nervousness was quelled, 'This man insulted us with great wit. Our response must bury them. We must make Zina clan a laughingstock,' he hesitated – and then confessed his self-interest, 'Otherwise we young men will find it difficult to marry...'

The silence in the room lengthened as they thought about a response that would be wittier and more devastating than Solo's coup de grace. '*God*,' murmured Ushie at length, taking the easy way out, 'why didn't you just leave the poor man's bollocks alone!'

'I have an idea,' said Amuzu again, cutting off Elder Zetabu's explosion, and he narrated his plan to his gathered kindred. When he was done there was a respectful silence and they looked at him with gratitude.

'It will cost us dearly,' observed Zetabu with deep satisfaction.

'I will have to sell my harvest early,' grinned Ushie.

'I could borrow against the takings of my minibus,' said Iha, then he slapped his thigh and hooted, 'bloody hell! I should sell the wretched bus!' the longroom roared with laughter.

Magama looked around with alarm as the enthusaism spread, he knew that the cost of the new plan could easily see his son into university, but he knew better than to pitch the academic accomplishment of a child against the weightier issue of clan pride. With his bad back, nobody would look to him to contribute money so the least he could do – to retain a modicum of the sympathy of his clan – was to show some enthusiasm. 'Fantastic,' he cried with a sinking heart, 'simply fantastic!'

***

By the following morning the news of the Butcher's revenge had spread all over Waterside. The disgrace of the Ishu clan was complete – and lasted an entire week. Those men who had missed the meeting were clued in on The Plan and when their wives returned home in tears from the mockery of their peers they maintained a stolid silence.

By weekend Iha departed for Onitsha with the savings of his clan and returned with a black bull in the back of a pick up. By the time he arrived at Zetabu's house a large crowd of invitees had gathered before the longroom. An errand boy was sent to fetch Solo. He had been told that a bull needed his attentions and he arrived with his contingent of three apprentices and a bag full of skinning knives. Three festive canopies covered the forecourt of the Ishu longhouse. It was filled by the men of the Ishu clan and dozens of invitees from the Zina clan.

Solo took up his kings blade and approached Zetabu. It had been a machete in another life, but years of sharpening had thinned it to an inch at its widest. 'Do I cut it up for a grill or for peppersoup?' He asked, giving the blade a final lick of the flintstone in a professional flourish.

'Peppersoup,' said Zetabu, in a voice that carried, 'I actually bought the bull for my wife, but she only needs his bollocks. As for me and my clansmen, we will have peppersoup...' he paused. His kinsmen watched his performance hungrily, admiring the pitch of his voice, which carried every last syllable of the drama to the ears of the gathered crowd, and his imperious bearing which contrasted with the casualness of the words that arrived, almost like an afterthought... 'Do you have a burial date yet for my friend?'

'Your friend?'

'Your late elder who died seven months ago,'

'Oh,' said Solo. His confusion was understandable, for the late Elder of Zina clan had been an implacable foe of Zetabu's, 'No, not yet... you know how these things are... he left no sons so the burial falls squarely on the clan.'

'You haven't bought a bull yet?'

'No, no, no,' said Solo, brows beetling in confusion. The bull was the single largest burial expense of a Waterside burial.

'So he's been in the mortuary since...'

'April. Since twelfth April when he died. About this bull of yours...'

'Seven months in the mortuary...' pronounced Zetabu gloomily, '...I should hate to die and be left seven months in the mortuary...' he looked glassily around the canopies, '...while my friends are eating and drinking peppersoup...'

Solo stopped sharpening the machete. He did not know where this was going but he was intelligent enough now to realise that he was in the middle of an intricate set piece that was unlikely to end in his favour. He looked around and caught the eye of the acting elder of Zina, who could not become a substantive elder until the late incumbent was properly buried. He did not like what he saw in that gaze. He suddenly wished he was elsewhere.

'What say you, kindred,' shouted Zetabu, 'we could have ourselves a nice pepper soup feast today, with plenty of meat to take home... or we could help our brothers in the Zina clan to bury their elder, who has been in a deep freezer for the last seven months?'

'*Seven months?*' said Iha incredulously, 'That's a lie.'

'I won't keep my fish in the freezer for seven *weeks,*' lied Ushie.

'Let's bury their elder for them,' said Pito.

There was a chorus of *bu-ry! bu-ry!* from the gathered kindred of Ishu. From the ranks of their guests, there was a deathly silence. Zetabu turned to the butcher of Zina, 'That's my decision. The bollocks goes to my wife, the rest of the bull I dash you and your clan, for the burial of my good friend.'

He turned and took three paces away before he paused, like one that remembered something: 'Of course the bollocks are yours by tradition... how much do you want for them?'

The butcher's articulation failed him, but he managed to shake his blade in a negative. Zetabu inclined his head and smiled his sarcastic thanks before leaving the venue of the aborted feast, ahead of his kinsmen. As Magama was wheeled past the open, scandalised mouths of their Zina invitees, he felt seven feet tall, and he realised that his kinsmen had been right after all. The pride of Ishu was more than fully restored. His boy's education could wait. The neatest trick was that at the burial of the Zina elder on the morrow, the Ishu kindred would still eat their peppersoup, and they – alone amongst the mourners – would enjoy the feast. Indeed, they would still be gloating over it by the time his son finished university.

ACCIDENTAL MAN

Chief Olobiri was recruiting thugs for the Harmattan elections when I first met Ista. This was in the time of the peace, before The Feud that eventually drove Madam Ganishu from her matrimonial home. Chief Olobiri was slowly rocking in the courtyard. He was due for a meeting with the Afini of Aafin, but had just finished three skewers of Madam Ganishu's roast goat meat and was currently engaged in the only physical activity he was capable of.

Ista was suddenly in the courtyard. The first thing that struck me was his stillness. He was like an old man who had borrowed a young man's body for the weekend and didn't quite know what to do with all the energy. I knew right away that he was deranged; maybe it was his tortoiseslow eyes. Maybe it was the dreadlocks growing from his chin. Or maybe it was the way he stood there shamelessly, a grown man, with tears actually running down his cheeks.

'*Yeees?*' drawled the Chief, who was not a very sympathetic person.

'I want to kill people, but I don't want to go to jail,' Ista's voice was rusty and disused, and seemed to issue from a much larger man. 'I'm ready. Anybody at all.'

'Is that all?' yawned the Chief. There was some mockery in his voice. He looked around the vast yard of Nazareth, at the three minibuses beside the boys quarters, the large chicken coops, the huddle of goats and the glut of lanky men gathered around Attack, who was regaling us with stories of political campaigns in the good old days when they went rioting with cans of petrol instead of ordinary batons; he had the largest mouth I had ever seen, Attack, and a voice to match. The Chief's eyes flitted speculatively over his men and fell, and fixed on the dog. He shouted at Bulldog, '*Nama!* Give me that thing.'

Bulldog dragged up the pole at the end of the Chief's pointing finger. More building material than weapon, it was a leftover length of wood from Madam Ganishu's kiosk, and formidable with it. The Chief gestured to his applicant who took the weight of the plank and rested it on his shoulder. The crowd around Attack looked up, but he continued talking, and we continued to laugh.

'Let's start with the dog,' said the Chief, 'it must not die immediately, okay? That's the test. Let it suffer. Five or six blows, then finish it off.'

'You mean for me to kill your dog?'

The Chief, picking his teeth, did not deign to reply. Ista turned resolutely to his task without another word. A tense silence now descended on the yard. Attack's mouth stayed open from his last uncompleted sentence, for there was only one person he feared more than Chief and it was Madam Ganishu. Her fondness for the dog was the only chink in the gruff exterior she presented to her household.

Nothing much happened for a while.

Gradually, life returned to the courtyard. Soon afterwards, The Block was taking a fresh bale of cloth to her seamstresses in the boys' quarters, and found the frozen youth in her path. As the wife of the prime regional politician, she was used to finding strange, lost men all over the place and she took it all in stride, '*Oi,* ' she grunted as she passed, 'give chance for road, go put that thing for corner there.'

That seemed to do the trick. She made a face as the dog followed Ista, tail wagging expectantly, 'this my *ashawo* dog too dey like follow stranger!' she complained cheerfully.

What was really odd, that evening, was how none of the half-dozen hard-as-roast-corn men out there laughed or cracked the obvious jokes they would crack in retrospect, years and years later. Just then, we were too swamped with relief that the Block's dog was still alive. And perhaps, we also felt Ista's pain.

Chief Olobiri, who had shown no interest in the mongrel's execution, now struggled to his feet, tightening his belt as he psyched himself up for the visit to the Afini. He appeared surprised to see the dog still alive. 'This killing of a thing is not easy, not so?'

'No sir,' mumbled Ista. As he returned from putting away the plank, I saw that his cheeks were wet. Once again, amazingly, no one made the obvious jokes.

'Lekan!' yelled the Chief; but his driver, having misjudged his master's condition once again, had slipped off to 'watch a home movie' with one of Madam Ganishu's girls.

'You're Goldsmith's son, not so?' said the Chief.

'Yes sir.'

'Where's that your bastard of a father?'

'At his house. With my wife.'

'Don't worry. I know somebody who will kill your father for you;' he paused significantly, 'His name is death. Okay? Have patience, he will come sooner or later. What's your own name?'

'Ista, sir.'

'Hmm,' the Chief said and lost interest. He yawned again, looking indecisively around. Ganishu emerged from the seamstress' room. She was a retired schoolmistress who had shed all her polish to embrace her role as local political wife. We called her 'the Block' because of her effortless way of killing some of Chief's more lunatic ideas. It had nothing to do with blocked Fallopian tubes, maternal instincts, or anything of the sort. 'Dearimi,' he said, 'I think I will go and see that old goat.'

'The Afini?'

'Yes.'

'Go well,' she grudged, disappearing into another room in her warren.

'Can you drive?' he asked Ista, A nod. 'Go and bring round the green Mercedes,'

'But, Sir...'

'Shut up,' said the chief in his first real flare of impatience,

Presently, the Mercedes drove up. Man-Palace, who was on fol-low-follow duty, folded himself into the front passenger seat and yawned as the Chief fell into the back seats in an eddying of suspensions. 'Ogoli, take charge here,' he called through the window as they drove off.

Ogoli was one of the Chief's more senior henchmen. He was wiry, faithful but more than a little dim. Attack was the usual choice to look after things, but his dodgy arithmetic had recently let him down badly in an attempted embezzlement and he had fallen out of favour for the moment. I was also the usual stand in for Lekan, and I had done nothing, that I remember, to explain why I should have been passed over for a new braggart who wanted to kill people but stumbled at a dog.

But I wasn't cross. I swear.

We could see Ogoli swelling, filling out his billowing clothes as he took the Chief's chair – his first mistake, for the Chief never permitted anyone to sit on his chairs.

A few minutes later, he made another, fatal one.

A cocky man had just slouched in, fortyish, balding and exud-ing a clammy turpitude. He wore black trainers, and a black leather jacket that was clearly borrowed – or stolen – from some-one with much shorter arms. He was sweating liberally and he wanted a job.

'You see that plank?' began Ogoli, aping the Chief's drawl.

'I no wan' carpenterwork,' warned the applicant. He looked around at us, clearly wondering if he had the right compound.

'You see that dog?'

'Ha!' gasped Attack, a warning that Ogoli misinterpreted as jealousy as he pressed on with his interview. There was a mo-ment of disbelief, then we sprang, too late, to the defence of the mongrel. Mercifully it did not need a second *thwack*. There was another frozen moment or two, then we stampeded for the gate, the brave crop of Chief Olobiri's private army, leaving Ogoli and his applicant to their fate at the hands of the Block.

***

It was Chief Olobiri's fifth attempt at the Senate and we were waiting to see what would go wrong this time. There was no question but that he was the most influential politician in Uguru District. Every time he backed a candidate for the House, the elections would proceed boringly to a finale. Yet every time he stood for himself, as he had four times in his long career, something catastrophic would go wrong at the last moment. So far, there had been two coups, one appendectomy, and an election petition that took five years to determine, by which time his opponent had finished the four-year term in the Senate. This last time it was a cholera that a drunken doctor misdiagnosed as AIDs. The Chief had withdrawn from the race to die, only to recover his perfect health, and seething fury, after his replacement was sworn in.

This time, the only serious candidate was businessman, Gaius Deh. Dr. Jatu was the incumbent looking for a second term, but he was going to lose his deposit. He was the nonentity of a lecturer who had been anointed by the Chief when he thought he was dying of AIDs. Unfortunately, Dr. Jatu had developed a taste for bombastic speeches on the floor of the Senate. He had also grown delusions of grandeur and political clout. He had resigned from the Chief's UHP to stand as an independent. The name Jatu still provoked laughter in the market. It was going to be a rout.

I ran all the way to the Afini's palace. The incumbent traditional ruler of Aafin was Gilbert Etan. When the post became vacant twenty years earlier, there had been a host of candidates for the position. – That was until Gilbert Etan's papers arrived. Gilbert Saka Etan, as every Aafin child knew, was the most famous Aafin indigene in the world. He had left Aafin in his twenties, when the town was still a village, and emigrated to America where he made a name for himself. He was a professor of something or the other, and as if that was not enough, owned a dozen big hotels. Someone had added up the stars in all his hotels (however dubious the merits of that exercise) and announced that he had thirty-six stars: one for every state in Nigeria.

So when his nomination forms arrived with US postage stamps, there was substantial scepticism that a man that had not visited Aafin for thirty-five years (at the time) would want to retire to the sedentary job of traditional ruler of the town. Where did this sudden love for Aafin spring from? Plus, (and this viewpoint was peddled by the most die-hard contenders for the traditional stool) would he still remember any customs at all?

Still there was a secret thrill in every Aafin heart that so important a personage would consider the town's chieftaincy a worthy retirement berth. It was clear that Aafin would immediately get a five star hotel, to begin with. No Aafin contender could offer so propitious a dowry, or put his self-interest so blatantly above the common good; and although Gilbert Saka Etan did not have a campaign to speak of, his contenders grudgingly withdrew from the running.

In the event, Gilbert Saka Etan, the hotelier, did not turn up. On the day before the selection of the Afini, Gilbert Etan arrived from Kano. He had gone straight to the palace, where a worried meeting of the council was in progress, and announced his arrival.

'Welcome,' they had said resentfully, waiting for him to leave so they could resume their important discussions.

Only one person on the council had recognised him. He had been away for that long. The councillor had pushed up his spectacles. 'Is that not Gilbert Etan the vulcaniser?'

'*Senior Vulcaniser*, SCOA, Kano,' he had corrected pugnaciously, 'although some people also call me "Saka".'

'So you're still alive!' they chorused.

By then it was too late for more credible candidates to jump back into contention. Gilbert Etan (whose scatterbrained daughter had posted his forms after returning to her waitress job in New York) became the next Afini by default. Twenty years had calmed him, and he was less wont to attempt the physical chastisement of his subjects. To give him credit, he was better than the last Afini, who was so old he had slept through the last fourteen or so years of his reign; still he was not, as most of his erstwhile rivals for the throne were quick to point out, by any means the real Saka.

It was dusk when I arrived. The palace, which was still under construction, was two hundred metres from the river beach. The Afini lived in the completed wing and saw visitors in the unfinished one. The green Mercedes waited under a giant mango tree. It was empty and there was no sign of the new driver. In the distance, Man-Palace sat attentively on a scaffold, his head was lodged cleverly and I could just make out the rattle of his snores. Through the criss-cross of scaffoldings I could also make out the Afini and the Chief, sitting on sandcrete blocks, in intimate conversation over a keg of wine. The Afini subjected his richer visitors to dire discomfort in the hope of increasing donations for the completion of his palace.

I dared not interrupt the meeting. It was enough that I was going to prevent the Chief from returning home that night. I sat on the bonnet of the car to catch my breath.

'What's your name?'

I started and looked up. He was sitting in a branch of the mango tree.

'The Condor,' I said. Ten minutes passed and I asked, 'Is it true?'

'What?'

'About your father and your wife. Are they really slee...'

'Mind your own business,' he said.

So I did. An hour passed. At first I resented the lack of conversation, but the darkness grew and I was grateful for that warning that there was a human in the tree. When the Chief emerged from the palace and Ista dropped from his branch, it was still all I could do to keep from taking to my heels.

***

Something came up after the meeting with Afini that required the Chief to leave for Ukpella immediately. I took the message home to the Block, close to midnight, but she was already asleep. There were broken glasses and fragments of the politician's photographs in the yard. I cleared them away and buried the dog in the back, behind the tomato beds. I dragged the shovel to and fro, although I did not look up at her window. She did not stop me, so it must have been okay with her.

By morning, she was still raging. She was pounding spices in a small mortar. With a household like hers that was crawling with servants, this was a chore she did not need to do; but we all understood that it was good therapy for her rage. I greeted carefully, but she did not respond. Then, when I was several paces away, I delivered the message from her husband. She glared at me, pounding a few violent imprecations into her spices.

She must have known that the Chief was my father. Yet, how could she have. It was inconceivable that I could have lived in the yard if she did. It was a childless home. People said it was called Nazareth because, despite her age, the Block was still waiting for her Promised One. Every now and again, she got a pet, on the wick of which she nursed her aging maternal flame. The Chief on his own part showed me no favouritism, in public or in private. When he fired his thugs during the Ephraim Investigation into Election Violence, I had not been exempted – and he had not cared or asked how I survived the two months of homelessness. When he visited after my mother's death he had been quite clear: there was to be none of that 'papa' nonsense. I was to be exactly like one of the *boys*, or I was out.

I was one of the *boys* now, had been for six years. I had rioted for him, beaten political opponents for him... In many ways he could never be my father any more. He was too much my master for that; and a lad cannot have everything. I keep my eyes open, my mouth closed, and most times people forgot I was around. I lived there at Nazareth, in one of the distal rooms of the boys-quarters. The Block's girls lived in the rooms that faced the courtyard, so that she could monitor their traffic to her heart's content.

***

There was a signboard near the gate that said 'Chief (the Glorious) Olobiri'. It had been there eight years since a grateful senator presented it to the Chief in response to a newspaper editorial that criticized him for using the style, 'The Honourable'. The Block had knocked it down on the first evening of her rage. Two days passed and Attack propped it up tentatively. Hours later, on her way to church, she knocked it over with her handbag. Attack raised it overnight and the Block karate-kicked it down as she returned from seeing off the Chaplain who had come on a futile mission of matrimonial intercession. The metaphor of the signboard continued for a week and three days before she grunted, '*Oi*, find small cement and repair that stupid signboard, *joo*.' Before the concrete on the base of the signpost was dry, Attack sent Bulldog to take the good news to Chief.

There was something like a small festival when Chief returned from Ukpella. He had sent ahead the biggest goat I had ever seen for his wife to make a little stew for his visitors. The excited women had gone to call Ganishu. She had walked around the handsome, tethered peace offering, an imperious he-goat with a beard that swayed in the breeze, and announced it too fine a specimen to kill. It was taken to the backyard and introduced to her flock, while she sent to the slaughterhouse for some portions of goat meat for the peppersoup.

Chief's visitors were Tagul elders. Tagul was fifteen miles south of Aafin, along the Sagiso river. It was the second, smaller town in Uguru District, but it had not produced a senator in the fifty years since the creation of the district. In the past, they had been content with cash apologies and future promises, but now they had a viable prospect: an uppity businessman who drank hard and spoke loud, whose name was Gaius Deh. He had not formally announced for Senate though. He would not have dared without Chief's blessings. But they were going to be much more expensive to buy off this time.

Ganishu was a politician's wife. It did not matter that she had not smiled in her household for a week, when the cars of the elders started to arrive at Nazareth, she danced outside to receive them, hugging each in turn, her laughter ringing out and filling male hearts with romantic regrets. She flirted brazenly, with an openness that neutered her innuendoes and made her more respectable than prim hostesses. When the elders asked after Chief she affected anger, asking whether their visit was to see her, or her old husband. They laughed heartily, forswore Chief Olobiri, and went along with her joke. Every other ancient was her sugar daddy. She feigned anger with visitors who could not eat a second meal, or drink a third bottle of beer, and went everywhere dogged by trays of food and drinks. She recognised everyone by name and made a special point of hugging those who had most recently been wronged or slighted by Chief. That kept her pretty busy.

The party really took off when Chief arrived. He was dressed in the most outrageously blue robe I had ever seen, decked with a cap of luxuriant red, and he waited until his wife danced out to receive him. Music was never in short supply in Aafin. The best musicians could make more money in a drunken minute than a carpenter could earn in a week. Once the occasion manifested, instruments would appear from cracks, pockets, and cupboards. They surrounded the couple now as Chief Olobiri danced around his wife, plastering her with currency notes from the bulging master pocket in the front of his garment. The musicians sang themselves hoarse, and were duly compensated.

It was well after dusk before the appetite for dance was sated. A few inexperienced revellers had over-indulged and were helped to the buses, but the majority of visitors from Tagul were weathered negotiators, old hands in the art of appeasement. They knew that the 'settlement' of their stomachs was but a foundation.

The party retired into the hall. It was Chief's favourite room in the house. The outside was nondescript, but inside was a heavily curtained, chapel-like dome with black sofas that surrounded the spectacle of Chief's Olobiri's throne. That throne required an occupant of considerable ego and Chief Olobiri was that man. It was a visit to that room that persuaded the Afini of Aafin of the need to build a fitting palace to clarify the identity of the real traditional ruler of Aafin. The walls bore photographs of Chief and sundry dignitaries, although some choice ones had disappeared since the death of Madam Ganishu's dog.

As they entered the hall the occasion acquired an air of sobriety. They seemed to recognise that a moment of levity had passed, that a time of consequence was upon them. An air of ritualised solemnity hung in that room, something akin to the awe one felt in the bamboo groves by the banks of the Sagiso River. The only person that seemed thoroughly at ease was Chief Olobiri.

The Block approached, flanked by a clutch of her maids. She took a tray of ceremonial kola from one of them and knelt before her husband. He took it, blessed her, and broke it. The maids passed around the kola and retired as Madam Ganishu took her seat, a much more modest throne, beside her husband.

None of us *boys* were in any doubt about the real power in the household. There were issues concerning which we simply did not bother with Chief's opinion. Yet, it was also true that Chief Olobiri's cough reverberated to the boundaries of Uguru District and beyond, and Madam Ganishu would never dream of slighting her husband publicly. It was an arrangement that stymied me for several months, but clearly there was enough power to go round in that union. I watched her sit and cross her legs, the top foot quivering like a battery-operated toy that would go on for hours at a stretch. Her eyes narrowed and she switched on her church half-smile, which could sit attentively on her face forever, while she ironed out sundry issues of her extensive household in her mind.

I wished, guiltily, that she were my real mother.

That burden was Lalito's. Her life had come apart when I arrived, the unsought love child that interrupted a convent education and trapped her in a disreputable schism for all her life. The church expelled her, her parents locked her out, and I'd been born and raised in that ether of resentment that surrounded Gagan Inn on Ntoi Road. I knew my maternal grandparents, knew the sprawling cottage where they spent their lonely, respectable retirement, and loathed them. Recently, when they courted me with visits and proverbs I'd kept my distance. I had lived on-and-off at the Gagan Inn for much of my life, inured to the surreptitious hampers that arrived some nights from Nazareth, only guessing at the means by which my mother paid my school fees in the year I didn't make the scholarship. Then my sixteenth birthday came and Chief himself arrived late on the night of the accident that claimed my mother's life, walked around her body and put a wad of currency notes in my hand. Everyone else thought he was playing the local politician, but *I knew*. Lalito had told me; and although he had never, would never acknowledge it, I knew.

The only scowl in the hall was Gaius Deh's. I watched him closely throughout the proceedings, wondering if he truly expected Chief to step down for him. All four senators who had represented Uguru District in the past three decades had done so as Chief's friends and surrogates. It was far safer to withdraw and sit in the wings until the inevitable happened and Chief had to find an urgent stand-in.

The speeches began. So far it was a hangdog catalogue of historic grievances, Tagul projects and contracts that went to Aafin. I'd heard it all before. Eventually, Chief would give the sign and we would bring the bag of money from the room under the stairs. They would grumble some more, Chief would dispense some proverbs, and then reluctantly go out himself. He would stay thirty minutes and come back with some more money, at which point the game would have to be over.

I watched eyes struggling to stay open, then succumbing gently to the post-feast sofas in that most amenable room. I flitted silently, to and fro, topping up glasses, then Gaius Deh rose abruptly.

'I don't have time again,' he snapped rudely, cutting off the elderly droner who'd had the floor for the preceding twenty minutes, 'how much will it take?'

Madam Ganishu's eyes started open, her top foot arrested mid-wriggle. All across the hall, discreet dozers roused with alacrity. The elders sitting closest to Gaius Deh tried to rein him in with whispered counsel, but they only provoked him into a louder demand: 'How much! One million, Ten? Tell me!'

Chief Olobiri laughed long and deliciously, like one that savoured a prize joke. We looked carefully in the tenor of the insult, in the stakes of the game, for the joke, in vain. It was at times like this that I prized my Olobiri education; the sort of lessons no university could have taught me. This was the laughter with which the politician deferred the humiliation of a heckler from a public to a private venue of the politician's choosing. 'Is more than money,' he said eventually.

Yet, if I was impressed, Gaius Deh was nothing of the sort. The laughter worked up a raging fury in him. 'Talk!' he demanded, 'Is it dollars? Is it pounds? Tell me! Me, I don't write cheque! Is cash I'm talking about! Tagul are not paupers that you can buy everyday! Talk!'

The silence in the room was broken by the Block. The half smile was gone from her face. She walked quietly up to Gaius Deh, looked him up and down, and, just when we feared a cataclysmic act of violence, she snatched his half-drunk glass of beer from his surprised hand, passed it to the ever-present maid behind her. Then she stalked quietly from the hall.

The battle-line was drawn then. Without a word, the woman had taken the insult on her man's behalf, withdrawn her hospitality, and Chief could do nothing but follow through, or lose face. I felt the eddying of malice in the room. I was in the middle of something exciting and dangerous. I should be fleeing. I could do nothing but wait, and watch the unfurling of standards.

Chief Olobiri's voice was whip-thin, a voice to which laughter was alien. It sliced through the air, and the Tagul elders ducked to avoid its arc. 'I said is more than money can buy.' He snatched his own red cap and flung it on the ground – a travesty in its own right, on a normal day – then he took a grip on a lock of his thick hair and yanked it angrily, 'HUMAN HEAD!' he bellowed, 'That's the price! Your head or my head! That's the price!'

Several elders from both Aafin and Tagul jumped to their feet, enacting the tried and tested machinery of mediation. Two men rescued the cap, dusting it down fastidiously between them, a hubbub of earnest voices grew and fell, Chief Olobiri, turbulent with rage, was pressed into his throne and smothered with platitudes and praise. Gaius Deh, for all his own propitiators, remained standing. His stubborn spine seemed to have fused into one unbending bone in his waist, yet when he spoke again, he was more chastened. His angry words seemed oiled and earnest, 'Nobody needs to die. What am I doing with human head? Eh? I am a businessman, but what is fair for Aafin is fair for Tagul. Is it a lie? Fifty years! *Haba!* Nobody needs to die…'

'Bastard!' yelled Chief Olobiri, who was quite aware that the tiff could not be settled too quickly. The insult had been offered before his wife, before too many witnesses. A quick mediation was utterly out of the question. A total falling out had to happen. After that, a peace delegation had to come from Tagul. On a day to be negotiated subsequently. It was going to have to be a month-long quarrel at the least. It was in that garrulous process of appeasement that the proper hierarchy of rank could be re-established. Otherwise he would have young monkeys jumping up to insult him left right and centre. 'Bastard like you!' he cursed, 'What's pushing you? Common oil contract that you got yesterday? Bastard you! I was a tycoon before your mother born you!' They pressed him to his throne again, and the elder in his front, who had taken the full benefit of his angry spittle, retreated to deploy his handkerchief.

Gaius Deh's voice, when he continued, was strained. It was clear that the chorus of "bastard" was chipping away at the businessman's self-control. 'I've not abused anybody, yet,' he warned.

It was also clear that he was losing this exchange: although there was a mass of grovelling Tagul elders interceding with an imperious Chief, four or five angry men shushed Gaius perfunctorily. The businessman turned to the doorway and snapped his fingers at his waiting boys who left promptly. 'I've not abused anybody,' he repeated doggedly. 'My own is what is best for everybody, whether Tagul or Aafin. A man does not quarrel with his destiny.'

'What is that you're saying?' yelled Chief, ' Who does not quarrel with whose destiny? Open your whole mouth and talk like a man, bastard you!'

'The whole Uguru District knows that your destiny is not in that

Senate. It is not a matter of human head. Even if you stand unopposed something else will happen. Four times already…'

He swallowed and petered into a humming silence. *The Great Unsayable* had suddenly, unaccountably, been said publicly. Every eye in the room swivelled onto Chief, 'So, is your own cockroach destiny that will stop me this time, eh?' he asked quietly.

Four Tagul youths entered the hall, dragging two brown sacks. The first they took to the fore of the hall, before Chief's throne, where they poured such a cascade of currency notes that switched the allegiance of many a heart in that room. They took the second bag to Gaius Deh, where they roughly supplanted the ring of elders around the businessman.

Money was what you threw at the feet of prostitutes, not chiefs. Certainly not Chief Olobiri. Something had happened to the chicken overnight that transformed it into a new, terrifying creation; the eagle had to be wary. I knew what was in the second sack. The clang of ironware that emanated from it dried my mouth involuntarily. There was going to be that other type of trouble. I sneaked to the back and fled to fetch Attack, but he was only paces away from the door, and he stalked in with ten *boys*. Madam Ganishu would have called them. I let them crowd past me and followed.

'You can count it if you want,' Gaius Deh was saying insolently, 'that's what you paid Tagul elders for our birthright last time – and the time before that. Plus interest! If is not your destiny, even cockroach will stop you, and God knows I'm bigger than cockroach,' he raised his voice dramatically, and his hands above his head, '*I don't want human head o! Everybody can hear me now o!*' Then he dropped his hands, his voice, and stared down Chief Olobiri. 'But me, I'm not afraid of you, of anybody.'

With that he pushed his way out, flanked by his men, his shoulders barging aggressively against everyone in his way. The momentum ended at the door, where Attack was standing. Alone he was enough to hold the door; but he was not alone. Every time I saw Attack laugh, I thought again: *this is the largest mouth I have ever seen.* When he laughed it was full of teeth and the jokes were larger, funnier than life; but when he scowled and gritted his prognathous jaws, he was hell proximate; and to stare into eyes like his was to be seared with his malevolence.

Gaius Deh was not fazed. He turned to the throne, palpating his crotch with the insolent, audible scratch of unruly fingernails on angry linen. 'Everybody here is carrying the thing that makes him a man. Can we go in peace? Or shall I prove my manhood.'

He was armed then. It was the ultimatum before the bloodletting. I began to tremble, desperately glad I was at the door, in prime position to flee when the shooting began. Once again I wondered why I was still serving Chief. I'd more than repaid the note he gave Lalito on my eleventh birthday that got me into the Federal Government College. Chief Olobiri rose in a cold rage. His voice rushed at me. 'Condor! Get me an egg.'

I wanted desperately to ask "a what?" but I did not dare. Instead I fled to the chicken coop where I swiped one of Ganishu's eggs, a mortal crime in normal times. I hurried back to the hall. He snatched the egg and hurled it to the floor, inches from Gaius. The fury of the egg bomb spattered strands of albumin, stains of yolk, on nearby clothes.

'If that egg can become whole again,' cursed Chief, 'then the two of us can see ourselves after today. Sagiso says so! Go!'

It was a terrible, *terrible* oath. Much worse than anyone expected. I had never witnessed an egg oath in my life, and did not know anyone who had. It was the sort of thing that eddied to-and-fro in Uguru folklore until you were not sure it had ever happened before.

Attack stepped away from the door with alacrity, but Gaius Deh's feet were suddenly leaden. He laughed, but it was a hollow sort, lacking the conviction of Chief's earlier peals, for even he could see that matters had gone too far. Once he left that room he would never again stand in the same room with Chief. But to retreat then required a grovelling he probably did not have in him, and would have been in vain anyway. Besides the Tagul elders were on their feet, ready to walk out with him. Chief had been their political mentor for decades, but the egg oath had crystallized their primal, clannish loyalties. He had to go through with it then. And he did in style, with all thirty-eight Tagul elders that came for the meeting with Chief Olobiri, a greater political harvest than he had dared hope.

That was the beginning of The Feud. Within days the communities were split down the middle. Almost everyone supported Chief on the matter of the senate seat. There was a sense that the old man had a right to sit in that bloody house before he died, after all the dolts and brigands he had sent there. But roughly half the district sympathised with Gaius Deh on the matter of the egg oath. As far as Uguru people could see, there was enough space in the world, even for worm and elephant.

That worm and elephant proverb was first used by The Block that very night of the egg oath. There was nothing private about Chief's quarrels with his wife. Although they usually happened in The Bedroom, they were conducted at violent volumes to the music of breaking things. Despite her own ferocity, Madam Ganishu always drew the line at political bloodshed. In that sense she was all bark and no bite. She had exacted a promise from her husband to lose elections rather than spill blood. It was not a promise he ever intended to keep, but the egg oath showed his hand a tad too publicly, it was the clearest intimation of imminent bloodshed and any indigene of Uguru knew that too well.

'Who started it?' roared Chief from the bedroom, 'who was it that seized his beer?'

'There's difference between seizing beer and breaking egg!' she thundered back, '*Nama!*'

'Me? *Me*, Chief? You call me *nama?*'

Yet, when she moved out the very next day, we remembered that the Block's parents were Taguli after all. It was signal to Uguru District that the world was coming to an end.

The next few months were a little difficult: the Uguru markets at Aafin and Tagul were burnt, along with six houses and eight cars. Two men died in the riots that began to happen with the regularity of wildcat discos back in the old days. Even Ista took the opportunity of the confusion to attack his father with a machete. They both ended up in adjacent hospital beds where the contested wife was forced by overworked nurses to feed both husband and ex-husband.

The riots worsened. It was the sort of thing Taguli husbands had been waiting for, all those years, to put their arrogant Aafini wives down a peg or two, but it quickly went out of hand and not a few cross-border wives followed the Block's lead, taking indefinite vacations from their matrimonial homes. One in four residents of Aafin was Taguli. Most of the Main Road shops in Tagul were owned by Aafinis. It was easy enough to riot, to loot and burn a shop or two, but on the mornings after the markets closed there was no milk for the tea, no beans for the pottage. Minibus travel became impossible. Halfway between Tagul and Aafin, between eighth mile and ninth, the buses would regularly spin over onto the shoulder, doors would fly open, and the Aafini/Taguli fisticuffs that had broken out between commuters would explode onto the road spreading among the commuters – and the occupants of passing minibuses shrieking to a halt to join the fray.

In the midst of all that feuding, the violent elections came and went. The results were cancelled and the election was deferred indefinitely. The Olobiri jinx had struck a fifth time. It did not end the feud for it was clearly also the start of a Gaius Deh jinx. The businessman, who had massively overspent his election budget only to see victory snatched away, was moved to call a meeting of Taguli elders. There, after an impassioned speech peppered with the twinned words "Olobiri" and "bastard", he also broke an egg and swore a terrible oath.

That ratcheted up the tension. All the schools closed. The district was like a war zone and people carried machetes in satchels on errands to the market. It was in that climate that the Afini called me into his palace one evening. We met in his private rooms, in fearful secrecy. He had one question for me: 'Will you betray your master, for the sake of Uguru?'

For a moment I wondered how he had singled me out of Chief's *boys* for the approach, then I nodded.

'Come with me,' he said.

We drove that night into Tagul. It was a journey through byroads and even then, fraught with danger, and I had no idea where we were headed until we arrived at the palace of the Abani of Tagul. He was a much older traditional ruler than the Afini, and he had a real palace, a cheerful, lighted place where I sat in a wide reception lounge, eating cassava wafers with a silent man I recognised from Gaius Deh's party many months before.

The two traditional rulers were in conference for hours on end. Finally they came out. They took fresh oaths from us, and sent us on our way. Back in Aafin, I did not sleep till morning. Until I stood before the Chief I was unsure what I was going to do. He was my father, after all, even though he treated me like just another hired *boy*. Yet I was going to have to be loyal to my community, or to him. It had to be one or the other. I stood before him just before dawn, and when he asked what I wanted, I told him there was a plot to kill him, and one of his closest bodyguards was complicit. He was immediately on his feet. It was the flavour of the times. 'Who? Who?'

'I don't know.' I whispered, looking behind me with a fear I did not have to fake, for if Attack discovered my plot I was probably dead anyway, 'the man who knows wants to meet us on the first ferry this morning. He wants fifty thousand for the name.'

'How did you...'

I looked at my watch. 'The ferry is in ten minutes, Chief.'

It was as the Afini had planned. There was not time enough for him to think clearly. There was only time enough to put fifty thousand naira in the great front pocket of his robe and drive to the jetty. In those circumstances he left the house without a bodyguard, something he hadn't done in years and years. I don't suppose Chief could have taken the word of anyone but me – or perhaps Attack, on a thing like this. He grilled me throughout the five minutes of the drive, but my story was simple and I stuck to it: I'd overheard the talk in a minibus. I had struck the deal with the man. His text had appeared on my phone some minutes before: He would met Chief in the ferry. That was all I knew.

We were the last to board the ferry. In the half-light, it was teeming with the Afini's stooges. Just before it pulled away, I remembered that I'd forgotten the key in the ignition. I hurried back to the car – and sat there, ignoring Chief's calls, for the two minutes it took the shadowy hulk of the ferry to pull away from the jetty.

I watched the stooges jump from the ferry and swim ashore, one after the other. I watched the sun rise slowly, heard the campaign truck pass, blaring the Afini's message. Presently, Attack arrived, breathless, with his posse. They saw the ferry, which was now 'broken down' in the middle of the Sagiso. Attack stripped to his shorts, but the Afini was there, with a line of men on the beach to prevent just that. Attack put his clothes back on, snatched the keys from me and spat in my face.

We started the march to the Coral Beach.

After two hours in the middle of the Sagiso, the pilot 'managed' to restart the engine. It did not head downriver on its regular schedule. Instead its bow turned towards the Coral Beach, to the disused jetty where a great and restive crowd was gathering. They had arrived from the streets, markets and parks of Aafin and Tagul. Both rulers had spread the word that Chief Olobiri and Gaius Deh were having a showdown on the ferry. The atmosphere was charged. It was the largest gathering of Aafini and Taguli since the feud began and the very air was flammable, waiting for a spark.

It was fully daylight when the ferry berthed at Coral Beach. Besides the crew of the ferry, there were only two passengers left on board, Chief Olobiri and Gaius Deh, and they were not locked in the mortal combat required by their terrible oaths. Indeed they did not look as though they had exchanged many angry words at all. The Uguru crowd was perplexed. One Warri newspaper had proposed to settle the feud by buying Gaius and Chief a dozen crates of eggs apiece. Foreigners never seemed to get the thing about an egg oath. Now, as we watched our leaders debark clumsily in a canoe that should not have been big enough to hold them both, we wondered if we got it either.

Spontaneous boos from Taguli and Aafini alike dissipated the tension in the crowd, resounding, in political ears, like death knells to certain careers. The politicians tried to be elsewhere quickly; but it was a long walk from Coral Beach to anywhere. They were stuck in the heckling company of erstwhile supporters suddenly chagrined at the thought of the blood they had drawn and the homes they had burnt on behalf of politicians who didn't have the common decency to beat themselves to a pulp when they had a chance. The multitude melted away in every direction, like pus seeping away from the lanced boil of The Feud. At first I was borne along in the Aafini current, then I caught the stony stares of the *boys*, and Chief's frosty eyes, and my feet grew roots.

I had not thought beyond my moment of chivalry to the days and months that would come after. Suddenly, those weeks and years hit me and I was struggling to breathe. The war was over, but so was my old life as well. I'd saved Uguru, but the Afini and his grateful clique was gone, probably jockeying to fill the new political vacuums in Uguru province. There was no heroic moment; there was no pension plan for my dead career. It was just that moment of shame; then the kick I had not seen coming, the punches to the small of the back from *boys* that had, until that morning, been my only family, and that hot, scabrous spit from Attack, that still burned like acid. My loyalty to community had cost me dearly.

Then, slowly, something like relief began to rise through the shame. I was twenty-one to Attack's forty-five; I did not need to stuff another ballotbox, to burn another car... for Chief, for anyone... I still had time to find myself, to move on from *boy*hood, from the arc of fallen mother and twisted father...

'*Oi,*'

I turned.

'What's that your name again?' The Block was resplendent in green, as imperious a presence as ever. Suddenly, I *knew* who had given the Afini my name. She would have known that her husband trusted me enough... but how could she have known that I could have betrayed him?

307

'The Condor.' I said, breathlessly.

She made a face. 'I mean your real name.'

'Nkiti,' I felt strange. I had not spoken the name in years.

She humphed, 'Which kain name is that? Your mother must have really vex with somebody. I'll give you a nice Taguli name: *Manisi.*'

I continued to stare. Her effrontery sometimes took away the breath. It was not everyday someone presumed to change your name, especially when she no longer fed and sheltered you.

The crowd was quite gone. We were alone by the riverside, alone with the worried whine of the ferry's screw as it tried to extricate itself from the green clutch of seaweed. Her flirty laughter boomed, the sort she normally reserved for political bigwigs, 'Shame on you, Manisi, you didn't even ask about me!' She gave me her bag, 'But, you're a good boy; come and see my new house.'

She turned and set off but I weighed her bag on the spot. It was easy to follow: there would be shelter and a houseboy's fare at the end of the journey, but I had just cut loose from Chief's wake. I would not follow his estranged wife, be her good boy. Besides, she was an Olobiri; one of these days, they might make up, and where would that leave me? Or perhaps she would get another dog... I had spent my last six years being loyal to a lie: a father that played the master at arms length, who returned the proud GCEs I showed him with an indifferent grunt. Another easy lie beckoned. I dropped the bag. I was nobody's houseboy any more.

The Block stopped and turned to me. I took a deep breath, filling the interstices of my emptiness with rage enough to stand up to a Madam Ganishu Olobiri. She must have seen my eyes, for she approached in mincing steps until she was standing very close. I was closer to the Block than I'd ever been before. So close I could smell the strength of sweat, the scrub of soap. 'Manisi,' she said softly, 'remember those baskets from Nazareth? That wasn't Chief. That wasn't politics. That was me. For fifteen years I made sure that Lalito did not have to sell herself, to feed you.'

'It's a lie.' I whispered defiantly.

'Will you say you didn't know?' she said, accusingly, her low voice dropping lower still; a political carapace cracked open and the fierce eyes of a schoolmistress pinned me back, 'I've seen how you look at me. Why was it that… of all the *boys* that passed through that my house, it was only you that worked like my son, in my garden, in my poultry...' she paused, her lips twitched, 'didn't you bury my dog for me?'

I took a deep breath, 'What's the meaning of *Manisi*?'

'The promised one.'

It was a good thing then that the riverbeach was deserted, because I was suddenly afflicted with Ista's incontinence. My face slowly fell apart. We wept together, for what seemed like years, and I saw how one could be a man and still the boy, then I took my mother's bag and we went home.